Praise for Islands

Amazon Reviews

*"If you only read one book this year - make
sure it's this one! a beautifully crafted story
with characters you will care about as they
could so easily be you and I. Difficult subjects
that touch us all are dealt with a rare level of
honesty, integrity and understanding."*

*"Downloaded this today and have just read it
in one go. Page turning, plot secrets revealed
with unexpected twists. Brilliant capturing of
the pain of invisible loss."*

*"Absolutely loved this book. Flew through it
from start to finish."*

*" I wept at its honesty when I read its first draft
because this is a book which does not shy away
from handling big issues."*

You can sign up to be notified when Gwyn's next book is published, and to receive special offers:

http://www.gwyngb.com

You can also connect with Gwyn online:

Twitter: @gwyngb

Facebook:
https://www.facebook.com/GwynGBwriter/

Pinterest: https://www.pinterest.com/GwynGB/

Instagram:
https://www.instagram.com/gwyngb/

Website: http://www.gwyngb.com

Islands

Gwyn GB

CHALKY DOG
PUBLISHING

Published in 2016 by Chalky Dog Publishing

A CIP catalogue record for this book will be available from the British Library

ISBN 978-0-9955165-1-9

We are each of us islands, every one an individual, full of secrets and experiences no other can see or understand.

1

25th February 2008, London

Sometimes no matter how hard you try to forget, or how far you run, the past catches up with you. It catches up with Katherine in the hallway of her London mews house, and it comes in the form of a letter from Jersey.

Although it's a shock, in many ways she's also relieved. Thirty-two years of trying to forget she'd killed her best friend, Anne, has been very wearing on her conscience. The timing of the letter couldn't be more coincidental. Two days earlier the world's media had descended on her home island which is now the scene of a major child abuse and murder inquiry. Jersey is struggling to come to terms with its hidden past. Katherine knows it's time to face up to hers.

The process begins Saturday - the day starting just like the previous weekend and the ones before it. With no work commute Katherine indulges in a short lie in bed followed by a bit of window shopping; meandering along the high street, weaving in and out of the crowds. After her usual Saturday lunch, Covent Garden soup with ciabatta from the artisan bakers on the corner, she potters around her patio taking in the sounds of next door's TV. The rugby is in full swing, and the smell of washing tumble-drying wafts from their kitchen vent; a thin mist of homely comfort.

A few houses away comes the sharp rap and rasp of DIY action, and from the big white townhouse at the end of her garden the shouts of children playing table tennis escape from within. On her little patio Katherine allows herself to be carried on the tide of everyday human activity ebbing and flowing around her.

She tidies up the remains of winter debris, putting the leaves back into the flower beds to rot and hiding the twigs in the bin where the refuse collectors won't see them. When the February chill makes itself known she retreats inside, her thoughts turning to the night out she has planned and the prospect of a long, hot soak in the tub. Knowing she won't be in later she turns on the BBC's News24 channel to catch-up with the world,

'*A child's partial remains found at a Jersey care home*,' is the headline running along the scrolling strip at the bottom of the screen. She freezes. Just the mention of Jersey is enough to make her forget about getting ready to go out and instead stay perched on the edge of her Laura Ashley sofa. Watching. Listening.

What she hears over the next two minutes shocks her to the core. Physical and sexual abuse of children as young as five, the possibility of children having been killed, abuse that had gone on for decades without anyone noticing - or at least without anyone caring. To accompany the report, she sees images of the Haut de la Garenne care home itself. It's somewhere she vaguely remembers passing on car and bike journeys when she was younger; or seeing in series of Bergerac when the children had gone and the film crew took over, turning it into the fictional Bureau des Etrangers. How ironic the police are back, but this time for real.

Then the report shows views over Gorey Harbour to Mont Orgueil Castle, just a couple of minutes from the former children's home, and her stomach twists with its familiarity. Every other time she's seen this view, on film, in magazines, in real life, it's always been picture postcard beautiful; the imposing granite castle rising up where sea meets land, trimmed by a quaint harbour of colourful buildings and bobbing boats. Now, whether it's the accompanying words of the reporter, or the way it's been filmed, it looks almost sinister.

This isn't the Jersey she recognises from her childhood. Moments from a lifetime flash into her consciousness, their contradictions stirring something in her. She's shocked her home island could have hidden a different side to it, a nasty dark side - but something else gnaws at her.

Over the next two days a chronic aching invades her bones making scars itch in her heart and dark thoughts prowl her mind. The aching culminates with the letter, until she knows there is only one thing to do; go home and face up to the death she caused - and to those she's left behind.

2

June 1976, Jersey

The flower is tiny, fragile, pink; or is it perhaps lilac? The petals thin, silky velvet. Tiny veins pattern their surface merging at its heart where the stamen rise, vulnerable, offering their treasure of golden red pollen to each passing bee. To Katherine its thin stem rising up from the ground makes it a survivor, most of the grass around it has already turned brown. She likes that about the flower, so tiny and yet indomitable in the face of nature's harsh cruelty. She almost goes cross eyed staring at it, squinting with eyes screwed tight against the white light of the sun.

There is nothing else in her head except for the image of that flower and the burning heat which seems to swell her brain and make futile all attempts at other, more useful thoughts, such as what might be in tomorrow's history exam. When was the Munich Agreement signed, September 1938 or 1939? And most importantly, will she see Darren Le Brocq tomorrow at Sands Disco?

'Every time I close my eyes all I can see is

Mark Vibert in his black trousers,' Katherine's best friend Anne sighs. The two of them lie prostrate in a field near to Katherine's farmhouse. They've been making the most of the sunshine. It's the end of June and although they don't realise it yet, they're going to get sick of the heat. This is the summer of '76 and it will be the longest and hottest since records began.

Anne has been 'in love' with Mark Vibert for a good six weeks, which is a record for both of them and doubtless a result of the fact she hasn't yet spoken a word to him. It hasn't stopped her talking about him, or from writing out his name 100 times in some kind of teenage ritualistic hope it might attract him to her. Her patience was rewarded earlier today when she saw him and he looked straight at her - an acknowledgment of her existence. A result. Since that moment the doubts have set in.

'He obviously doesn't fancy me otherwise he would have come over.' She throws her thoughts out to Katherine, hoping she'll return with something reassuring. This is well practiced group therapy, necessary teenage support.

'He was showing off, being cool. He didn't have the chance to come over and ask you out did he?' Katherine replies, prompting Anne to murmur in reluctant agreement.

Katherine can't see her friend's face

because she's lying on her stomach with her head buried into her almost olive brown forearm. She's always been jealous of her natural colour, ever since they were little toddlers playing in the nursery garden in the summer sun: Anne in her pretty sleeveless summer dress, Katherine in long flappy sleeves and a large annoying sun hat. Katherine never turns more than a pale tan, blonde hairs shimmer across the surface of her skin. She can't stay out in the sun as long as Anne with her black hair and skin that tans so easily, but it's never stopped her thinking of Anne as if they are sisters. After all they've more in common than Katherine and her own sister, Margaret.

'Yes, but that bitch Louise de la Haye was trying to get off with him,' Anne whines. Katherine thinks for a moment searching for the right reassuring words. She's momentarily distracted as some children run past up the lane giggling and laughing, probably coming back from the beach all salty and tired, buckets, nets and spades hanging from their little sandy arms.

'If he snogs *her* then he's not worth it, is he?' Katherine triumphantly replies. Of course that isn't really her talking, it's her mother. Being a teenager she and Marie don't always see eye to eye, but she can be relied on as a bank of ready solace when Katherine can't think of anything else to say. It does the trick; Anne goes back to daydreaming about Mark Vibert. Katherine uses the ensuing silence to reach out and pick the tiny flower, planning on pressing it between some tissue later.

The field where they lie is being rested by the farmer, Mr Binet, who rents the land from Katherine's mother. At the start of the year it had been a brown, empty scar from her bedroom window, but nature has been quick to reclaim it as her own. Grass, dandelions, buttercups, hogweed and the tiny fragile pink flowers now adorn its surface; coloured jewels that have bobbed and floated on the waves of green since Spring. Now even nature has faltered in the face of the relentless scorching of the sun.

'Katherine, tea time,' Margaret's voice shouts across the field from the yard, breaking into their thoughts.

It's Katherine's turn to sigh, 'I'd better go,' she says to Anne.

'Yeah, sure,' Anne replies, 'I'll see you at school tomorrow.'

'Yup, just one more exam and we'll be free - no more school, no more Miss Batterford, no more uniform.'

Anne smiles back at her, brightening. 'We can talk about flat-hunting tomorrow night.'

'Yeah, don't forget 8 o'clock at Sands, if you want to see Mark,' Katherine adds. 'I just know him and Darren are going to be there. I'm sure of it. My horoscope said next week's going to be the start of a new phase in my relationships.'

'And they're not going to be able to resist us,' laughs Anne, 'I'm wearing my pink skirt and new top dad bought me last week. Party time. See you tomorrow.'

Katherine watches as Anne jumps on her bike and cycles across the bumpy field to the road. She's so often wished she was Anne with her free spirit and sense of adventure. Nothing seems to faze her. Where Katherine hangs back shy and embarrassed, Anne will fling herself into the occasion, chattering and making friends. Her parents are just so much cooler about things than Katherine's mum, Marie, who keeps a tight rein on her daughters.

Katherine and Anne have been inseparable ever since Anne chose Katherine to help give out the free milk on their very first day at nursery school. Anne willingly volunteered for the role of distributing the drinks to all the new faces and she picked Katherine, who was quietly crying in the corner, as her comrade. It was the start of a permanent union - through nursery, primary and now secondary school. Where other friends had come and gone, their partnership remained unsullied.

Being friends with someone as outgoing as Anne definitely has its advantages, not least the fact they both got to meet some of the Radio 1 stars when they were over for the Summer roadshow because Anne blagged their way backstage. Plus, she's not shy around boys. In fact, Anne has already 'got off' with one or two, something which at first made Katherine extremely jealous; but only until her friend willingly shared every minute detail of the experience with her, demonstrating "the kiss" with a cushion.

Anne shares absolutely everything with Katherine. When her father brought back a bottle of Charlie perfume from one of his trips to America, she'd made sure she let Katherine have a squirt every morning at school. 'We're best friends,' she'd said, 'We have to smell the same so everyone knows we're best mates.'

Katherine walks back alone across the field to her home, the whirr and whistle of wind through feathers overhead making her flinch slightly as a pigeon soars past. A dog barks not far away, muffled by the distance, but she can still tell it's the sound of a large dog announcing somebody's arrival on its territory. It's answered by the sharper yap of a terrier, slightly closer this time, and an accompanying shout from a human voice. In the distance is the clanging rumble of a tractor, its metal teeth digging into the earth, its chains and machinery banging metal on metal as it works. The sounds carry for miles despite the stillness of the afternoon - or perhaps because of it.

'Hi,' Katherine cheerfully announces her entrance into their kitchen causing her mother and sister to look up. Her mother is at the stove stirring a large pan, whilst Katherine's younger sister, always the homebody, has on an apron and is kneading dough on the wooden board.

'What have you been doing?' her mother casually asks.

'Oh just lying in the field, having a break from revision.'

Her mother looks up at her, studying her face. 'On your own?'

'Yeah,' Katherine comes back rather too quickly and her eyes dart away from her mother's scrutiny. A sigh comes from the direction of the stove, and her mother returns to her stirring. Katherine is never sure if she gets away with her fibs or if her mother sees right through her and just decides not to take things further. It's not as if Katherine likes lying to her, but her mum just goes off on one if she's been hanging around with Anne.

'You know it upsets her,' Margaret whispers, as she sits at the table. Margaret is an involuntary accomplice in Katherine's liaisons with Anne.

'Shhhsh,' she replies and throws a quick glance their mother's way. There's never been any good explanation as to why their mother doesn't like her seeing Anne outside of school. All she says is, 'Because I said so, that's why!' which isn't really any kind of a reason at all.

'I can't believe it's your final exam tomorrow,' Margaret, ever the pacifier, diverts the conversation.

'I know, I can't wait,' Katherine leans back on the chair, throwing her blonde hair off her neck and closing her eyes. She's still hot from being in the field.

'We'll have a celebration supper tomorrow for you,' her mother joins the conversation, Anne seemingly forgotten.

'I can bake a cake,' Margaret chips in.

'Thanks,' Katherine sits back upright and smiles at them both.

'I'll go to the shops on the way home from work then,' her mother says. She's proud of her daughter's achievements and isn't afraid to show it. It's at moments like this Marie misses David the most. Her husband, David Gaudin, had been a doctor, though perhaps not a very good one because he failed to diagnose his own chronic blocked arteries and impending and very untimely death from a massive heart attack. He left Marie in somewhat of a pickle financially. The house and land had been left to her by her parents, but finding the money to keep their two girls clothed and fed hasn't always been easy. The land brings in a small rent, but when a hole developed in the roof during a bad storm a couple of years ago, Marie had to sell one of the fields to a neighbouring farmer. The rest of the time they make ends meet with her part time job in the post office.

'Let's hope I pass,' Katherine's voice brings Marie back to her kitchen.

'Of course you will,' she quickly replies, 'you've got your father's brains - thank goodness. I never did very well at school. Not like you.' She turns to smile at her daughter. Where have the years gone? What she sees is a young woman not the little girl in her heart. She knows Katherine is itching to spread her wings. Marie's been teetering on that tiny rocky ridge so many parents find themselves on, caught between wanting her to soar away and find success, to follow her dreams, and her own selfish yearning not to lose her. Then again, another part of her wishes Katherine would leave Jersey for a while - get away from Anne. The sooner that friendship ends the better as far as Marie is concerned.

3

Feb 2008, London

Katherine stays glued to the news about Jersey on her TV screen. She has a strong urge to call Margaret and seek some reassurance from her sister that her memories aren't false, the island being portrayed isn't the one they'd grown up in. Instead, as is usual these days, she holds back afraid of the reception. Reluctant to chance her emotions. She calls her friend and cancels their date. The thought of socialising, talking small talk, whilst all the while her brain is elsewhere fills her with dread.

The television news has left her with an uneasy feeling, a tight knot in her stomach and a sense there's a shadow just behind her shoulders. Her brain is searching for something, anything which could link her Jersey to the one in the news report. She drinks a glass of wine, then the rest of the bottle. It doesn't help her sleep well that night.

Next morning the news from Jersey is the first thing to enter her mind when she wakes up. She lifts her head to look at the clock. It's early, only half six but she's restless. She decides to get up and go to the newsagents, find out if the papers have picked up on the story.

It is a bright dry day, although the February chill sharpens the air as she steps out of her front door and pulls it shut quietly behind her. The tiny mews is deserted except for a neighbour's fat tabby cat curled up on the doorstep of its home waiting to be let back in. It half lifts its eyelids as she walks past, but doesn't deign to offer her any further recognition.

The mews is on the outer edges of London's West End. Not too far away the hum of Tottenham Court Road can be heard, which even at this early hour on a Sunday, is filled with traffic. Memories of Jersey's quiet roads and peaceful countryside trickle into her mind. The sunlit, narrow green lanes in her head contrast with the wide, drab, brick and concrete thoroughfare in front of her.

When she reaches the small newsagents it's already full of people. The tiny shop's walls heave with shelves of newspapers, magazines, comics and trading cards; a sea of words and pictures crammed in, all competing for the eye's attention - broken only by heavily populated racks of confectionery and cigarettes. Stacked on the floor are the British Sundays, swollen with their supplements and advertising brochures.

Katherine quickly scans the front pages.

The story hasn't made it there yet. It doesn't take her long to find it inside. "Body found amid fears of child abuse ring on Jersey," The Independent on Sunday's headline snarls at her. She gathers as many papers as she can carry and shuffles forward in the crowded shop, repeating 'Excuse me,' over and over to everyone she has to push past to reach the queue. As she waits she reads on, "Detectives said they expected to discover more bodies at the former Haut de la Garenne home in St Martin."

She hears the man in front order some Dunhill Lights with his tabloid. Katherine stops reading, it's made her feel sick. She's shocked to the core - that something like this could have happened just down the road from her home. She fumbles in her pocket for her purse, desperate to leave the shop as quickly as she can. It's almost like she's guilty by association; at any time she might feel a tap on the shoulder and be asked questions. The tone of the reports in the papers are all accusatory; insinuating everyone in the island had been in on this terrible secret, hiding the abuse, allowing it to continue. She was there at the time but she knew nothing. How could a child, let alone several children, have gone missing without anybody noticing; without somebody querying where they'd gone? Surely there must be records, even if many of the children at Haut de la Garenne came from troubled homes?

Katherine's thoughts turn darker still as she searches her memories for any signs of this 'hidden' abuse. If it's all true, could people she knows be involved? Somebody she's trusted? Still trusts? As she walks home, burdened by more than just heavy papers, faces rush in and out of her memory: challenging, taunting.

If she hoped the newspaper reports would ease the disturbed feeling she's had since last night, then she's disappointed. The Sunday Times gives the island as bad a press as all the rest of them, "Parts of a child's skeleton have been found buried under concrete," it adds, "The body is believed to date from the 1980s."

She devours all the papers re-reading and cross-checking, and then sits almost motionless thinking about what she's read, about growing up, about all the people she's left behind.

Her living room is silent, the only noise in the house an occasional clunk from the heating pipes or radiator. The double glazed windows don't allow the outside world to seep into her still existence. She becomes aware of the silence and strains to hear something, anything. The effort almost makes her ears ache with the overwhelming white noise of nothing; the sound of the newspaper pages turning a welcome relief.

She skip reads the latest on the search for missing nine-year-old Shannon Matthews in

Dewsbury. Police have widened the search and are now looking in ponds and sewers. The only headline she wants to read in this story is she's been found. The television images of her distraught mother's anguish have already upset Katherine with unsaid fears of what fate could have befallen the little girl. She can't know that in just a few weeks' time Shannon will be found safe and well with a relative, and her mother's crocodile tears will turn real as she's arrested by the police.

It suddenly dawns on Katherine she misses Jersey. She looks around at her little house seeing it afresh. There's nothing holding her here, no pets to worry about, no cat or dog, not even a goldfish. After John left she'd avoided becoming attached to anything, or anyone for that matter. What is she still doing here? How has she ended up staying in London for so long? At first it helped ease the pain, distanced her from the constant reminders, but then? Then it probably just became habit. At least she'd like to think that was it, rather than she was scared to return, scared to go back and face up to things. Surely enough time has gone by now, all wounds healed, scar tissue barely noticeable. She can return to Jersey with her head held high - a success.

Only something holds her back. She can't quite put her finger on what it is, but it is there in the background holding on to her. Until she can figure it out she can't possibly hope to set herself free.

The Monday morning post brings the unexpected catalyst for her return. When Katherine steps through her front door after work, the initial surprise is seeing the Jersey stamp on the envelope at her feet. She scoops it up and immediately opens it, disgorging its inner secrets in her Farrow & Ball Oxford Stone hallway. Pulling the letter free she is taken unawares by the stale odour of cigarette smoke. Seeing the signature of her dead friend's mother at the bottom makes her heart lurch and causes her to dump her handbag and keys unceremoniously on the floor.

"Dear Katherine,' it begins, *'I hope this letter finds you, and when it does, it finds you well. I am not so well. I'm told I have just weeks remaining. There are things I need to tell you, things which should have been dealt with many years ago in relation to the events in the summer of 1976. I know you have no reason to show me mercy in my final days, but if you could find the opportunity to visit me there are things I know Anne would like me to have said to you. I await your decision. Yours sincerely Elizabeth West."*

Elizabeth West. She hasn't thought of that name in years. To see Anne's mother's name on the letter in front of her makes her head reel.

Katherine believes there are only two living people who know the truth about Anne's death - herself and Anne's mother. Now she is dying and wants to talk. The decision to return to Jersey is made.

4

June 1976, Jersey

Katherine is so close to finishing, or should that be starting? One more exam and that'll be it. She'll be an ex St Helier Girls School student and a grown-up, ready to work and take her place in the world. She is sick of revising, sick of sitting at her tiny desk in her bedroom looking out over the same boring fields. There has to be more to life than this, more to fill her days than schoolwork, or hanging around the house.

Her bedroom walls are covered in a multitude of distractions: posters of Donny Osmond and David Essex, plus an underground map of London which she's virtually memorised. There is a sheet from "Jackie" showing twenty different styles to try with long hair. During the weeks of revision Katherine has experimented with every single one of them, plus a lot more variations besides.

Where there aren't posters there is her wardrobe - a big, double-doored mahogany beast of a wardrobe which dominates the room. She wants to paint it, brighten the place up a bit, but her mother won't let her.

'It's been in the family for generations, you'll ruin it,' she'd said.

'Exactly mum, it's time for a change, a bit of modernisation if you ask me,' but Marie hasn't asked her and so the wardrobe stays its natural dark reddish-brown. The doors of the wardrobe never close - not for any mechanical reason but because of the mass of cloth intestines which hang from its gut, spilling out onto the floor and spewing over its door handles. Katherine likes to think the mess in her bedroom is another trait she's inherited from her father - his maverick style of order.

From Katherine's window the fields all around are multi-coloured greens and browns, broken only by the smattering of white hogweed heads or yellow clusters of buttercups. To the right a darker, more sombre, green of potato plants. In front is a bright summery emerald sea of lettuces and to the left a chocolate brown expanse stripped of its fruits which are already sailing across to England labelled "Jersey Fresh", destined for the shelves of a chain of greengrocers.

Katherine isn't looking out of her window. She's managed to find a welcome distraction from revision in the form of a fashion catalogue she discovered buried underneath her desk. She's already spotted an outfit she knows Anne will love so she's torn out the photo to show her, folding it carefully and putting it in her school bag which sits under her desk ready for the morning.

A fly finds its way in through the half opened sash window, then begins banging and buzzing at the glass to get out. Katherine stops to watch it, wondering if it feels pain each time it knocks itself. What goes through its tiny mind as it repeats the same action over and over again? Does it have a mind? She toys with the idea of rolling up her catalogue and squashing it but she begins to feel empathy; both of them trapped inside her bedroom, desperate to escape into the big wide world. Instead she uses the catalogue as an escape aid, guiding him up the glass and over the wooden frame to where fresh air and freedom await. For Katherine, escape isn't so simple. For her there are only the history revision notes on her desk.

Finishing her last exam is nothing compared to how excited she is about going to Sands. Rumour is Darren and Mark go there every Friday and she's not about to let this opportunity to impress them go by without a mammoth effort. She's raked through her entire wardrobe checking every single hanger, picking up all the stuff from the floor where dresses and tops were enmeshed with shoes and handbags, most of which are now piled on her bed. She has finally chosen the perfect outfit. There's a buzz inside of her. Life is just about to start. Just around the corner she can feel excitement and adventure waiting. She is *so* ready for it.

5

Feb 28th 2008, London

'Margaret, it's Katherine.' There's silence for a second or two. Katherine pushes the phone closer to her ear straining to hear something.

'Katherine! How are you? ...It's been a while.'

'Yes I know. I'm sorry.' More silence, the nature of their adult conversation. Katherine grinds her teeth; the habit her dentist has tried desperately to stop. 'How are you all?'

'Oh we're fine, we're fine. I suppose you've seen the news?' her sister asks.

'Yes. I can't believe it. Is it really true?' Katherine momentarily forgets to be defensive.

'Well, the Independent reckons they've found the body of an eleven to fifteen-year-old. It's just awful. Everybody here is so shocked, I can tell you,' Margaret's voice falters.

'I was too. I mean I just had no idea anything like that could have been going on. They're talking about possibly seven children being buried there. How could nobody have missed them? Children can't just disappear like that surely?' Katherine asks her sister but doesn't expect the answer.

'I don't know Katherine; I really don't know...Is that why you called?'

'No. Actually I was calling because I'm coming over to Jersey,' Katherine feels the common ground slip away. Returning to her defensive position she waits for her words to create their impact.

'Really?' Margaret sounds genuinely surprised, 'Great...work is it?'

'No. Not work… I'll tell you about it when I come. My flights are booked, next Monday. Don't worry I'm not expecting you to put me up or anything, I was going to book a hotel...'

'Don't be ridiculous,' Margaret jumps in, 'Are you not staying at yours? With John?'

'No, I thought best not to.'

'Well, you must stay with us, this is as much your home as it's mine after all. You don't really want to stay in a hotel do you, away from us?'

Katherine thinks the idea is more than just a tempting one, but she's boxed into a corner. She should have said it was work and then Margaret wouldn't have pushed her so hard to stay with them.

'Only if you're sure Margaret,' she replies, 'I wouldn't want to cause any trouble.' Her sister hesitates at this, and Katherine wonders what's going through her mind.

'I'm sure. What time do you get in?'

'Monday morning at eleven.'

'OK I'll be at the airport to get you.'

'Oh you don't need...'

'No arguments. Eleven o'clock I'll be there.'

Katherine and Margaret speak little, but scale a mountain of emotion.

There have been so many reasons for Margaret to be annoyed with Katherine over the years, and she knows it. She's been a rubbish auntie, a crap sister, a negligent daughter and then there's John. So many reasons not to return home.

After the phone call Katherine sits for a while in her peaceful living room, wondering if she's doing the right thing, conjuring up the landmarks of her childhood with all their resulting emotions. Their school doesn't exist anymore. St Helier town is quite different with modern offices towering over the last of the family run shops and Havre des Pas is past its tourism prime; but around the island the beaches have stayed the same. The tide may shift the sands but essentially they don't change. When she'd last been over to Jersey, for her mother's funeral, they'd queued up for hot chocolates at Big Vern's Cafe in St Ouen's bay. Next door the Sands nightclub has gone, now self-catering apartments, but the setting was enough to turn the sweetness of the chocolate bitter in her mouth. It was tough being there, back where it had all begun.

6

June 1976, Jersey

Sands is a white building set just off St Ouen's beach. A fairly ugly building for such a beautiful setting. When Marie drops Katherine off for the evening she can see people have already spilled out of the disco onto the golden beach. Usually they're not allowed to leave the club, but the slight sea breeze tonight has proven too much of an attraction for the groups of teenagers who have broken away from their dancing to pose and cool off outside.

Katherine waves her mother off and then waits for Anne. Tonight is the culmination of a thousand teenage dreams. Her exams are over - that means the end of school and the start of a new life of independence. Together with her best friend she is about to embark on a voyage of discovery: boys, work, being able to make her own decisions about life. This night is the climax to all those months of revision, to all the plans and ideas she and Anne have talked about. They're going to be on cloud nine tonight and nothing's going to touch them - unless it's Darren or Mark!

Katherine's early as she's eager to ensure

her mother has left before Anne gets there. The last thing she wants is a scene with her mother. She's told Marie she's meeting some girls from school - and she isn't lying, not really.

As it is, Anne is late. Katherine chooses a spot in the car park to wait where she can see all the comings and goings at Sands. The entrance to the club is seaward, but there is already a small queue forming to get in through the heavy wooden doors propped open for ventilation.

She's desperate to get inside and keeps checking her watch. It's twenty minutes past their arranged time, and over half an hour since she arrived, before she sees Anne's dad's Volvo turn into the car park. Katherine watches as Anne gets out and walks towards the nightclub. She doesn't look up as her father quickly reverses to leave. There is no wave from his daughter, her shoulders are rounded.

'You're late.' says Katherine bounding up to her, waiting for an apology. She's bursting with excitement expecting to see the same energy and enthusiasm mirrored in her friend. There's no apology and no excitement. It throws her at first. 'I thought you were wearing your new top?' she asks Anne, trying to draw her out, but her friend just shrugs and looks down at the floor. 'What's going on, you OK?'

'Yeah I'm fine,' Anne replies.

Despite the fact Katherine can see she's

anything but fine, she decides to ignore it. This is a night she has been looking forward to forever and no-one is going to ruin it. 'Come on then, we've finished our exams, cheer up and let's party,' Katherine grabs Anne's hand and tries to chivvy her along.

Outside, standing under the surfboard sign announcing the Sands' entrance, is a bouncer who looks them up and down. From inside comes the sound of Abba's "Dancing Queen."

'You two eighteen?' he asks with a gruff London accent.

Katherine looks to Anne for one of her usual cheeky responses, but she says nothing. 'Yeah, we've just finished our A levels,' Katherine quickly replies with a confidence that surprises herself. There's no way anybody is going to stand between her and the night out she has planned. He doesn't look fully convinced but waves them in.

A wall of sweaty heat hits them as they enter, it's a dancing sauna packed with a couple of hundred young people. The two bars on their left are the main focus of the lighting - rectangular holes of bright white challenged by a multitude of bobbing heads trying to catch the bar staff's attention. The dance floor at the back is marked by swirling coloured lights and it's in that direction they head as soon as they get inside.

It isn't easy to wriggle through the throng of

sweaty bodies to the tiny dance floor which is sticky underfoot and so cramped you can barely sway let alone let rip and become a dancing queen. Nonetheless they start a dance, of sorts, and Katherine notices although Anne is beginning to cheer up, she's still not on top form.

Weeks of anticipation and exam revision mean there's going to be no stopping Katherine from enjoying herself tonight. She carries on regardless, eyes sweeping the whole room, searching for Darren or Mark - hoping the latter might be a cure for Anne's blues.

Three dances later and they're already flagging in the heat. Some boy, quite tall, a couple of years older than Katherine, and not bad looking for that matter, asks her for a dance. He looks like a cross between the guy who plays Starsky and David Essex. She says no. He's decidedly sweaty, probably just a tourist, and besides she's saving herself for Darren - the only man in her heart. The boy looks dejected for a few minutes, then two records later she spots him smoochy dancing with another girl. Katherine's a little miffed he'd gotten over her so quickly but his behaviour reinforces her suspicion he's just here on holiday.

Katherine's getting really thirsty and so motions to Anne she needs a drink. They begin their battle to the bar, dodging the hard core dancers, heading towards the white light. It's then she sees them. Mark first, then Darren. The pair of them together, standing looking at the dance floor. They've probably been watching them all this time. Her heart does a triple somersault.

Darren looks as fabulous as always. He's a well-built lad, product of a farming upbringing. He's got a short sleeved T shirt on which accentuates his shoulders and biceps, plus a pair of stone coloured trousers which only just seem to contain his muscular legs and arse. She can't believe their luck. The two of them stood together. She alters their course slightly and charts a path that will take them right past the boys. Just to be inches from them, breathe the same air as them, is going to be exciting enough.

Then it gets better. As they draw level Darren splits away from Mark and leans over touching Katherine's arm. An electric tingle screams its way to her core.

His voice is in her ear, 'Do you two want a drink?'

There's no hesitation, she's lived this moment a thousand times already in her dreams. She knows exactly what to say. 'Yes thanks, that would be great. I'll have a Martini and lemonade please. Anne what would you like?'

Anne has a look of utter shock on her face.

Katherine hopes hers isn't recording what she's thinking quite so graphically. 'Same thanks,' Anne blurts out.

Darren says something to Mark, they exchange a few words glancing over at the girls, and then Mark turns and walks to the bar. Anne and Katherine exchange a wide-eyed look of amazement with each other before moving into the spot he's vacated to avoid other people pushing past.

Darren attempts some conversation, 'Haven't seen you in here before?' Katherine thinks he says, but talking isn't really working, she can barely hear him, and her throat, which would have preferred a glass of water to a Martini, is so dry she can barely shout above the noise for him to hear. On the plus side it means he has to lean in right up close to her, their cheeks occasionally brushing against each other, the feeling of her soft skin against his adolescent stubble making her heart beat even faster.

Mercifully for Anne and the art of conversation, Mark returns quite quickly with the drinks, putting them into their hands and simultaneously grabbing Anne's free one with the mimed suggestion they all go outside to cool off. Katherine would have walked through fire if Darren suggested it. She isn't sure if Anne has cheered up, but she seems as willing as she is to go along with the new turn of events and Katherine is as sure as hell going to enjoy every minute.

The bouncer isn't happy about them leaving. 'You're either inside the club or out,' he says, but it doesn't deter them. They are however, not allowed to take their glasses outside, and so the four of them are forced to down the ice cold drinks in one go. After the bite of the cold on the roof of her mouth, the warm rush of alcohol quickly goes to Katherine's head. The combination of heat, dehydration, and the thrill of the moment creates a light-headed floaty sort of feeling she's unfamiliar with. She follows Darren, his rough hand clasping hers, as he leads her to the beach.

They kick off their shoes the second their feet touch sand, relishing squishing the tiny cool grains through their toes, digging in deeper to find the fresh damp sand beneath. The tide is out; the calm sea waves barely audible in the distance. Jersey's massive tidal reach means the sea line is now hundreds of yards away from where it had been just six hours before and only the occasional splosh, as a wave catches another awkwardly, makes its way up the beach and through the throbbing competition of the disco.

The boys lead them along, Corbiere lighthouse direction, past shadowy humps of other giggling chatting groups littering the sands, the odd wisp of smoke rising up. They continue towards the edge of the teenage tide where dark shapes of couples lie prone together, no words rising from their entwined forms.

Finally, it is relatively quiet except for the thump, thump of the disco along the beach. The four of them drop down onto the sand, separating slightly into two couples, beginning an awkward teenage courtship. Katherine is still feeling a little woozy from the Martini so she isn't surprised when Mark informs them it was a double. Anne and she giggle awkwardly, swapping silly comments between each other for support. As the darkness begins to melt their shyness, the conversations become more personal and their voices drop to whispers.

'You're at La Vielle Farm aren't you?' questions Darren. Katherine nods. 'Thought so, seen you round there a few times, I sometimes go over with dad to the Binets. You go to St Helier Girls don't you?'

She nods again. 'Well I did,' she quickly qualifies, 'we've just finished our exams. You work for your dad now right?'

It's Darren's turn to nod. There's silence for a few moments and she becomes aware of his breathing whilst her mind struggles to concentrate and find something else to say.

'I like your top,' he says awkwardly, nodding at her blouse which she'd agonised so long over wearing.

'Thanks,' she mumbles. Then inspiration hits. 'You must have had a tough time of it this year, what with the drought,' she tries, and hits on a good topic.

'Yeah, it's bloody awful. Nothing's been growing, fields are dust. Had a Centenier round this week cos Dad's been damming one of the streams.'

'Yeah I heard the Honorary Police are cracking down,' Katherine adds. Mr Binet had been talking to her mother just a few days ago.

'Made Dad unblock it, said he'd be fined heavy otherwise,' Darren looks off in the distance dejectedly. She tries to bring him back.

'Should have been good for your strawberries though, all this sun?'

'You're kidding right? No. They ripened too quick, had to chuck a whole load away, and they're too small, not enough water. We'll make a big loss on those too.' They both sigh and look out towards the nothingness of the sea. She's beginning to wish she hadn't brought the subject up, it's depressed him.

Above them the sky is marbled black and grey, and the white segment of moon hangs admiring its reflection in the water. Katherine is aware Anne and Mark seem to have moved further into the shadows. She tries not to let that, and the thought of what could be about to happen, panic her and searches her mind again for something to fill the silence. She isn't being very imaginative. All she can think of besides him, is the drought and the hot summer - mind you that's all anyone's been talking about lately.

'Why don't you cuddle up to me?' he suggests, his voice softening. He shuffles up closer to her and puts his arm around her shoulder.

She is in a state of excited tension, sitting stiffly, not sure what to do next and too nervous to take a guess. Her body feels like the string on a bow pulled and ready to fire. He kisses her gently on the cheek and her left hand which has been hovering, comes to rest on his thigh. It is solid beneath her fingertips. Alcohol rushes to her head, and blood to other parts of her body she's not been fully aware of before. She turns to say something, yet another inane comment about the drought, but he catches her unawares placing his mouth over hers so only a little squeak comes out. He kisses her softly at first, testing. Then when he finds her willing, takes her head in his hands and kisses long and hard; thrusting his tongue into her mouth, touching hers with his, searching, caressing. Inside of her a whirlwind is building.

He gently pulls her down onto the sand so they are lying facing each other. As she falls back her hand slips down from its safe spot on his leg and brushes past his crotch. She nearly gasps as she feels the hard shape in his trousers. It's her first encounter with an erection and its presence is both threatening and exciting.

Darren runs his hands down her back, every movement sending her skin into raptures. He is kissing her again. Sensual, passionate, wanting.

Then it happens.

7

March 2008, London

A week after the letter arrived, Katherine sits in the departure lounge at Gatwick airport watching the multi-coloured, multi-national waves of people swelling and subsiding as they drift from the flight information screen to Duty Free, from snack bars to sunglasses kiosk; until they all eventually slip away to a boarding gate somewhere and the promise of a new destination. Usually she likes that about airports: the constant flow of anticipation, whether a holiday, seeing old friends, or just the welcome familiarity of returning home. Right now though Katherine feels adrift in a world turned hostile.

She may have left Jersey but it has always been her rock. Brush away the tax haven tarnish and find the real Jersey underneath and whether she admits it or not, she's been secretly proud of her home island: its beauty, independence and history. Now every time she hears Jersey mentioned everyone tuts and shakes their heads, 'Terrible news,' or 'Not so perfect after all.'

The week's papers have brought yet more

revelations about the abuse at the children's home. Katherine feels her island's shame and expects to return to a Jersey under siege.

When it's her turn to make the journey to the departure gate she quietly stands in line before handing over her boarding pass. She sees the security photograph come up on the screen - a middle aged woman, moderately attractive but nothing special. The kind of middle aged woman who can just blend into a crowd, become virtually invisible in a sea of people: mousy hair that was once blond, skin that's lost the glow of youth, eyes reflecting weariness, not life. She takes back her boarding card and disappears into the waiting lounge.

Britain can look so pleasant from the skies. As the plane rises up into the air over Gatwick, she looks down on a spread of mosaic fields, different shapes, and different hues of green. You can see where big business farms, large chunks of land given over to one colour. Nearer to the towns are smaller fields adorned with the wooden shapes of Jesus's birth - home to the tiny insect sized horses which dot the landscape. Row upon row of houses interspersed by the odd park, or the prosperous ascent of office blocks in the town centre. You can't see the graffiti or the rubbish in the streets. You can't smell the fumes from the ever pumping artery of a motorway or hear its incessant drone, it's a sanitised view of Britain.

Up into the clouds for what feels like only a few minutes, on top of the world, nothing between her and the sun. No other life forms, a space where anything seems possible, and nothing seems possible.

The captain announces the descent to Jersey.

Back through endless white, the stuff of dreams and songs, until suddenly there is the sea; clear aqua green and blue, sparkling in the sunlight, broken only by the odd fluorescent buoy held to its surface by a rope, heralding the approach to land and a return to man's domain. There's no sign of waves, the movement amid the calm water only betrayed by a white tail reaching out from behind the buoys. Then beautiful sandy beaches stretching out as far as the eye can see, lined by the green of fields marking the sea's boundary. A giant fertile granite rock rising out of the ocean.

Beneath Katherine is a perfect miniature world. Tiny little granite houses with manicured gardens and glinting blue swimming pools. A farm laid out neatly with Lilliputian animals and tractors in its fields. Then it all rushes towards her, swelling in size, and the huge sandy expanse of St Ouen's beach comes into view. As the plane carries on towards the runway Katherine's mind goes back to that night at the Sands nightclub, as it has so many times in the years since. She can still remember the emotions, even the sounds and smells. As the tyres bump down onto the tarmac and the pilot switches the engines into counter thrust, she's back there again - wondering what she could have done differently.

8

June 1976, Jersey

Darren's passion is thrilling every molecule of Katherine's body. Their kissing has grown more urgent and he's moved closer still to her now, her body magnetised by his; the pair of them entwining each other as though trying to weld into one. This, thinks Katherine, is what making love must be.

Then suddenly from behind comes a slap, followed by an indignant 'Fuck!' from Mark Vibert as Anne's shadowy figure scrambles off, running away up the beach.

'Anne!' Katherine shouts after her, but she's gone.

'What's all that about?' Mark says, standing up and holding his hands out in embarrassment. 'Prick teaser,' he suddenly yells after Anne, more aggressive now he realises they are staring at him in shock. 'I don't know what her problem is. I didn't do anything,' he qualifies to them.

Katherine rises to Anne's defence. 'You must have done something to upset her,' she finds confidence in her concern.

'I did nothing for fuck's sake,' he almost

shouts back, 'we're getting all cosy, she's kissing me and then slap. I get it across the face. There's something wrong with that girl.'

'I'd better go after her,' Katherine turns to Darren.

'Aw come on, she'll be fine. Stay here, I bet she'll be back in a few minutes. Mark can go look for her, can't you Mark?' but Mark only grunts back reluctantly.

Katherine isn't so stupid as to think he actually wants to go after Anne. She hesitates, her mind cart wheeling options and possible scenarios. She's been waiting for this moment, to be alone with Darren for forever, she doesn't want to go...but... it's no use, the moment has gone. At least for now.

'I'm sorry, I have to go,' she says to Darren as she stands, picking up Anne's discarded sandals and handbag as well as her own. She pauses, waiting for Darren to say he'll call her, that he's had a lovely time and why don't they do it again... something. Surely after kissing her like that he'll want to meet up. He must like her a lot. She waits for him to ask for her phone number, for a tender goodbye.

'OK, see you then,' is all she gets. As she heads off into the darkness after Anne she turns round and sees the pair of them walking back towards the club, without so much as a backward glance.

It's not surprising she's really annoyed with

Anne. She's completely ruined everything. All this time Katherine's spent waiting to get a chance like this with Darren and Anne goes and throws some stupid tantrum. She'd been in a grump right from the start. She of all people knows how much Katherine likes Darren. Is she completely and utterly selfish or what?

Stomping in sand isn't easy, but Katherine manages it. A part of her thinks it's very unlike Anne to behave like this, especially as she's supposed to like Mark too, so maybe something is up, maybe he really did do something to upset her. It's this last thought that keeps her walking.

There is a huge expanse of beach for her to search, Anne could be anywhere; she might even have disappeared up a slipway, or the steps that lead up to the Five Mile Road.

'Anne, Anne, it's me. Where are you?' she stomps on, swearing as she stubs her toe on a large stone and occasionally looking behind; just in case Darren and Mark have had a change of heart and are coming to help. The beach is empty.

After what seems like forever in the darkness, she finds her. Katherine had nearly walked past but she hears a snuffle and sees a huddled shape sitting in the corner of one of the old gun emplacements. Anne's definitely crying so despite her own disappointment Katherine errs on the side of sympathy.

'What's the matter? What happened? What did he do to you?' the dark shape simply sniffles back. 'Look...do you want me to call your parents?' Katherine continues.

'No,' says Anne forcefully. She leans forward out of the shadows, her face illuminated by the light from the pub up on the road above. She looks unusually pale and her cheeks are wet. There are dark circles under her eyes accentuated by the road top lighting. 'No, you mustn't. You mustn't say anything to them. I'll be fine.'

Katherine isn't convinced. 'I thought you really liked Mark?' she offers, tempted to add, *like I like Darren,* but thinks better of it.

'I thought I did,' is all Anne replies. The silence yawns between them. 'He started to grope me. I didn't like it.'

'Grope you? What did he do, did he force himself on you?' More silence, 'Anne did he?'

'Sort of...Yeah...' is all she mumbles.

Katherine isn't quite sure what 'groping' entails, but it's obviously serious enough to upset Anne quite badly. She's also not sure what to do next. 'Maybe we should tell the police then?' she offers.

'Don't be ridiculous,' Anne snaps back, 'They'll just say it's my fault for being on the beach with him, that I let him. It'll be my word against his. Or they'll call me a silly little girl who's making things up.'

Katherine doesn't know what to say now, the ferocity of her friend's reply takes her by surprise. 'Do you want to go and get a drink?' she offers. It's something she's heard on TV shows when something shocking has happened.

'No,' the dark huddle replies. She's stopped crying, but her voice is choked with misery.

'Shall I call a taxi then?' as Katherine asks she fumbles in her pocket to make sure she's still got the ten pence her mother gave her earlier for the phone box.

'Yes,' is Anne's weak reply and she stands up, clambering down from the rock shelf onto the sand. Katherine would far rather be walking back in the opposite direction to go and find Darren, resume where they'd left off, but Anne needs her, and so she heads towards the stone steps leading up to the road and the La Pulente pub where she can call for a taxi.

Anne barely speaks or looks her in the face whilst they wait, or even once they're in the cab. Katherine isn't sure if she is upset or embarrassed. Either way they sit in virtual silence for the whole of the journey home. Her mind keeps going over and over the events on the beach. She can't help but enjoy the memories of her time with Darren, but she searches for any signs that she could have heard or seen something was going wrong with Anne and Mark before they heard the slap. She can't.

Katherine doesn't want to forget a second of her evening with Darren: his touch, the taste of him, the smell of him. She discreetly dips her head towards her left shoulder - she can still catch the scent of his aftershave on her top from where she'd lain against him.

Then her attention is caught by the reflection of Anne in the side window. She sits staring blankly out into the darkness.

9

March 3rd 2008, Jersey

Katherine's mind is full of memories, worries and regrets. As they touch down at Jersey airport she is swamped by a tsunami of the past: that evening on the beach, Margaret, their mother, John and the ghost of Anne. She almost expects to see them as she looks out of the plane window, lined up to greet her like a scene from an old "This is Your Life" programme.

Whilst her fellow passengers busy themselves with gathering belongings, checking the netted seat pockets in front of them and pilfering the in-flight magazines, Katherine sits thinking. The dong of the seat belt sign turning off sounds around the cabin and everyone rises from their places - an ovation of passengers. Katherine remains, soaked in her memories, steeling herself for what is to come.

She waits for the rest of the passengers to shuffle forward to the doors, one by one, before standing at the top of the steps, taking in the island air and plunging downwards, dispersing. Katherine is almost reluctant to leave the plane, but she picks herself up and moves through the airport building barely glancing at the images of beautiful beaches or the promises of the wealth management ads on the walls.

Into the arrivals hall she joins around thirty others, a flock of herons pond-side, gathered around the luggage carousel waiting for the siren to sound and the rubber belt to squeak its circular path.

As she waits she flicks through one of the free Jersey Recommended guides; spotting familiar names with more contemporary faces: de Gruchy the department store, Durrell, no longer the Jersey Zoo she'd grown up with; and Mont Orgueil, or Gorey Castle as most people call it, newly re-furbished. A modern facelift for an ancient visage now open to foreign visitors, instead of trying to repel them from Jersey's shores. Katherine thinks perhaps she might like to visit it, do a bit of sightseeing. Revisit a few of her *good* childhood memories.

Finally, she has both of her suitcases on a trolley and she points it towards the big sliding doors which lead out into the Arrivals greeting area. The last time she did this it was for her mother's funeral, and a red eyed Margaret had been waiting for her, looking tired and pale.

This time Katherine quickly spots her sister, hovering at the side behind a metal barrier, conveniently protected from any urge to rush forward and embrace her. She has a healthy glow about her but, even after all this time, Katherine can sense the tension in her sister's stiff hug and kiss of welcome.

'Hello Katherine,' Margaret says. Even her greeting comes across as having required effort.

'Hello Margaret. How are you all?' her response is in turn stilted. Twenty-one years of unfamiliarity has had its toll on their relationship.

'We're great thanks. I just need to pay for the car park over here, and then we'll head home.' Margaret points to a ticket machine just to the side of where they stand and the pair separate, almost relieved by the need for its mundane distraction.

Margaret's car is an old Mercedes estate that, had Jersey got an MOT system, would almost certainly fail and not be on the roads. In the back is evidence of many family days spent at the beach. A well-used boogie board, sand, wet suit and towels. All are shoved over to one side to make room for Aunty Katherine's big cases.

'James uses the car sometimes,' Margaret explains away the debris in her boot.

'How are the children?' Katherine questions, prompted by the evidence in front of her, but as she says it she realises it sounds more like a business woman asking a client, than two sisters talking. Margaret's children are almost complete strangers to her, she hasn't witnessed their growing up or shared in their lives.

'They're all great thank you. Sara is just finishing her second year at Uni.'

'My God! I can't believe she's been there two years, so that must make her…'

'Twenty.' Margaret says it rather too quickly. 'Last week.'

Katherine who has been trying to sound interested and knowledgeable about Sara is knocked completely into touch. She's missed her twentieth birthday, some Godmother she turned out to be! She's silent for a few moments, but refuses to give in.'What's James doing?' They're pulling out of the airport now, heading past the bowling alley and big luxury car garage, before turning right down the hill towards Beaumont and the coast road.

'He's taking his exams and is going to have a year off before applying for University.'

'That sounds exciting. What's he going to do?'

'Get a part time job and spend the summer in Jersey on the beach, is the plan. Most of the time he's at St Ouen with his mates. After that, he's applied to a couple of ski companies to become a chalet rep. He's looking at doing law eventually, so we'll see. Sophie has started at St Clement school, it's lovely; a really nice new building, just across the road from the old one.' Katherine nods her head, digging up forgotten images in her mind of the old school. 'So, how's things with you?' Margaret's tone is clearly fishing.

Katherine knows she must be wondering why all of a sudden she's decided to return home, 'Fine thanks, work's going well,' she's not ready to share her thoughts and plans yet; and if she's honest, she's not really sure what they are anyway. Something catches her eye in the side pocket of the door, it's a smooth round pebble, purple-ish red in colour and speckled with lots of different pastel colours, a small granite egg. Katherine picks it out and turns it over in her hands. It's quite beautiful in its simplicity.

'That's one of Sophie's finds,' Margaret qualifies, stealing a quick glance from the road to look at her sister. 'We're always having to repatriate shells and rocks back to the beach, otherwise we'd have a house full.' A young Margaret wandering a beach gathering pebbles and shells appears in Katherine's mind, a childhood memory freed by the trigger of a new generation.

They're turning left onto the coast road now, and Katherine glances at her sister as she drives. Her dark hair is beginning to show the odd grey hair at the front, and the years of Jersey's sun tanning her olive skin has allowed the wrinkles to etch their mark on her face.

Katherine can't help but notice Margaret also seems to have put on more weight, even since the last time she saw her. Not that she's obese or anything, just a spare tyre or two around her middle and, at a guess, Katherine would say the tops of her thighs rub each other. She started getting heavier after she stopped her post round, all that cycling had kept her fit. Admittedly Margaret has always been slightly chunkier, but it's become more obvious as they've got older.

It's a shame, thinks Katherine, it means Margaret won't be able to borrow her clothes. She knows her sister can't afford the stuff she buys. Today Margaret's standard range M & S jeans and top look distinctly utilitarian compared to her own sleek designer trousers and cashmere jumper. She wonders if that rankles with Margaret. Then again, she always was a homebody compared to Katherine.

10

June 1976, Jersey - Margaret

The day after Katherine celebrated the end of her exams at Sands nightclub, it soon becomes obvious to her sister she is phone watching. Margaret had been shopping with their mother, leaving Katherine in bed, and she is still nowhere to be seen even after they'd returned home. That is perfect as far as Margaret is concerned because she's looking forward to having the whole kitchen to herself while their mother does some overtime at work.

She runs her fingers along the row of white tin storage jars on the dresser, full of flours and sugars, rice and raisins, choosing what she needs. All her ingredients are placed on the oak worktop which has probably been there almost as long as the house. Butter comes from the fridge, which shakes and rattles with a shiver each time its motor kicks into action, or turns off. Its white door is rusted and chipped around the edges from years of use. The chrome handle fell off ages ago, and to open it Margaret has to dig her nails into the rubber seal of the door and tug. Consequently, the seal has started to come away from the door where they've missed the right spot and the grey rubber is cracking with age; but it's like an old member of the family now. She can't imagine it not being there.

The kitchen is Margaret's favourite room, soaked in the aroma of generations of cooking. In the winter she'll come and sit in the wooden armchair by the Rayburn to snuggle and read a book. Now, in the height of summer, she stands on the kitchen floor with bare feet - letting the stone flags draw the heat from them. She's been known to lie on it after a particularly hot walk home from school; staring up at the wooden ceiling or at the wall, where there is an old sepia photograph of their grandparents standing in the yard in traditional Jersey dress. Her grandfather is proudly holding a Jersey cow with a rosette on her collar. She's a beautiful animal with the big soft eyes and long lashes of her breed. A chain adorns her small forward facing horns. Her grandmother wears the customary white cloth bonnet and apron, both of which are still folded away carefully in a trunk in the attic. She's holding a wood and metal bucket which Margaret always imagines to be full of milk. At her grandmother's feet is a small girl with a white pinafore and little stick legs protruding from the bottom of a black skirt – their mother. She's clinging to her mother's leg, peeking out from behind her skirt, nervous like a shy kitten.

Sometimes Margaret will take down the silver framed photograph which sits centre stage on the sideboard – it's their father. She loves this image of him. He is laughing, just slightly turned away from the camera, cheeks flushed and his blond hair ruffled slightly as though he'd just run his hands through it. When Margaret concentrates on that photograph she can still hear his laugh, his voice, but only just. Their echo is disappearing with time and she's often scared she might lose them altogether; wake up one morning and not be able to see him when she closes her eyes, or hear his voice. She worries she'll forget the way he teased her when she was little, pretending to steal her nose, putting his thumb between his fingers to show her he has it. She would cry in protest feigning upset and tears, calling for mum or Katherine to help until, eventually, laughing he would pop her nose back on, giving it a kiss for good measure. They don't often talk about their father, but they all still miss him.

Their mother said she'll cook a cottage pie on her return so Margaret takes off her pinafore and heads out the back door to her little veg patch where she's been dedicatedly tending to her rows of runner beans, peas, carrots and potatoes. Desperately trying to protect them from the relentless thirsty sun.

As soon as she opens the door the change in

temperature hits her face. The yard is heavy in the heat of the day, so hot in fact, even the birds are quieter than usual. Before she's crossed it she's begun to miss the cool of the big granite farmhouse behind her, its walls built of solid stone which even today's relentless sun can't penetrate. She loves the granite of their home. It isn't a soulless dull grey; it almost seems to have a life of its own. Shimmering shards of quartz captured within it, each block an individual with its own shape and contour. One with flashes of rust and pink, another almost black. All around her the house and barn rise up solidly from the ground. Reassuring. Permanent.

By the time she's returned to the cool of the kitchen, strands of her dark hair stick to her cheeks and forehead. She searches in one of the drawers for a hair band, pulling her long hair off her face and releasing the heat trapped against her neck.

She is just about to start baking when the phone rings. Even before Margaret can put down her measuring spoon, she's already heard her sister's feet pound down the stairs. There is a murmur of voices, the phone goes down and Katherine appears through the door.

'You got a pen?'

'There's one over there,' Margaret points to where their mother makes up her shopping lists. 'You're keen to get to the phone, who was it?'

'Oh just somebody for mum that's all.' After a quick scribble Katherine is gone again, back up to her bedroom and her music.

Margaret is left to her kitchen once more.

11

March 3rd 2008, Jersey - Margaret

No one could miss the tension in the air and Margaret, driving home with her sister sitting next to her, feels like she's just picked up a stranger. It seems to her Katherine is behaving like some kind of visiting dignitary which is getting on her nerves. She can almost see her sister look down her sophisticated London nose at her.

'Once I've dropped you at home,' says Margaret, 'I'll have to pop out again to pick up Sophie, and I've promised James I'll get him from the surf shop. He's taken his board to be repaired.' That will show you who's important in my life, she thinks. She can almost feel Katherine bristle next to her, no doubt put out by the fact her sister isn't going to be running around after her.

'No problem,' replies Katherine in her clipped tone which no longer carries any indication of the Jersey accent she once had.

'Have you eaten? I've made you some lunch,' Margaret continues, 'I'll be back by about four anyway. It'll give you the chance to unpack and chill out before the children arrive home.' Margaret isn't going to let her accuse her of not being a good host.

'Thanks.' Katherine replies. She's staring out the car window as they drive by tall office blocks which dominate the St Helier skyline. 'There's a lot more building been going on since I was here last.' The road they're on has been reclaimed from the sea. Off to their right is The Waterfront, a totally reclaimed part of the island which now sports apartment complexes, a multi-screen cinema and swimming pool.

'What's going on with the Weighbridge?' Katherine's voice rises with surprise, the first hint of any emotion Margaret has seen since she arrived. They're just a little further on and about to leave St Helier behind and head through the tunnel to the East of the island. To their left is an open area of tarmac which appears to be being excavated. Last time Katherine was here the bus station stood in front of the Royal Yacht Hotel. Now the hotel has been completely revamped and the area in front is full of yellow diggers, men in hard hats and various States of Jersey vans.

'They're turning it into a kind of park,' replies Margaret 'There's a new bus station on the Esplanade. So... how long are you here for?' Her tone struggles to belie the true extent of her interest. She's been dying to ask, but purposefully stares straight ahead at the road and avoids Katherine's gaze.

'I'm not sure to be honest,' she pauses, thinking, 'I got a letter from Anne's mum.'

'Really?' Margaret glances quickly at her, shocked. 'What about?' Her hands grip the steering wheel tighter and she hopes Katherine doesn't notice her jaw harden and the colour drain from her face.

'She's dying. Wants to see me, talk to me about something, about the year Anne died.'

Margaret struggles to find the words to respond.

'I think I owe her that,' adds Katherine.

'You don't owe her anything,' replies Margaret, trying hard to keep the venom inside of herself.

'Now you sound like mum.' Katherine hits back.

'Well maybe mum was right about a few things…' The sentence has more than one target and Katherine knows it.

'Look,' says Katherine interrupting, 'I'm not here to start an argument. I've come over to see you all, I know it's been a long time, but I'm going to see Anne's mum at some point too. I need to.'

Margaret doesn't answer, then a thought crosses her mind. 'There's nothing wrong is there?' she asks.

'There's nothing wrong.' Katherine smiles, the first sign the pair of them might be more than just acquaintances sharing a car journey.

'Does John know? He hasn't told me if he does.'

'I emailed him.' There is silence in the car for a while as the two women contemplate what Katherine has just said.

Margaret is fuming again, "emailed", her sister can't even be bothered to speak to her own husband - one of the nicest men she knows. The way she's treated him! As for Anne's mother, well that is one hell of a bucket of worms. She certainly doesn't deserve anyone's respect, dying or not. Katherine should have gotten over Anne's death years ago. Why dredge it all up now? What does she want with her sister? What if Anne's mother tells Katherine the truth? There are some secrets which should stay buried.

Margaret feels herself bite too hard on her bottom lip, the earthy taste of blood serving to re-focus her mind on the road ahead.

12

June 1976, Jersey

The morning after the night at Sands, Katherine is dreading the questions from her mother as to why she'd come home early. She stays in bed, even though she isn't really sleeping, alternating between day dreams of Darren and remembering the nightmare with Anne. She keeps one ear out for the phone, he is bound to ring sometime today and she's going to be ready.

When she hears her mother and Margaret leave in the car to go shopping, Katherine gets out of bed and heads straight for the phone in their hallway. She calls Anne.

'You OK?' she asks as soon as she hears her voice on the other end.

'Yeah. Sorry about last night. I know you really like Darren but...' Anne trails off.

'So what exactly did Mark do?' Katherine presses, a little annoyed Anne has taken until now to finally realise she'd ruined her evening.

'Just started touching me up...you know,' she replies.

Katherine doesn't, this is all new to her. 'Are you sure we shouldn't tell the police or your parents, somebody...'

'No.' Anne comes back vehemently. 'I've told you no. They'll just say it's my fault. Please you must promise me, swear to me you won't tell a single person about this. Please Katherine. Nobody, not Margaret, not your mum, not anyone.'

Katherine can tell she means it. 'OK,' she reluctantly replies. There is nothing but the sound of the phone whirring for a few moments. 'So, did he rape you?' Katherine isn't exactly sure what rape constitutes, but she's got a fairly good idea and it's serious. She knows Darren and she started to *make love* last night, his tender kisses and gentle touches showing just how much he cares about her, but Mark - well he'd obviously done something completely different altogether.

'I don't... well, I guess.' The fight has gone out of Anne's voice again. 'He put his hand under my skirt and blouse. I kept pushing him away, but he kept on coming back again.'

There is further silence between them as Katherine tries to take in what she's just said. The thing is, she can't help it, but the thought of Darren's hand on her skin is an altogether pleasant one; there must have been more to it than that.

'So,' Anne breaks the silence, 'how did it go with Darren then?'

Katherine ignores the fake cheerfulness of

her friend's voice, desperate to share her experience. 'Oh Anne, he's just so gorgeous. His legs, they're solid muscle, and he's such a good kisser.'

'When are you going to see him again?' Anne is trying to sound interested.

'I don't know.'

'He's got your number though?'

'No, things were a bit fraught after you left,' Katherine feels a tad guilty at the silence that comment elicits but what did Anne expect? Why is she asking her about Darren, questioning his feeling towards her? He obviously likes her after his display of affection. Maybe Anne's jealous.

Katherine's fear is Darren's been put off by what happened between Anne and Mark - whatever it was. It's certainly going to be awkward if they start going out together, but they'll figure it out. Love conquers all, right?

13

March 3rd 2008, Jersey

Standing in their farmhouse Katherine has the feeling she's arrived on an old film set; a stranger in familiarity. A viewer who has somehow found themselves inside a movie they've watched a thousand times.

Coming home is always a massive trip down memory lane for Katherine. Although Margaret and her family are all around, the essential core of the house has stayed the same since they were children. There are some new wall coverings and carpets, some more modern pieces of furniture and technology has invaded, but it's still easy for Katherine to close her eyes and remember back to when they were children.

The kitchen is probably the least changed room of the house, the main difference the new appliances: a dishwasher and a shiny white fridge/freezer instead of the old one. The chopping board is still in residence, oiled and cared for, the scars and dents from years of use badges of honour on its surface for the thousands of dinners in which it has played a role. Their father's photograph remains centre stage on the sideboard, surrounded by smiley images of the children growing up and watched over by their grandparents on the wall. It has always been, and remains, the heart of this house.

Once Margaret leaves to pick up Sophie, Katherine takes the chance to look into her old bedroom, now Sara's. It's a lot neater than when it belonged to her. There's a new bed made up ready for Sara's return from Uni but the old mahogany wardrobe still dominates, still unpainted; its doors neatly shut hiding its soft insides. The windows have been double glazed to keep out the draughts and there are more houses visible from the bedroom window. A small neat estate of multi-coloured dwellings rises on the far right of the horizon. The fields are still there in the foreground - only they're like shimmering pools of water reflecting the grey sky. All uniformly covered in plastic sheeting to protect the valuable Jersey Royal potato plants growing in the soil beneath.

Katherine turns back to look at the bedroom. This could have been her daughter's room. In the car Margaret's busy schedule with her family re-awakened the old scar, reminding her of a life that isn't hers. She's come to terms with the cards she's been dealt, but their edges are sharp, still able to cut if she handles them without concentration.

Standing in her old room it's strange to

know their mother won't call her or appear at the door. She knew Marie was disappointed when she stayed away in London and, as she put it, 'Chose a career over family and love'. She'd warned her she'd be a lonely old woman in a big City, more than once trying emotional blackmail for having to suffer her daughter living so far away. 'I hardly know you these days,' or 'We never see you.' Perhaps Katherine should have told her, but the moment just never seemed right. She'd become defensive and they wouldn't talk for a while. Then life, or rather death, took away the choice.

Her mother's presence is missing from the house. Katherine can feel its loss, but she also knows Marie would be horrified at the thought of her going to see Anne's mum - and she'd make sure Katherine knew it. There are several loose ends to their relationship and one of them is the question which will never be answered: why did Marie dislike Anne so much?

14

August 1976, Jersey

Before hot July finishes with the world it makes one last big effort to leave its mark. A massive earthquake hits China on the 28th of the month. Hundreds of thousands are killed, and television screens are dominated by images of the misery of the bereaved and homeless. In the UK it's the water shortage and the summer heat that continues to dominate minds, and on August 13th a state of emergency is declared in Jersey; followed by water rationing. The drought has gone on for so long the Fire Chief warns of near desert conditions massively increasing the risk of fire. Farmers are desperate, their cattle thirsty, crops failing all over the island and the Government is talking about compensation packages to help them through the worst.

For Katherine the water shortage is a peripheral annoyance. Whilst she waits for her exam results she's got a Saturday job at Dorothy Perkins in town. The ad for a 'Part Time Fashion opportunity' had been in the Jersey Evening Post, and she'd gone straight in to see the manageress.

'A two-week trial at seven pounds a day for a shift, that's eight forty-five until five forty-five,' she reported back to her mother. She's been there three weeks already, and loves getting the little paper packet full of cash at the end of each day.

Since that night at Sands the only time she's seen Darren or Mark is when they've walked past the front of the shop. She's glad they can't see her because she's too embarrassed to speak to Darren. She'd spent days waiting for the phone to ring, hoping he'd get in contact, making excuses when he didn't - but there was nothing. She feels humiliated. It's obvious he'd only been after one thing, just like his friend. How can she have got it so badly wrong?

Mark is a different matter. She has so often in her head walked right up to him and told him what she thinks of him. She's rehearsed her lines over and over. Now she knows what they're both like she can't believe she'd ever doubted Anne. She should have been there for her, done something more to help instead of being wrapped up in her own silly crush.

Anne seems haunted by the experience, almost a different person since that day. Whenever they see each other her friend seems fine for a bit, they'll be chatting away, trying on a new eye shadow, or lying in the field planning what they're going to do once they've got their results - then suddenly a look will come over Anne's face. It's like the shadow of clouds before a storm and each time Katherine sees it, she knows it's the precursor to her growing quiet and distant. She loses her every time. Anne won't tell Katherine what's wrong. She asks if it's Mark and Anne denies it, but she knows it must be. She's never kept anything from her before and it's straining their relationship. It makes Katherine feel angry and guilty. When Anne calls her up to arrange to go out she keeps finding excuses. Anne's just not fun to be around anymore.

The weather is the one thing that hasn't altered for weeks; no months. Every morning Katherine wakes up to the same view of sunshine burning in through the curtains at her bedroom windows. The sashes are open as much as possible but no air disturbs the dust on the windowsills. Today is no exception. The air is thick, dense, as though the oxygen has been mixed with cornflour to make it sticky and heavy. Blue skies might be a sight to look forward to in more usual times but, after six months of virtually no rainfall and incessant heat, she longs for the sight of a black cloud and a cool hard breeze to blow it in. The heatwave has the effect of making the summer seem endless. She can't imagine being cold, or remember wanting to lean against the Rayburn for warmth. The feeling of sluggish, overbearing heat seems to have taken over all her senses.

Today is different though. Today they get their exam results. It seems strange going back to school, empty of the babble of girls, disjointed without the constant timely reminders of the school bell. This strange lonely echo of a place seems somehow in keeping with how she's felt lately in her friendship with Anne. Things just aren't the same between them, the bond has been damaged and she's not sure why or how to repair it; but Katherine dutifully waits for her at the entrance. Little gaggles of girls bustle past her. She exchanges hellos and the odd chat until Anne flies up to her on her bike, her face red from the heat.

'Sorry I'm late,' she gasps, 'Dad's away on business, there wasn't a bus for an hour so I cycled. God I am so scared, aren't you?' She smiles at her, the old Anne smile, and Katherine feels herself instantly relax. The barrier which seems to have been between them since Sands is gone. It's almost as though time has been reversed – the pair of them back at school, before Sands, when their friendship was the one thing they believed they could rely on.

'No problem,' Katherine says, grabbing her hand, 'Come on, let's do this.' Just like the old days they walk together through the door into reception where the results have been posted up.

Katherine feels her heart beating. This is it, the moment she's been thinking about throughout the weeks and weeks of revision. English Lit, Maths, Geography, History, RE.

'Oh my God, five A's and four B's!' Katherine exclaims, clasping her hand to her mouth, eyes wide with excitement and disbelief. 'That's great, even better than I hoped. How have you done Anne?'

'Five C's, two B's and two fails, that's good. Better than I thought too.' They give each other a hug and rush round comparing results with the other girls in the hall which buzzes and bubbles with teenage excitement. Now they have *qualifications*, pieces of paper that can be the tickets away from their boring teenage lives and onto something new, something better. Katherine is riding high. A Goddess on the crest of her knowledge. She has nine O levels, she has a future, she is somebody.

'So, when are we going to get that flat?' Anne turns to her. 'There's one come up in town near de Gruchys.'

'Not just yet, next year maybe?' Katherine tentatively replies. 'I should be able to get my apprenticeship with an accountancy firm with these grades, but it'll mean low wages whilst I'm training.' Even as she speaks she can see Anne's face change, betrayal emblazoned across it.

'But you're already working at Dorothy Perkins. We said we'd do it as soon as we got our results. I've been applying for loads of jobs.'

'It's only part time Anne, and I don't want to do it forever. I want a career. With my grades I should be able to get something good, but it means making some sacrifices at the beginning...' She trails off at the sight of Anne's face. 'Look I'm not saying we won't do it, I want to, but you've got to understand, it's just not practical right now. We couldn't afford it.'

'I see. Fine,' is the only reply. The barrier has returned, 'I'd better get going.' Anne turns, 'See you around then,' and she is gone without another word.

As Katherine walks home the sun burns the top of her head, and a headache bulldozes into position behind her eyeballs. Her brain feels fit to bust. She is elated, the stress of waiting for her results is over. She feels as if she's grown five inches taller, proved herself to the world, proved she can do what she sets out to do and this is only the start. Tomorrow she will begin applying for the apprenticeships, she's already made all the necessary enquiries. There is a pile of forms at home waiting to be filled in, and her O'levels will be just the start of her success. Katherine Gaudin has arrived in the world! But she is also fuming. Fuming about the fact this moment she wants to remember for the rest of her life has been ruined by Anne: again. By the guilt she now feels: again. By bloody Mark Vibert who has attacked her best friend and left her broken and depressed.

When Katherine sees Darren walking towards her there is no possibility she is going to hold back. She knows she promised Anne not to say anything to anyone, but Darren was there, he knows what happened already.

If only Katherine had held back. If only the next two minutes could be erased from all their memories. If only the next two minutes hadn't ended up being the two minutes she regretted for the rest of her life.

15

March 3rd 2008, Jersey

Katherine helps Margaret get dinner ready for Sophie. The little girl is shy around her aunt at first. By tea time she's into the 'showing off' stage and it has to be Aunty Katherine who sits with her while she eats. It's been a long time since Kathy was in the company of a child. She sits next to Sophie looking at her soft white skin, the gossamer blonde waves falling around her face creating a celestial effect, filled with energy and luminescent youth. Afterward Sophie is allowed half an hour of television before bath time and a bedtime story from her aunt. Katherine finds herself standing at the kitchen sink with her sister, a tea towel in one hand, looking out over the yard.

She isn't sure what she feels right now, back here in Jersey. Perhaps it's a lifetime of trying to ignore her emotions, or the shock of returning home and finding very little has changed. Maybe even that she hasn't changed as much as she thought. On the outside yes, but the inside? The fields may have different crops in, the hedges and trees taller than they were, but as she looks at the scene in front of her all she can see is herself, Anne and Margaret as young girls lying on their backs in the sunshine trying to put their small world to rights. How different would things have been if Anne was still with them? Still her best friend? If she'd been there to help Katherine through her troubles? How different would things have been if the truth had come out about her death? Nobody ever said why or how, everything was just hushed up. The truth just didn't seem to matter.

A Blue Tit springing out of the nesting box on the wall opposite catches Katherine's eye. The box has been there for as long as Katherine can remember and is black and green with age, but still clearly provides a comfy dry home for the tits. The pair can't be the same birds she watched coming and going as a child but maybe it's their grandson or great-granddaughter with their new mate. An endless cycle of birth, life and death. It's too early for it to nest yet but the little bird is obviously surveying the local accommodation, perhaps trying to grab the family home before its siblings arrive.

The granite walls of the barn are splashed with the green leaves of the Campanula flowers which live in clumps in the cracks between the stones and are just waking up after their winter sleep. By May and June, they'll be a mass of bright violet blooms. Some people don't like them because they damage the walls, but Katherine has always enjoyed their vivid show of defiant life amid the unyielding rock.

The kitchen window curtains have changed. Gone are the slightly frilly faded brown and pink that had been their mother's choice of adornment. In their place is a brighter fresh pale yellow blind which is currently rolled up to the top allowing a full clear view of the outside. The Crittall metal window frames are warped and draughty and in need of a change, but Katherine remembers when they replaced the rotting wood and had been innovative and modern. In the top left hand corner of the window is the honeysuckle waving its tendrils outside in the breeze and to the right a giant Yukka plant which once grew indoors in Margaret's sitting room, before growing so large it was relegated to the garden. That was five years ago and it's now a giant of a tree adding a Mediterranean feel to the yard.

Margaret and Katherine's talk is to fill the awkward silences which keep appearing amid the chink and clunk of the washing up. Margaret places the plates and cutlery into the dishwasher but she's used several pans for Sophie's dinner and in preparation for their own meal of beef stroganoff, which sits slowly cooking in the Rayburn.

'You remember Simone Le Cain don't you?' Margaret cheerily asks her, 'You know the one with the really long pigtails in your year at school.' Katherine's face is blank. 'Wore those really thick glasses with red frames.'

'No...no I don't.'

Margaret looks a little annoyed.

'But what about her anyway?' Katherine asks trying to retrieve the situation.

'I can't believe you don't remember her.' Margaret shakes her head, 'it doesn't really matter now then, it was only that she's one of Sophie's teachers.'

'Oh! How strange,' exclaims Katherine trying to sound interested. There is another awkward silence. 'What time is Robert coming back?' she asks. He's usually home a lot earlier than this.

'About half six probably. He's not a postie anymore. You know that don't you?' Margaret looks at Katherine sideways, but she's staring at the pan in her hand, carefully wiping off every trace of water as though her life depends on it. They both know the answer to that question and Margaret continues with an air of rapprochement in her voice. 'He was promoted to being a supervisor, and now he's a senior supervisor so he does regular hours. More money, and means he's not out in all weathers, but I think he misses the round in a funny kind of way.'

'Less responsibility as a postie?' Katherine

suggests, but then immediately wonders if Margaret will take that the wrong way. 'You know... the freedom of cycling around is a lot different to managing people and doing loads of paperwork. Staffing issues are the bane of any manager's life!' she tries to qualify.

'Mmmmh.' Is Margaret's response, she can't talk because she's gritting her teeth so hard.

Katherine isn't sure if she's agreeing or not, but she errs against digging herself in deeper and shuts up. Margaret simply fumes into the washing up bowl, clattering and banging the dishes a little harder than she should and wishing she'd never mentioned Robert isn't happy. She feels as though she's betrayed her husband's confidence, made it seem as though he isn't up to the new job in front of the 'successful' Katherine.

Margaret steals a quick glance at her sister - she's a stranger. She's no idea what's going on inside that head of hers: what her life has been like in the years she's been in London, who her friends are, what motivates her and why she's back? That last question dominates Margaret's thinking. It has the potential to completely turn their lives upside down and she is powerless.

This person she grew up with, shared a family and this house with, is like a cuckoo among them now. Their nest is the issue - it's half Katherine's. Their home, the only home

Margaret has ever known, might have to be sold.

'It's just a house darling.' Robert had said last night, trying to calm her. 'What's important is our family, the children, our memories. If we had to sell, then there would be plenty to buy us something else.'

'I don't want something else.' Margaret replied like a petulant child. 'This has always been my home, Mummy and Daddy's, Grandpa and Grandma's, and beyond. It will be bought by a developer and turned into a housing complex for finance workers.' Robert just doesn't understand how much these granite walls mean to her. She also doubts very much that Katherine understands either. She wanted to leave their home, their island and the life they all shared. It must be a millstone around her neck, a reminder of everything she doesn't want in her life. The island must seem so small and parochial after cosmopolitan London.

Then again, there is another smaller voice inside her head which keeps trying to remind her Katherine has never once asked for a penny of her inheritance. She's never questioned that Margaret's family, and John, live rent free in the property that is theirs jointly. That little voice just doesn't fit with the Katherine she sees, the Katherine who hasn't taken an ounce of interest in her nephew and nieces, not even in her own husband for years. The selfish woman who turned her back on her family and her home without a second glance.

Katherine is concentrating on the jar marked 'Sea Treasures' on the windowsill in front of her. It's a large clear glass Pyrex jar full of little pieces of broken pottery and pretty shells, beautifully coloured granite pebbles and blue and green glass. All of them have been caressed and carried by the sea until their edges wore smooth. Margaret's always looked for the smallest of details, even on the beach. Whilst Katherine would be off searching for adventure and excitement climbing rocks, Margaret was the contented child wandering across the beach picking up interesting things. She could tell you what shells are found on which beaches, oyster shells in Grouville bay, winkles at St Aubin. Katherine has never understood her sister's contentedness, her own life has always been a search for fulfilment and the next challenge. She's never understood it - but there have been many times she's longed for it.

16

August 1976, Jersey

Darren Le Brocq saunters along the road: t-shirt flung over his right shoulder, his chest puffed out. Back straight. He's parading his muscles which undulate and throb beneath warm, smooth suntanned skin. Even his gait is perfectly tuned to allow each brawny thigh enough time to flex and bulge under his shorts. This is a young man strutting. Then he spots Katherine. She isn't sure if it's embarrassment for never having called, or for what his friend did to Anne, or perhaps it's simply the expression on her face, but suddenly he looks awkward. His saunter becomes ragged. She's not even opened her mouth and already she's having an effect. It's fodder to her anger, proof of his guilt. Her prey is two yards in front of her.

'Your bloody friend has got a lot to answer for,' she exclaims vehemently. 'Did you know he attacked Anne at St Ouen's, virtually raped her on the beach?'

Darren's face is a picture. Incredulity is the only way to describe it. He was most definitely not expecting that. 'Don't be ridiculous,' is his first reaction, 'she was going along with things just fine and then flipped, and besides nothing much happened...'

'Nothing much happened!' Katherine's voice comes out strangulated by the pent up anger, 'So why did she run off crying if nothing much happened? He attacked her.'

'Oh for God's sake you prissy little virgins have no idea; you can't go around saying things like that. You should be careful what you say.'

'Are you threatening me?' Her confidence turns into defensiveness.

Darren throws up his arms, exasperation on his face. 'I'm just saying perhaps you need to talk to your friend and find out exactly what did happen because she's lying.'

With that their altercation is over. He walks off, quicker than before, and leaves her to silence and the long walk home in the heat.

The burden of her argument with Darren is too heavy for Katherine to bear, she needs peace and quiet in which to contemplate their conversation. After she's told her mother her exam results, and tried desperately to feel as elated as she had done earlier, she takes herself off to bed with some headache pills. In the still of her room, the accusations and questions are ticking time bombs in her head; a huge pulsing grenade of a dilemma throbbing along with the pain behind her eyes. What has she done? Is it true? What should she do now? Of course the right thing to do would be to tell Anne, to talk to her, have it out with her.

The doubts whirl around her mind. Is what Darren said right? Did Anne lie to her, let her think something far worse had gone on? Why would she do that? Jealousy perhaps? Is that why she finds it so difficult to be around Katherine, why she's so moody - guilt?

A part of her wants him to be right, wants it all to be Anne's fault because then Katherine will know why Darren never called her. It wasn't because he didn't like her, it was because of Anne. Yet there's another part of her which fears she's betrayed her friend even more by mentioning it to Darren, and now she's compounding that betrayal by doubting her. The emotional and moral dilemma is an unwanted cuckoo in her mind, and refuses to leave.

17

March 3rd 2008, Jersey

Margaret breaks the silence at the kitchen sink with a shared topic of conversation -the investigation at Haut de la Garenne. 'Have you seen the JEP today?' she asks her sister, always first to offer the olive branch.

'No, what's the latest?'

'They're saying the remains they originally found are only a skull fragment.'

'Really? But the papers said it was a skeleton, a body.' Katherine replies, interested in what her sister is saying.

'I know. They've found some kind of bath in the cellar, they've got a photo of it. Looks like a cow trough to me, but it says some of the victims described being lowered into a deep dark pit, put in a large bath of cold water and abused.' Margaret continues.

'It's awful. I don't want to believe it's happened here.' Katherine shakes her head.

'The whole thing is awful. All of it. Any of it. How can abuse like that go on without somebody doing something… but it does and it's everywhere.' The emotion shows in Margaret's voice.

'Do you ever wonder if someone we know was involved, you know like friends of Mum and Dad's, or someone else?' Katherine asks, looking at her sister.

'Yes of course. It makes you question lots of things, think again about situations.' The pair of them shake their heads again and sigh, common ground at the sink at last. Margaret continues, 'Mind you, lots of people say they were bound to find bones on the site, there's a dolmen nearby, they used to burn and bury their dead there, but that was thousands of years ago.'

Katherine nods. 'I remember that, and didn't old Vi say the Germans took over the place in the War?'

'Yes, she did, didn't she,' Margaret replies.

'But the thing is,' Katherine continues, 'with today's forensic technology they must surely be able to tell if it's a bone from ages ago, or one from the 1980s.'

'Of course and there wouldn't be so many people coming forward claiming to be victims of abuse unless something bad went on.'

After this conversation the periods of silence return. Katherine stares out of the kitchen window again. She's contemplating the yard which doesn't appear to have changed much: the same solid granite walls enclosing it, the same barn door which has been mended, a panel replaced and repainted here and there.

The soft scrunching of a car's wheels arriving through the archway into the property catches her attention. She hears it slowly pulling up and peers around the right hand side of the window expecting to see Robert, but instead a police car comes into view. She tenses, a natural reaction, an inbuilt fear there might be bad news coming their way. The officer gets out. He's got his back to them but is in a fluorescent yellow vest which simply reads 'Police', there's no uniform.

'Looks like an Honorary,' she says to Margaret, who is also watching - not the policeman but Katherine's face. 'I'm sure everything's ok.' she quickly adds assuming Margaret's expression is one of concern in need of reassurance.

'You know that's John don't you?' Margaret simply replies, and the second she says it Katherine can see it. He still hasn't turned, shown his face, but she can see the run of his shoulders, the thick hair just beginning to grey, and his walk. How can she not have known it's her husband?

'I hadn't realised he'd joined the Honoraries.'

'I did tell you,' came the curt reply, 'about a year ago now, but you probably forgot with so much on your mind.' Katherine feels exactly the way the remark is intended to make her feel, but she doesn't show it. It's starting to filter back now, yes, Margaret had told her, because she remembers she'd thought how typical of John to volunteer his time for his local community. She'd imagined him as a Centenier or Honorary police officer, carrying out his duties; directing crowds at events, responding to minor accidents and incidents, and all in that slow calm way in which he seems to deal with everything life throws at him.

It makes her remember the time in London, just before he'd left. She'd screamed at him, wailing at the top of her voice, calling him selfish, pulling at his clothes, pushing him, trying to get some reaction, make him fight back, make him fight to keep her. He hadn't of course. He'd stayed calm throughout, talking to her in a soothing voice; attempting to put all sides of the argument on the table. Even as she'd been screaming at him she knew it was her not he who was being selfish, but she hadn't been interested in calming down. She'd wanted something to happen, something to snap and break her link with the past, to sever her emotions from the excruciating pain she still felt. He was the closest person to her. He was completely involved in it and it was against him she directed all her anger. Only he wouldn't break. He never has.

'So, are you going to say hello?' Margaret sounds annoyed at the fact her sister is still standing there. 'Tell him you're here.'

'Yes, yes of course I am.' Katherine replies, but not through choice. Facing up to John right now is the last thing she wants, especially as she knows Margaret will be watching their every move.

John is just letting himself into his cottage - their cottage - as she walks out. He turns and looks up before she can say anything and the shock of seeing her is obvious.

'Kathy!' he exclaims, his hands falling to his sides as though all the energy in his body is being used to deal with her arrival. She takes him in, the soft eyes, still sparkly even if they're slightly less bright than they used to be and more sunken in his weathered skin, which carries the creases of age and sunshine. His wide strong body, the big hands and titan nose, still handsome. Still able to make her stomach lurch. She carries on walking towards him although she isn't quite sure what makes her legs work. The awkwardness would have been obvious to a blind man. They opt for a double kiss on the cheek in greeting.

'I didn't realise you were already here,' John continues after her brief hello.

'No... I'm sorry I should have let you know when my flight was in.' Katherine looks down at the ground.

'Why? You don't have to get my

permission!' There is an awkward silence in the wake of his defensiveness and she looks back up to his face seeking the emotions behind the words, '…Are you here just for the weekend?' he continues impassively.

'No I'm staying for a while.'

'Staying?'

'Yes, well I'm not sure how long, we'll see.'

John swallows hard. 'I see. That's good news Kathy. Will you be wanting the cottage then?'

'Oh God no, no, I'm not … I'm not sure what I'm doing yet, I'm just going to stay with Margaret for a bit, get my bearings, you know.'

'OK. well it'll be nice to have you around again for however long it is.' Katherine isn't sure what's behind that statement. Does he mean it, or is he just saying it because it's the thing he should say?

'We should catch up sometime soon…' she ventures, not exactly sure what it is she wants or if it's a good move.

'We should. You know where I am,' John rattles his keys again, unlocking his front door, 'Just let me know when you're free.' This time she clearly detects years of waiting and disappointment in his voice, and a definite sense he doesn't believe she will; that it's her who is simply saying the things she thinks she should.

As she turns away she catches a tiny glimpse of the hallway that was once theirs. The carpet is the same, but there's a different picture on the wall. She wonders how the cottage has changed, if it's changed much. What happened to all the things she decided weren't important enough to come with her when she left years ago? Did John get rid of them? When? When did he decide the time was right to throw them away? She longs to push the door open and go inside, but that's not an option. It's his house, his home, and so instead she turns and starts to walk away. As she goes she catches sight of the old Jersey cow cream jug on the kitchen windowsill. It sends a shock-wave of memories through her body so with each step she's walking through the treacle of their shared experiences. So ends her first encounter with John, her husband, the man she has loved, and lost.

Katherine walks back slowly, her emotions too ragged to be able to face Margaret and her hostility straight away. Why has she come back? Why didn't she just leave things alone, stay safe in her London hideaway far from the emotions which now pummel her body with each re-awakened memory?

She lingers in the yard smelling the air, fresh but thick with the sticky salt of the sea. All around her are familiar things. She's glad not much has changed since her childhood, the yard, the house - they all bring comfort but there's also pain. Pain she has tried so hard to forget. Unfinished business, incomplete conversations and relationships left hanging. Like flies in a spider web.

18

1981, Jersey

Theirs is a courtship practiced for generations, a gentle maturing of the senses, an awakening of emotional and physical awareness. Not like the quick fumble she'd mistaken for love on St Ouen's beach five years before. John Le Marquand had come to work for Mr Binet the farmer who rented land from her mother. Mr Binet is in his late sixties, and although not emotionally ready to let go of his farming business, physically his body is telling him things can't go on like they are much longer. His two children, a daughter called Sarah, and a son, Adrian, aren't interested in farming. Sarah has married a bank manager and gone to live with him in Kent, whilst Adrian trained to be a lawyer and now has a very nice house up in the parish of St Mary with his new wife. Mr Binet senior is sad that after generations his family will no longer be in farming, but he's realistic. The world is changing. So, whilst his heart catches up with his head, he's employed young John Le Marquand as Manager. Mr Binet tells Marie that John has come highly recommended by a friend of his in St Brelade, and he doesn't disappoint. John is twenty-five, Katherine nearly twenty-one.

It's been a difficult few years for Katherine since Anne's death. She started work with an accountancy firm and threw herself into it, desperate for a distraction to keep her mind off her friend. The burden of guilt she carries is always there, a continuous pain within her; and even years on it remains, a coiled tapeworm inside her. Should she forget, should she dare to enjoy life just that bit too much, she can feel it tighten, constrict, demanding attention. She even withdrew from the teenage social scene, scared in case she bumped into Darren or Mark and distrusting of others.

It's during one of Katherine's dark days she first sees John. The depression doesn't happen so much by now but occasionally something will trigger it. Today she's been tidying her room and has found an old school exercise book covered in messages from Anne: notes about their friendship, about boys, about things they would do after exams - and a little heart with Mark and Anne written inside. So, Katherine ended up on her bed staring at the ceiling, going over and over the events at Sands, trying to work out what could have happened, if she could have helped, and what if she hadn't said anything to Darren the day of their exam results. Perhaps if she'd run after

Anne at Havre de Pas beach the last time they'd seen each other. If she'd tried harder to talk to her, to support her. In her head Katherine's still stuck there, paralysed, watching events unfold.

Margaret pops her head around the door and finds Katherine lying on her bed.

'Hi could you come and help me with this skirt I'm making please?' she asks, but Katherine can tell by the change in her face that Margaret realises her sister isn't going to be of any use for the rest of the afternoon.

'In a bit.' Katherine replies, although she knows neither of them expect her to be going anywhere.

John has been with the Binets for a couple of days and he comes into their yard to introduce himself. It's his voice that reaches through the black fog and into Katherine's ears, filling her head with thoughts of youth and banishing the images of the past. He sounds young, but not too young. A lovely voice, soft, but at the same time deep and manly. A real Jersey man with the accent of the island so many tourists mistake for a South African lilt. It pulls at her, drawing her from the bed and to the window where she stands just peeking around the granite wall framing the opening. He has his back to her, talking to her mother who is smiling, a look of girlish pleasure on her face.

Katherine's come to recognise this in her mum, a hidden sexuality she's only recently started to notice. It's been about ten years since their dad died. Their mother slowly emerged from her grieving, re-hydrating her sexuality like one of those dried sea sponges you see in the tourists' shops abroad; at first hard, scratchy, almost brittle and then swelling becoming soft and pliable again. She never lost the tenderness of maternal love, but as a woman she'd withdrawn into a chrysalis like state. Right now, Katherine longs to see what her mother sees, giggling and chatting with this young man whose back is tall and broad, his hair hidden under one of the hats which are de-rigueur for farmers out under the sun all day.

Katherine must have peered around the window just a little too much because her mother spots her, suddenly waving and calling her name, and he is turning round. She has no choice but to lean out of the window and say hello. The moment he sees her he smiles, there's no mistaking the fact that what is going through her head and heart, is also going through his. She's instantly attracted to him, and is also suddenly grateful she's up in her bedroom, separated by space and a thick granite wall so he can't see the sloppy clothes she has on. As it is her thoughts go instantly to her hair which has come to look like a pile of beached seaweed of late.

He takes his hat off and runs his fingers through his thick black hair. His features are strong, and although she can't tell his eye colour from her vantage point, they sparkle at her. He's handsome, rugged and he smiles straight into her eyes.

Margaret is engrossed in sewing her skirt and listening to some pop chart programme on their mother's old Murphy portable radio. She's surprised to say the least when Katherine suddenly appears at her bedroom door and asks,

'Right, so if I help you with your skirt, will you help me with my hair?'

John gives Katherine a new lease of life; he is her target, her goal to achieve. In the following weeks he pops into their kitchen increasingly frequently, helped in some large part by her mother.

The moment Marie meets John she knows he is just what Katherine needs. He has a maturity that comes not with age, but from character. A man who considers life, not rushes through it eager to take all he can. His kicks don't come from persuading another girl to kiss him or go to bed with him, his pleasure is gleaned from what he creates, what he grows in the fields. Not from what he devours. Katherine doesn't see this, she sees a handsome young man, but Marie can see in him the qualities her daughter needs, that of gentle nurturing and encouragement.

It doesn't take Katherine long to spot Marie's somewhat unsubtle matchmaking and she's sure John hasn't missed it either. If they all sit down for a drink her mother will suddenly have to go off and do something. If Margaret is with them she's always dragged away too.

Afterwards Marie will grill Katherine, 'What did he say? Has he mentioned a girlfriend? Did he ask you out?' Eventually he does.

They start dating a few weeks after Katherine first saw him from her window. On their first evening together he confides in her he's been wanting to ask her out from that first day but was worried it might not look good as he'd just started his new job. She's relieved, Katherine had begun to worry he's only asking her out because of the pressure from her mother.

They go to Le Hocq for a drink, sitting in the corner of the pub as far away from everyone else as possible, desperately craving some intimacy, some privacy for their conversation.

Afterwards they stroll along the beach, heading down the granite cobbled slip, next to Le Hocq Tower, and onto the sand. It's fresh, especially after the smoky bar, with not much of a breeze to talk about but the unmistakable stickiness of sea salt hangs in the air peppered with the tang of seaweed. In front of them the big brown rock which dominates the natural harbour is nearly surrounded by water, the tide silently sliding in. Some of the small boats, moored on ropes in the sand, have started to float and right themselves. The ones furthest out are just beginning to bob on the water, while others, closer to the land, still lay stranded on their white keels awaiting the sea's touch. The sky is red, the sun setting behind Green Island to their right. It's a beautiful spring evening.

John takes her hand as they walk so she doesn't trip over in the dark - or so he says. His hand feels big and rough against hers. The evening is getting chilly as the sun slips into the sea, and he envelopes her thin cold fingers in a warm socket of flesh. They chat and talk, giggle and laugh, walking on, clambering over rocks where the sea has taken away the sand; until they decide the beach has all but gone and a retreat up the nearest slipway is the most sensible course of action. Then he walks her home, stopping in the yard to say goodnight. He doesn't kiss her, just says thank you, but he does ask if they can do it again.

John has never been into dancing and loud discos, smoky rooms or drinking as much alcohol as is physically possible in a few hours.

Their dates are completely different to the ones Mark Vibert or Darren Le Brocq take their girlfriends on. They stick mostly to the pubs on the east side of the island, quieter, more rural than the ones in St Helier. John sees no pleasure in hanging out with the gangs on the Weighbridge in town, and Katherine discovers she enjoys this maturity, as well as knowing she'll be less likely to see Mark or Darren.

They often start off in a pub, but it's the need to be together in their own personal space which will usually see them out walking. Even in the bar they stay close, ensuring they're always touching, leaning into each other, almost stealing each other's breath. Not to hurt the other one but to take it, make it their own and then give it back again - blended. Watching everything about each other. Needing to. Needing to concentrate on every detail, every mannerism, every millimetre of skin, so when they are apart they can conjure each other up.

Katherine likes to sit, her Martini on the table untouched, drinking John in. The way his skin around his eyes creases like sun rays when he smiles. His mouth with lips that are capable of such tenderness and which, at the start of the day, are surrounded by soft skin, but by the end of it hundreds of tiny little bristles poke through his sun tan. His hair is black with a hint of brown the sun will do its best to find. When he gets embarrassed he'll fidget and look away, but she can always draw him back; gently bringing his face round to hers with just the touch of a finger.

Then there is the smell of him. He will clean up after a day out working so there'll be the slight perfume of soap, usually Imperial Leather, often a splash of his aftershave, and then him. Most delicious of all is the smell of a man, not sweat, not acidic, but musky, full of pheromones and testosterone - the natural chemicals of love and lust. She will seek out and latch onto them, trying to lose herself in their redolence.

More often than not John becomes self-conscious in front of his fellow farmers and islanders. Many of them will tip the nod or come over for a few words, breaking into their bubble and causing John to suggest they go for a walk where he can relax and enjoy their courtship alone. Sometimes they'll head off around the coastal cliff paths in the north, the stunning views of the sea and France wasted on them. Or they'll walk up the small path that leads past St Clement Church and its graveyard, after a drink in The Priory Inn at the bottom.

It's a fairly steep climb, but they'll walk slowly using the hedgerows as a distraction from the effort. Hawthorn bushes and small Elder trees line the banks, created many years ago to act as wind breaks for the fields and orchards of cider apples. The apple trees are mostly gone now, replaced by the green spread of Jersey Royals, and in late spring the tractors and the farm workers will be out well into the evenings digging up the valuable crop.

The footpath starts to grow narrower in the spring, nature's own taking over. Hogweed and Hemlock growing tall, their white blooms almost identical, but John points out the purple blotched stems of the poisonous Hemlock, and tells her how his cousin in Britain died from the plant after making a pea shooter from its hollow stem. His two friends survived, but he didn't. He was just six. Katherine makes a mental note to tell their children of the dangers, and feels a tingle of excitement at the thought of a family with John – and the act of creating it.

They walk past bindweed and grasses of all types, sometimes mixed with the brown heads of Ribwort plantain, or interspersed with the small green Lupin-like flowers of the Navelwort, the tiny yellow blooms of Alexanders, giant Dock leaves, and the small Dandelion-like flowers of the Sow Thistle. If she has to be a plant she wishes she can be the Ivy which entwines itself around the Hawthorn trees, clinging to their bark with tiny finger like tendrils. She would wrap herself around John, becoming a part of him - one living thing.

In autumn, the leaves fall from the trees,

and John falls onto one knee and proposes. Katherine delightfully accepts. On hearing the news Mr Binet announces his retirement from farming and suggests John approach Marie with a view to taking on her land himself, and if he wants, rent the land and equipment belonging to the Binet farm. It's a great opportunity, Katherine's mother is delighted and immediately offers the couple the dowager's cottage attached to the house. It hasn't been used in years and needs a fair bit of TLC, but John rises to the challenge, and within a few months they have a handsome two-bedroom home. They can't believe their luck. What more could they want from life than each other, a home, a livelihood. Except of course, a family of their own.

19

March 3ʳᵈ 2008, Jersey

Margaret watches Katherine walk out to John in the yard. She can't help it, but her sister's apparent complete disinterest in him infuriates her. What the hell is she doing back here anyway? How can she just turn up here after all this time and not even bother to make an effort to re-connect with her husband? If there's a man she never deserved, that's John. Why he has let her treat him like this all these years she can never understand. He even tried to move over to London to be with her, but she was far too busy lording it up with her professional friends to realise he'd been choked by the City. His feet are firmly rooted to soil, soil he can work on, and life in London was not for him. What Margaret never understood is that why, once he came back to Jersey, Katherine didn't put him out of his misery. Let him go, tell him she wanted a divorce, instead of leaving him just hanging on a tiny thin thread of hope all these years.

The Katherine who left Jersey twenty years ago was her sister, they were close, but she's not the same person as the woman who is out there now. This Katherine is distant, she's a stranger, she's been obsessed with nothing but her career and money for two decades. So, she's coming back home is she? Why? Is it to claim her inheritance? Has Katherine stopped to think about the impact of what she does? About what it could mean to other people? Of course even if she doesn't insist on selling their home she could say they have to pay rent. That would put an end to any hopes of James going to University, let alone Sophie. They'd never be able to afford the fees, but then Katherine wouldn't think about that would she? She has nobody but herself to spend all her money on. In fact, she seems to have positively avoided having to share, especially with a family of her own. She doesn't even seem to like children. The second Sara was born she did everything she could to avoid her. Margaret and Robert asked her to be Godmother in the hope of at least getting her to show some interest in her niece, but it never happened. She didn't even send the girl a card for her twentieth birthday last week, her with all her money and nobody else to look after, you'd have thought she could have at least remembered a card for her Goddaughter! How can two sisters be so different?

Then of course, if she doesn't lower herself to kicking *them* out of the main house is she going to try and evict John out of the cottage, his home for the past twenty-six years? He's built up a nice little business on the farm, it's been great to see the land being used by somebody in the family.

Margaret is positively seething by the time Katherine and John's brief exchange is over. She watches her sister walking back, looking all around her, taking it all in. What's she doing, sizing up what she's going to do with the place, what she's going to alter?

Thankfully Sophie takes Katherine out of Margaret's line of fire. She's left to bang around the kitchen muttering to herself while her sister reads a bedtime story to the niece she has barely ever met. By the time she comes back down Robert is home, a buffer for the growing tension, but even he can only hold back Margaret's wrath for a limited time. Fuelled by alcohol the cork inevitably blows later that evening.

It's Robert who is the innocent catalyst to the argument. They've eaten dinner and are sitting around the fire in the lounge drinking yet another bottle of wine, chatting about the island, talking about somebody they'd known when they were younger. Katherine is struggling to remember and Margaret has been getting more and more agitated.

Even Robert has noticed her knocking back the wine rather too fast and commented on it. He feels the tension building as his wife seems to be revelling in Katherine's difficulty to recall their old friend and so he changes the subject.

'So Katherine is there any particular reason why you've come back now, or did you just fancy a break?' Robert thinks it an innocuous question.

Margaret, seething by his side, jumps at the opportunity. 'Yes Katherine, why have you come back?'

Katherine looks a little stunned at Margaret's ferocity and Robert notices it too, turning to look at his wife. 'Well, I just felt it was time to catch up with everyone. You know Jersey's been in the news a lot lately and it just got me thinking that's all.' Katherine replies.

'Thinking about what? About your husband, about us, or maybe about this house?' Margaret viciously retorts, leaning forward in her chair, spoiling for the fight.

'Well... about everything really...but what do you mean Margaret, *about this house...*' Katherine is beginning to realise she's under attack.

'Well it's half yours isn't it?'

'Yes, but...'

'Don't tell me you haven't thought about getting your money out of it, with the land it could be worth a million each. You'd like a million wouldn't you?' Margaret is slurring her words slightly.

'Margaret I think you've had enough.' Robert tries to intervene, but he's no match for a sisterly argument that's been brewing for twenty years.

'I'm fine,' she snaps. 'So you telling me you haven't thought about the house at all?' She directs her latter question back to Katherine.

'Not in that way no.' Katherine looks from one to the other.

'In what way then? Don't tell me you still think of it as home, not after twenty years away. Twenty years!'

'Margaret are you annoyed with me because I went away? I don't understand. You chose to stay here; I chose to live away for a while…'

'Yes I chose to stay here that's right and I'm glad I did. I really am. I also chose to stay with my husband,' Margaret waves her hand in Robert's direction, 'To build a family, a home and I'm bloody proud of it too.'

'So you should be. You don't need to say that to me. I don't understand what's wrong? Why are you angry at me?'

'Because you walked out on everyone, Katherine.' Margaret's voice becomes more whining when she says this, 'Me, John, Mum, all of us. You've not been a sister to me, you just decided to leave and that was that. I have three children and you barely know anything about them. And what about John? Didn't you ever think maybe he deserved the chance to have a family, to be married to somebody who is there and cares about him … and Mum, how much did she see you before she died? It broke her heart. You barely ever came back to visit. You're selfish. Completely self-centred. Then you just bloody well turn up out of the blue.'

'Steady on love….'Robert stands up now.

'Butt out Robert,' is his answer.

'It's OK Robert, let Margaret say what she needs to say.' Katherine is staring at her sister now.

Robert slowly slides out of the room, keen to escape the battleground and avoid hearing things he thinks he'll be embarrassed about later. 'I'll leave you to it then,' he directs at Margaret, but she doesn't even give him a glance in response.

'Do you know what Katherine,' Margaret is in full flow now, 'one of your problems is you just won't let it go. You're here because of Anne's mother, not us. Still behaving like a bloody martyr over Anne's death. It wasn't your fault, everyone knows that. You were sixteen but you've made it your life to keep on mourning her, to not let go…'

'Perhaps there are some things you don't know about.' Katherine's eyes burn with a new intensity now. Her sister has found her soft under belly.

'Well perhaps there are lots of things *you*

don't know about too, and perhaps you should have concentrated on those who are still alive, the people who are your family instead.'

'You're drunk Margaret. I'm not here…'

'I am not drunk. You just don't like hearing the truth do you?'

Katherine throws up her arms in despair. She's drunk enough wine herself to have lost some of her own inhibition, and patience. 'Look if you won't even let me speak, then I'm not going to bother listening to you.' She flounces out of the room, just in time to nearly collide with James who has just arrived home.

'Hi Aunty Kath,' her nephew cheerfully offers; before seeing the look on her face.

'Hello James. Sorry I can't stay. Your mother's in there. Good night,' is as much as she can muster. Her sister's onslaught is beginning to sting and it's hurting big time. James looks somewhat surprised but she isn't going to hang around for small talk just to placate him. Another time.

20

1984, Jersey

She looks at it. It's quite possibly the most
wonderful thing she has ever seen. She could
kiss it, but perhaps that isn't such a nice idea.
Katherine is going to remember this moment,
the moment she first saw it, forever.

Today is without doubt the best day of her
life so far, although she might not put it to John
like that. Husbands seem to like to think that
you'd call your wedding day the best day of
your life. Not that she doesn't think her
wedding day was fantastic, it was, it was
completely wonderful, but this... This is
different. A wedding is exciting, beautiful, an
affirmation of something you've already
created, life changing yes; but this,
confirmation of a child growing inside of her,
this changes everything. Not just their lives but
it re-configures her very make-up, physically
and emotionally. The chemicals in her body
will never be the same again. *She* can never be
the same again. So many thoughts are spinning
around inside of her, so many possibilities, she
can't wait for John to get home. She will put
the pregnancy tester back in its box for now,

and then take it out later, watch his face transform.

Already Katherine's mind has gone over the moment a hundred times. She will start off by saying 'Darling, I've got some news for you.' His face will look quizzical, perhaps slightly worried at what she might be about to say, but then she'll announce, 'You're going to be a father,' and he'll explode with happiness, sweeping her up in his arms, before suddenly stopping and placing her gently down again in case he hurts her or the baby. After, she will run next door to tell Margaret and her mother. They'll be squealing with happiness. Her mother will head up to the attic, rooting around in generations of keepsakes, until she finds the baby things stored away from when they were little.

John will call his parents. Or perhaps they'll drive over there so he can tell them in person, see the joy on their faces at the prospect of being grandparents. They live in a bungalow in St Brelade and they go over and see them every other weekend, popping in for a cup of tea and a slice of one of the fabulous cakes his mother makes; or every once in a while inviting them over to the farm for Sunday lunch with her mother and Margaret. They're quiet, gentle people and Katherine feels so lucky that they've been able to fit into her family like missing pieces of a jigsaw.

Katherine puts the pregnancy test kit away in the little bathroom cupboard and heads back downstairs to their kitchen. It may be small, but she loves it with its brand new appliances and modern units. They'd chosen everything together, although John said, 'I want you to have whatever it is you want. All I want is for you to be happy.' He'd nearly made Katherine cry right there in the middle of the shop. So, she'd chosen the Calico cream paint of the walls, the Moorland moss tiles and charcoal grey marble effect worktops. They're both proud of the state-of-the-art lighting John installed. Some under the top units, some in the ceiling to illuminate the cooker, sink and table. When she has guests Katherine likes to just turn on the under unit lights to give the kitchen a cosy feel. It's filled with things her mother and Sally, John's mother, have given them. Spare pans and Pyrex bowls, baking sheets and a weighing scale, and an old Jersey cow cream jug which takes pride of place on the windowsill next to the little primrose plant her friend Trisha from work gave them as a house-warming.

Katherine sits down at the little leaf-fold table their mother took out of the family kitchen years ago when sitting the four of them around it became too cramped. She smooths the thick white plastic tablecloth with her hand; it looks like linen, but isn't. Underneath it the dark brown wood is stained, scarred by a big pale ring her dad inadvertently created with a hot mug of his favourite Darjeeling tea. On the other side are some neat little scratch lines from when the infant Margaret decided to gouge a pattern with her fork; all intermingling with a host of other family memories, now protected and hidden from view.

She looks at it with fresh eyes. They could squeeze another one in here no problem but another two would be pushing it. She can't believe that in less than eight months' time she'll be sitting here with a tiny little baby: her tiny little baby. Feeding him or her, rocking and soothing it, smelling the scent of its soft skin and baby milk. The excitement of knowing there's a little person growing inside of her; of not knowing what they'll look like, of waiting for new life to begin, is a wonderful feeling. She takes the calendar from behind the kitchen door and sets about working out when their baby will be due.

When John arrives home Katherine is singing along to a Police song playing on the small radio-cassette player in the kitchen. Steam rises from a pan on the hob and there's a pie in the oven which he'd know about even if he couldn't see it through the frosted brown glass door, as it's filled the whole house with a delicious buttery smell. John goes immediately to the sink to wash the fields from his hands, briefly kissing Katherine along the way. When he turns, towel in hand she's there waiting for him, smiling. He stops, looking quizzically at his wife who resembles a small child about to explode with excitement.

'I'm pregnant,' she can't help it, she just blurts it out, speech forgotten. The pupils of her eyes widen like black star bursts and she thrusts the calendar towards him with a big cross marked on it, 'We're due around the tenth of March.'

It takes a few seconds for the news to sink in and she's watching his face intently. 'Really?' he asks, 'Are you sure?'

'Yep. I did a pregnancy test when I came home from work. I'm two weeks late. I'm sure.'

The towel is thrown onto the draining board and John lurches towards her, arms outstretched, his face now a mirror of her own, and his body puffed to bursting with pride.

'That is fantastic...you clever, clever girl.'

He kisses her, his love enveloping all three of them.

It's difficult to say what Katherine notices first about being pregnant. Is it the general sense of her body being pre-occupied with something else? Or is it the effect of the massive hormone increase which not only makes her more prone to getting soppy at the silliest of things but also slightly fuzzes her mind. Then there's the tiredness. It's a different sort of tiredness to the 'had a hard day' type, or the 'burning the candle at both ends' type. It's not physical from the point of view of aching muscles, but it's as though her body just suddenly says enough is enough and demands a shut down. She has taken to going home for her lunch hour so she can get a half hour's lie down. Luckily she hasn't been too sick and she's managed to hide it from everyone at work. They plan to tell those outside of the immediate family after the twelve-week scan.

Every morning John fusses over her when she's feeling nauseous, although it's actually been worse in the evenings when she's tired. Her breasts are so tender it feels like her nipples are being rubbed by sandpaper, even with the softest cloth. The biggest change of all though has been the feeling that her body just isn't hers anymore; it's not just her brain, her soul living within its confines. Somebody else has taken up residence. From being careful what she eats and drinks, to the way she finds herself subconsciously rubbing her stomach, she's already begun mothering her unborn child. Her role in life has changed.

'Mrs Le Marquand?' The midwife standing at the waiting room doorway calls from her notes.

'Yes,' Katherine raises her hand, then instantly feels like she's back at school for register-taking. She and John get up to follow the midwife to one of the examination rooms. Katherine is so excited, but she's also nervous. Excited because this is the first time they're going to see their baby; nervous because she has some strange irrational fear she's not actually having a baby at all – that it's all been some kind of phantom pregnancy like dogs get. Then there's also the fear no mother wants to think about, that something terrible might be wrong with the baby.

'Hello I'm Debbie, do come in. Is this your first?' The midwife is lovely, softly spoken, at a guess in her mid-fifties with a bob of brown and grey hair that goes well with her blue uniform. Her face is lined, not with deep fissures, but more like pottery glaze which has crazed; her skin having already lost the firmness of youth. She looks anything but porcelain-like though, the plumpness of her cheeks combined with soft downy hairs gives the impression of an over ripe peach. She's almost ephemeral or too soft for this harsh world. Katherine wonders if perhaps she's soaked up an excess of other people's sadness because she looks like the kind of woman who will sit and talk, or listen, to you patiently forever - if that's what it takes.

The midwife runs through her notes and

then asks Katherine to get up onto the couch. 'Have you got a full bladder?'

'Yes,' she replies instantly. In fact, she feels as if she's got such a full bladder the midwife could well witness a dam burst if she's not careful.

Debbie takes a big squeezy plastic bottle, gives it a shake and then squirts warm gel onto Katherine's tummy. Her trousers are already down to her pubic bone and Debbie has tucked a paper towel over the top to stop the gel from getting onto her clothes. John smiles at her reassuringly as he sits on the bright orange plastic chair the other side of the bed.

'Let's have a look then,' Debbie says, taking the hand monitor from the scanning machine. She pushes it into Katherine's abdomen, pressing and moving it around, every now and then finding her bladder which is most uncomfortable, and then, 'Here we go,' Debbie smiles at them both and turns the monitor around so they can see. There on the screen is a shape just like the ones in the book and magazines she's been reading - a tiny little human. She can't take her eyes off it and feels John's hand reach for hers. 'Here look. There's baby's left arm and here, its right,' Debbie manoeuvres the scanner around, pressing this way and that into her lower stomach. The little baby on the screen jerks and jumps in response to the pressure. Katherine's so enthralled she no longer hears the screams from her bladder. 'Here's your baby's heart,' Debbie continues her anatomical tour, showing them their tiny offspring is all present and correct. 'Everything looks absolutely fine,' she smiles, 'it looks like you're eleven weeks and two days. I'll just take some more measurements.'

She uses the machine to print out some images, finally wiping the gel from Katherine's stomach. A grin has fixed itself to Katherine's face, she just can't stop smiling. As she rubs the last of the gel from her tummy she imagines just below the surface of her skin is their little baby, all safe and warm inside of her.

They leave clutching two grainy images of their first child and, after a dash to the toilet, exit the hospital officially as parents-to-be. Arm in arm. The joy of new life swelling their shared world with a thousand hopes and expectations.

Katherine begins to learn a new language, the language of pregnancy and child birth, which introduces her to words like 'trimester'. She's just completed her first, so she learns, and is now starting her second: the easiest of the three by all accounts. She discovers her baby is already fully formed, and now it's simply a case of growing bigger. The whole process is a wonderful mystery to her, a voyage of discovery. The most natural and normal function of a woman and yet it's the most wondrous. To think a little human being which will one day be riding a bike, playing on the beach, going to school, and eventually perhaps becoming a mother or father itself, is growing inside of her.

It's also a scary prospect. Katherine's seen enough movies with screaming, sweating, straining women supposedly giving birth, to know that it's a somewhat unpleasant and painful process. After a little gentle persuasion John agrees to go along with her to some ante-natal birthing classes. She books their place, plots the dates onto their calendar, and imagines how many weeks gone she'll be by then and what she might look like.

It's funny how you can go through life barely noticing something, or at least not registering that you've seen it, but then when it happens to you all of a sudden it's everywhere. Katherine seems to be surrounded by pregnant women and babies. She's never been a 'baby person'. The kind of woman who adores every single baby they see, stopping to coo over them, or even asking to hold them. She's never seen the attraction: until now. Now she's on the threshold of motherhood: she's sneaking peeks into every pram and pushchair that passes, smiling conspiratorially at other pregnant women, putting her hand to her tummy at the sight of new-born babies and checking out the relevant equipment and outfits of the respective infants. It's a new club, a new world she's entered and there are so many more discoveries to come.

A favourite topic of conversation between Katherine and John is the subject of 'The name'. Every now and then one of them will ask, 'What do you think about...' She's found it odd going through the naming process because she's quickly discovered who in life she really does and doesn't like. Names are tainted by association, and for both of them there are certain ones they'd never entertain giving their child as it reminds them of somebody they're not particularly keen on.

Margaret has given them a little Baby Names book in which she neatly inscribed, 'To help you choose, love from Bump's Aunty Margaret x.' It's one of those books that gives the meaning of names as well as a big selection to choose from. Katherine hadn't realised it, but her name means 'pure'; whilst Anne derives from Hebrew meaning 'God has favoured me.' She doesn't think he actually favoured her at all. Katherine toys with the idea of naming their baby Anne if it's a girl, a kind of tribute to her friend, her way of saying sorry; but she decides against it. The superstitious part of her worries Anne's troubles might transfer with her name.

Options they are seriously considering

include Emily and Rebecca, whilst John likes Charlotte and Alice. Katherine writes down their suggestions so they can see if there's one they both favour. On the boys' list are William and Thomas, Charles and Oliver.

Straight after her twelve-week scan she lets her boss and everyone at work know she's pregnant. Trisha immediately squeals, 'I knew it, I knew it,' and everyone congratulates her. Before long the Jersey bush telegraph has gone into overdrive and wherever Katherine goes friends and family acquaintances come up to her and congratulate her. Everyone seems to want to share in their good news.

The gradual swelling of her belly, which she so wishes would hurry up so everyone can see what she has known for months, and the shared expectations between her and John, make Katherine feel content. More content than she can ever remember feeling. There are times when she can just sit and do nothing, absolutely nothing except breathe and think about their new family. This marvellous feeling of being peaceful, serene and at ease with herself is something new, something she's never felt before and she likes it.

21

March 4th 2008, Jersey

Katherine doesn't wake up to clear fresh air after their long overdue family storm cloud had burst. She awakes in the spare room of her sister's home with Margaret's accusations crashing around inside her head, which throbs and aches from their constant battering; and perhaps also from the dehydration and disturbed sleep, the results of too much wine. One consolation is she suspects her sister, who had drunk far more, will be feeling much worse.

Katherine lies on the sagging mattress looking at the room, its familiarity now contemptuous. The sloping ceiling is still covered in the faded flowers of 1970s fashions, even the duvet cover, a paisley type affair, had been one of their mother's and it's an irritation. Perhaps she's made a big mistake coming back here. Right now she feels very alone, more alone than she had in London. Margaret has the advantage, she's got Robert to go over the argument with, calm her down, bring back some rationality and help soak up her emotions. Katherine, fired up and consumed by her own arguments, feels like an unwelcome outsider.

She's angry. Why is it that it's always after the argument she comes up with the right answers, precisely put, delivered with deadly precision to kill any counter argument? Now is no good. She has all the best retorts to Margaret's painful accusations, only Margaret isn't here. Why is it that those who know you the best, and are supposed to love you the most, can be the cruellest? Does her sister really think she would sell their home, kick John out of his? Does Margaret honestly think that badly of her? Is this what she's come home to? Or perhaps that's the point, she's been kidding herself - this isn't her home at all anymore.

She hears the faint sounds of family life rising from downstairs. Sophie's voice, shrill in its youth, travels well as too does the sound of her feet running from room to room, or up and down the stairs. As Katherine lies in bed, eyes half closed against the morning light, she suddenly realises those very same feet are now climbing higher, up the second flight of stairs to her attic bedroom. She listens. There's whispering, clinking sounds, and then a gentle knock at the door.

'Aunty Kath…Aunty Kath.'

'Yes Sophie, come in.' The door creaks open and the little girl carefully steps through its threshold carrying a large tray laden with crockery.

'I've brought you up some breakfast Aunty Kath,' she says beaming, 'There's tea, toast and some fruit for you.'

Katherine smiles at her niece and wriggles herself up the bed, stuffing the pillow behind her back as she watches the little girl totter across the bedroom, willing the bowl and jug on the slippery tray not to slide off and crash to the floor.

'Oh wow, that's fantastic Sophie, thank you.' She reaches out for the tray, eager to secure it, 'You're so kind.' Sophie smiles proudly and hands it over, then stands there looking at her aunt, smiling. Her beaming face makes the perfect olive branch: as if that isn't Margaret's intention! 'Would you like to share some of my toast and fruit?' Sophie nods excitedly and clambers onto the bed beside Katherine, her back leaning against the headboard beside her aunt's and little legs stretched out in front parallel with hers. Katherine puts the tray between them after carefully taking the tea off.

'How long are you staying?' Sophie asks turning to look at her aunt, a strawberry midway between plate and mouth.

'I'm not sure yet, at least a couple of weeks, maybe longer.'

'With us?' she asks excitedly, 'Here in this room?'

'We'll see.'

Sophie looks a little disappointed but seems to accept the answer. 'It's raining,' she says matter of factly, completely changing the subject as only children can. 'Mummy says I can go to Fort Regent later...will you come with us?'

Katherine looks at her expectant face, it isn't the thought of going with her, it's the prospect of having to spend time with Margaret that holds her back. 'I'm not sure sweetheart. I'll try.'

She hands Sophie half a slice of toast, smothered in home-made blackberry jam and cut in triangles - just the way her own mother used to.

An hour later Katherine is washed and dressed. She still has a slight hangover feeling of alcohol oozing out of her pores, but the Ibuprofen she's taken have eased the headache. She goes downstairs with the tray but finds nobody around. The kitchen is spotless, so she puts her breakfast things into the dishwasher and wipes the tea and milk spills off the tray. She is just looking around for its home when the back door opens and the silent room is instantly filled with Sophie's bubbly presence. Margaret follows close behind with some freshly pulled carrots from her polytunnel. When she sees Katherine she looks a little awkward.

'Morning. I'm taking Sophie to Fort Regent in a bit, do you want to come?' She says as nonchalantly as possible.

'Do you mean the swimming pool?' Katherine asks, the prospect of splashing around with a whole load of noisy children not exactly inviting.

'No. The pool was shut years ago. They've got one of those play area things, you know where the children clamber around inside a giant climbing frame.'

Katherine looks bemused and a little unsure, in her life it isn't something she's come across.

'We can just sit and have a coffee while she plays…. Anyway, we're leaving in ten minutes if you want to come.' Margaret extends her own olive branch, although Katherine can still see the sparks of last night's lightning strikes flashing in her eyes.

'OK.' Katherine replies, still smarting from all the harsh words. She wants an apology, not an invite to a play area. Nevertheless, ten minutes later she's at the bottom of the stairs handbag and coat ready as Sophie sits on the floor pulling her pink flowery wellies off and replacing them with shoes. She's humming a little tune to herself and looks up with a glow of innocence as her aunt approaches.

'Are you coming Aunty Kath?'

'Yes I'm coming,' she replies with a smile. She's not sure what Margaret's motivation is for the invite, to mend the bridges, or to have another pop at her, but she does know it will bring a smile to Sophie's face so she'll take the chance. She also wants the opportunity to put the record straight with her sister.

'Come on then, monkey,' Margaret says appearing from the kitchen, car keys jangling and her handbag swinging on her arm. 'Perhaps you might see some of your friends from school,' she continues opening the front door. Sophie doesn't need any further encouragement, grabbing her raincoat from the rack, she skips out to the car.

Katherine follows. It's been more than twenty years since she last visited Fort Regent. 'I don't suppose the skating rink is there any more, is it?' she asks Margaret as they pull out of the yard.

'No, God no, that went years ago, along with the little fun fair thing that used to be outside along the ramparts. Do you remember that?'

'Yes, I do,' she replies, wistfully. She and Margaret spent many happy days there when they were younger.

What happened? How did it all go wrong? Was it entirely her fault as Margaret said last night? Did she get so consumed by grief that she completely shut the living out? Perhaps if

Margaret knew all that had gone on then she would have understood why she'd had to get away, for her sanity, for her survival.

Even now when Katherine remembers those days, before and just after she'd left, they fill her mind with black smoky fog. With cold. A coldness that makes her bones ache, and claws at her, dragging her down into suffocating mud. Only she knows just how close she came to completely succumbing to its power. Those dark, dark days after John left her in London, how near she had been to giving in; to accepting that nothing was worthwhile. Life was pointless.

22

1984, Jersey

At week sixteen Katherine returns to the midwife for another routine check-up. John doesn't come this time, there's no need. Her urine tests fine, as too does her blood pressure, and she offers up her arm for more blood tests. Then she lies down on the couch whilst the midwife checks the baby's heartbeat.

'I feel like I'm getting my energy back now, which is great,' she chats to the midwife. 'And I'm sleeping better again too, although I suppose that will get worse again as I get bigger. I don't seem to be getting that big yet though, people keep saying that if they didn't know, they wouldn't be able to tell that I'm pregnant.'

It's then she notices the silence in the rest of the room and when Katherine turns to look, the midwife's face has changed. Just a few moments before she'd been smiling, relaxed and chatty, now a professional mask has fallen across her features and she's listening intently, moving the monitor around Katherine's belly but not keeping it still.

A terrible knot of fear grasps Katherine's

insides, twisting her intestines and wrenching her heart. 'Something's wrong isn't it?' she asks.

The midwife doesn't answer straight away. Her face unintelligible. 'I'm sorry.' she says at last. 'I can't seem to find the baby's heartbeat. It doesn't mean that something is definitely wrong.' She places her hand on top of Kathcrine's gently. 'But we need to get you in for a scan, take a look at what's going on.' The touch of her hand is enough for Katherine to know exactly what the midwife is thinking.

'Could the machine be faulty?' she asks, desperate to find a way out of the gaping hole of fear and misery opening up before her.

'I don't think so love, it was working just fine half an hour ago...but you never know. That's why we must get you in, double check. Would you like to call your husband while I telephone the hospital?'

Katherine nods.' When, when will the scan be?'

'Straight away love. They'll see you this afternoon.' She smiles sympathetically at her, reinforcing the touch of her hand. Katherine is falling into a whirlpool and being sucked down fast. What's happened to her baby? Why can't the midwife find a heartbeat? They'd had the scan, everything looked fine. How can this be happening? She slowly sits up and after the midwife leaves the room, Katherine walks to the desk to telephone John. She prays he's not out in the fields, so far away that he won't hear the phone ringing on the yard speaker.

It seems to take forever for him to pick up, every second feeling like a month, then she hears his voice.

'Hello, La Vielle Farm.'

'John, it's me.'

'Oh hello darling, I was in the barn. You finished at the doctors? Everything OK?' There's a tightening in Katherine's throat making it nearly impossible for her to speak. 'Kathy?'

'No… No it's not. John, she thinks the baby has died. The midwife can't find a heartbeat. They're sending me for a scan.'

'No!' is all she hears from the other end. She doesn't need to see him because she knows that she's just ripped his insides out.

Then his voice again, different this time, quieter. 'Are you sure?'

'She says she can't be sure, but I think she believes it's died. There's no heart beat John. Why? Why our baby?'

'Stay calm Kathy. It could be a mistake. I'm coming now, don't go anywhere.' The phone clicks and goes dead.

She sits for a while staring at it, at the little holes in the mouthpiece down which she's just uttered those dreadful words, 'I think the baby has died.' So easy to say, to send them off to

John's ear, but what a terrible effect those six simple words have on both of them. She's calm, very calm, but that's because she's numb. Katherine is desperately hoping the midwife is wrong, that something is faulty with her machine, that their baby is going to be bouncing around on the scanner screen again just like it had been four weeks ago. Deep inside, she knows, she's clutching at straws.

At first her womb shows up on the scanner monitor as an empty grey chamber. There's no sign of the little jerky baby whose image she carries around in her handbag. The little form which once seemed to fill the space they're now looking at. This space, which only a few weeks ago seemed capable of such miracles, creating and giving life to a baby, is now a cavern that has swallowed all her hopes and dreams. The midwife pushes the scanner right down, to the bottom, searching...and there it is. There's no mistaking that it's lifeless. It simply hangs there on the monitor, not responding to the pokes and prods, not moving. A little tiny human. Suspended. Dead. Her womb, the symbol of fertility and new life, is now its grey grainy grave.

From somewhere she hears the midwife say she's sorry, and feels John take hold of her hand. She turns away from the screen to stare at the wall with its posters of pink healthy babies and advice on what you should and shouldn't be eating during pregnancy, and the big sign that says smoking will damage your unborn child. What did she do wrong? What damaged her baby? Why has her baby died? She's looked after herself just like all the books said.

'Why?' Her voice seems to come from nowhere.

'We usually don't know why,' the midwife replies, 'It's very common you know, a big percentage of pregnancies end in miscarriages.'

'But I haven't miscarried.'

'Any failure of a pregnancy at this stage is called a miscarriage, it doesn't just mean that you lose a baby spontaneously.' The midwife patiently explains, pausing and looking to John for some kind of go-ahead to continue. 'We need to talk about what the options are now. We'd recommend that you are admitted and the baby is removed. From its size I'd say it died around two weeks ago, and as your body hasn't expelled it itself, there could be a risk of infection if we don't remove it.'

The midwife looks to John again and back to Katherine. 'I know it's a lot to take in, but the best thing would be for you to go up to the ward now. I'll call the doctor, get him to come and talk to you. Would that help?'

Katherine nods because she doesn't know what else to do. 'I need the toilet,' she says, slipping off the bed.

'Shall I come down the corridor with you?' John asks, but she shakes her head. She needs a few moments just to take this all in. Katherine feels for him, she knows he's upset too, that he's feeling helpless right now; but she's just got to get out of the room for a while, away from all the reminders of the last time they were in here. As she walks down the corridor she stifles the overpowering urge just to run, run away and try to make believe that none of this is happening.

She doesn't run of course. She's not even sure she's capable of running at this point, and even if she did she'd be running straight smack bang into reality. The longer she stays within these four walls the longer it's another world away from their real lives and she can hold on to that former life for as long as possible. Katherine doesn't want to return home and not be pregnant. This is just not how it's meant to be. She should call her mother and Margaret, but she can't bring herself to do it. She wants to keep this terrible secret just between John and herself. She doesn't want to hear the disappointment and worry in her mother's voice.

Faces jostle forward through the fog in her head. Smiling faces of all the people who have congratulated her over the last few weeks, each one further evidence of her failure. What will she say to them? She can't bear the thought of all those smiles turning to sympathetic looks. She needs to at least call her boss, tell him she won't be back in today, perhaps not for a few days. Maybe John will do that for her.

As the doctor explains what is going to happen, Katherine is on autopilot. She signs the consent form for 'The Removal of Products of Conception' and offers up her arm for blood tests and blood pressure monitoring. They sit awkwardly, waiting for the inevitable. She's not allowed to eat or drink, and John refuses anything for himself. He wants her suffering to be his, she can feel it in his touch; and there's a look of guilt in his eyes that she's having to go through this as he sits by and watches.

Two hours later Katherine is taken down for surgery, wheeled through the corridors on a bed by two porters. As she says goodbye to John, the anaesthetist tries to calm her and make her feel more at ease with some inanely cheerful chat. All she wants to do is scream. He asks her to hold the oxygen mask over her nose. The smell of disinfectant fills her nostrils. Then he puts the needle into the back of her hand. She doesn't want the needle in her hand. She doesn't want to be here at all. She's scared. Scared of what they are going to do to her. Scared of being unconscious. Scared of having to wake up afterward and deal with what will have happened. Her jaw starts to feel numb and tingly, then she feels woozy. She doesn't want to go to sleep...She doesn't want to have...an operation. She doesn't...want...them to...take away...her...baby...

Noise first. Mechanical blips and the gentle murmur of voices. Her eyes open to bright white light and fuzzy images. Where is she? Her mouth. The overpowering taste and smell of anaesthetic and plastic. The dryness of her throat. The heavy gas which seems to lie like a fog in the depths of her lungs. Then the feeling. The overriding feeling which suddenly dominates her consciousness - the soreness in her womb – and it hits her. She knows where she is, why she's here, what has happened. Her baby has just been taken from her - and she cries.

She cries for her baby, for her loss, silent sobs so as not to attract the attention of the nurses. Her tears, hot and full, escape the corners of her eyes and soak into the white hospital pillowcase turning it grey. The job is done. The problem sorted. She is not pregnant anymore.

If only she could have woken up to another life, a life where her baby still grows in her womb. Instead she's woken up an empty shell, her insides sucked and scraped out like a whelk. A few moments and it was all over. All she's good for is to be thrown back on the beach where the sea can smash and bash her until she's just another grain of sand. No life. No identity. No purpose.

Katherine thinks of Anne lying dead in her grave. Perhaps this is what she deserves, perhaps this is to make up for how Anne's parents felt when they lost her. Perhaps this is her eye for an eye. This is her reality now, lying in a hospital bed her womb throbbing and aching for its loss, just a sore bruised feeling where once her tiny baby lived.

Is this what grief tastes like? Will this artificial medical taste in her mouth be the signature of her loss? It's not the first time she's experienced death. First there was Dad. The shock of discovering her father's body. Completely still. An empty husk instead of the man who'd been so full of life and strength. She was cast adrift then, the rock torn from under her feet, tossed on a storm of emotions she'd found difficult to rationalise at such a young age. Then Anne's death. The signature of that grief was guilt, a gut twisting knot of guilt, clouded by remorse and by the fear that at any time everyone might figure out it was actually all her fault; that Katherine failed her friend and was the catalyst for her death.

This grief is different. This time a little piece of her has been hewn from the rest. It will never grow back, never be completely re-filled. Her grief throbs inside of her, a beacon to every sympathetic glance and whispered comment. All she wants is to melt into the corner, merge with the shadows and hide from the world.

Katherine leaves hospital the next morning, walking into the world a different woman from the one who left it yesterday afternoon. She hasn't yet experienced the cramps she's been told to expect, and physically she probably doesn't look all that different to most people.

'There's no reason why you can't try again as soon as you're up to it,' the smiling doctor tells her. She wants to shout back at him that she doesn't want to 'try again', that she'd been happy with the one she'd had, but she knows it's not his fault. It's not anybody's *fault* apparently, 'Just one of those things,' they keep telling her.

John has kept close to her throughout it all, holding her hand, his arm protectively around her as they leave the hospital.

'I'm so sorry love,' he keeps on saying, as though somehow he's to blame.

Perhaps they both feel responsible, both feel as though they've failed. The doctor has warned her about the inevitable crash of her hormones, that she's likely to be weepy; but he said this more to John than to Katherine, as though if she does cry he can explain it all away as some chemical reaction.

While she'd been in the operating theatre,

John called her mother and his parents. When they return home all reminders of her pregnancy are gone. The magazines, the information sheets, the little book of names Margaret gave them, and even the pieces of paper on which she'd written, 'Emily, Rebecca, Charlotte and Alice. William, Thomas, George and Oliver'. All that's left is a space on the coffee table where they'd once sat. The house is also spotless. She recognises her mother and Margaret's touch in the vase of flowers on the kitchen table, and the food in the fridge which hadn't been there yesterday morning. Half of her is relieved that she doesn't have to face all the reminders of where their lives had been just twenty-four hours earlier. The other half is upset at the fact their baby has already been erased in every way. Life can go on as though the pregnancy never happened.

As soon as they arrive in the yard Marie appears, taking her daughter into her arms and hugging her tightly.

'I'm so sorry darling,' she whispers into her ear. Katherine feels stiff in her mother's embrace; she doesn't want to accept her sympathy because it might soften the loosely latched flood gates of her emotion. She doesn't want to cry again. She wants to put on a brave face. Lots of people have miscarriages right?

An hour or so later Sally calls to see if there's anything they can do.

'I'm really sorry sweetheart,' she says to Katherine. 'I know exactly how you feel. I had a miscarriage in between John and Stephen. Not quite sure exactly how far gone I'd been, we didn't have scans in those days, but I can certainly remember when I lost it. The best thing is to keep busy love. I went to a dance the same night; I was determined to keep my mind off things. It's not good to dwell.' *Dwell!* Katherine thinks, *dwell!* She's only just come out of the hospital and already she's telling her not to dwell. But, she's been through this, she coped, and so will Katherine.

That evening they go to bed early willing the unconscious state of sleep to overcome them. Lying in their bed, as they have done so many times before, it just doesn't feel the same. It's the same sheets they were given for their wedding. The same green blanket her mother passed on to them. The same red and white checked bedspread they'd bought together one rainy Saturday afternoon at de Gruchy's sale, rushing home afterwards to christen it by making love; and then lying in each other's arms listening to the rain on the window. They're a long way from that afternoon. The world suddenly feels colder, less friendly. Their innocent hopes and dreams now tarnished by a cruel reality.

'I never knew my mother had a miscarriage,' John says into the darkness.

'She's never mentioned it before...' and his voice trails off. Katherine can feel his pain, but she's too enveloped in her own to be of any comfort to him. He doesn't say anything more, just hugs her and strokes her hair for a while until he falls asleep. She's left listening to the rhythmic sound of his breathing.

She expected her baby to fill her insides, to squash her heart with its life. Instead her heart beats unhampered in an empty shell, its pounding echoing around the space that feels so completely deserted. Why her? Why her baby? What is wrong with her body that it can't swell and bloom in pregnancy like other women's? They've been cheated. Defeated by something they will never know the identity of. Her 'Product of conception' will never be an individual in their own right; a person who will find their niche in society. That opportunity was offered and then snatched away. Her arms will stay empty.

23

March 4th 2008, Jersey

Little Sophie is the saviour of the car journey. Without her cheerful chatter the road to Fort Regent would be a depressing one for Margaret and Katherine, both still fuming after the previous night. What interaction there is between the adults revolves around the little girl, or their shared distaste for the situation at Haut de la Garenne. On their way they pass a television satellite truck, east bound.

'There they go,' says Margaret with disdain. 'Do you know what? My friend Carol rang this morning. Said her sister had some newspaper bloke knock on her door, one of the nationals, offered her money if she had a story to tell. They were going round the whole estate.' Margaret looks in her rear view mirror at Sophie who has stopped her chattering and is listening to her mother. 'You alright sweetheart?' she asks her. Sophie nods and resumes chattering with the two dolls on her lap. 'That Telegraph article the other day, the one that called Jersey an "Island of secrets and terror", questioned how many people here knew what was going on and didn't do anything about it.' Margaret clenches her jaw, checking the mirror again and choosing her words carefully. 'It's like they think we were all in on it.'

Katherine is relieved her sister's wrath is, at least temporarily, diverted and to a subject they both agree on. 'I know, but they reckon about a hundred and sixty people have come forward now claiming to be victims so maybe it is helping,' she says quietly to Margaret.

'I'm not sure,' Margaret retorts, 'some people think all the media coverage is actually going to make it harder to get convictions. You know, defence lawyers will claim there can't be a fair trial.' She sighs heavily, shaking her head. 'So awful and they think they're going to find more remains soon too; I hope they catch the...' she mouths an expletive to Katherine.

'Those who are still alive!' Katherine adds, 'Some of them have already escaped justice. And I do agree with you about the people who are crawling out of the woodwork, selling their stories and saying they knew it was going on and couldn't do anything. I'd move heaven and earth to stop something like that.' Margaret murmurs in agreement. Katherine continues, 'I guess society was different then, I wonder what mum would have made of all this.'

Margaret doesn't reply immediately and Sophie ends the discussion, breaking into the repressive atmosphere with a question, 'Can I have a snack at the Fort?'

Fort Regent is both familiar and transformed. Outside the dome still dominates the St Helier skyline, but inside the fixtures and fittings are nothing like the place Katherine remembers. The old fortifications have been completely refurbished with a selection of sports facilities. Today, the sounds of children echo around its great domed hall. The smell of coffee permeates the air and flashing arcade games sit opposite the huge black 1800s siege cannons that were built to repel French invaders, not space invaders. Through the new entrance hall stream tracksuited adults, some carrying racquets and sports bags; or white suited Karate cadets wrapped-up with multi coloured belts. While Sophie and Margaret sign into the play arena, Kathy finds them a table.

The climbing frame, a multi-coloured labyrinth of tunnels and ladders, slides and ball ponds, rises up to the roof. Inside children swarm like ants, their squeals and screams the result of freedom from their parents, a world in which only they inhabit, unless there is a problem; and the only barrier is the breadth of their imagination.

With Sophie happily off playing, Margaret deposits her daughter's shoes and coat at the table.

'I'll get us a coffee shall I?' she half smiles at Katherine.

'Yes please, a latte if they have one.

Thanks.'

Katherine sits watching the busy to-ing and fro-ing of the children, every now and then returning to their mothers for drink or food, comfort or a loo break. The mothers sit at their nest of table and chairs surrounded by mounds of little jackets and fleece tops, half full bottles of drink, colourful beakers, toys, Barbie pink glittery shoes, and bags full of nappies and wipes. This is a whole different world. A world Katherine will never be part of.

Margaret returns and places a mug of coffee in front of her.

'Thank you,' she says as her sister settles into the seat beside her. For a moment they both sit staring at the climbing area, Margaret searching for her daughter's face, Katherine sorting through the backlog of waiting sentences in her head.

'You wanted to know why I've come back. Why now.' she begins. Margaret doesn't say anything, just turns to look at her. Katherine is still staring forwards, choosing her words carefully. 'I think I probably should have come home some time ago, but I didn't for lots of reasons. I guess what pulled me back was all the media coverage about Haut de la Garenne because I just didn't recognise the Jersey I knew from our childhood with the way the island was being portrayed. I'm not wrong am I? It's just I always felt we had a happy childhood, a good one… apart from Dad dying so young of course. I needed to come back and make sure those memories aren't false.'

Margaret has been studying her sister as she talked, she shakes her head. 'No they're not false. No one I know recognises the island in the papers.'

'I'm not saying that there wasn't abuse,' Katherine continues, 'I believe those people, you can see it in their faces, but the image of Jersey like something from The Wicker Man, it just doesn't fit.' Margaret nods and Kathy looks at her. 'I did blame myself for Anne's death. You're right about me being hung up about that. I truly believe it was my fault… Things I said and did in the weeks before…' Margaret opens her mouth to interrupt, but Kathy isn't finished. 'You can say that I haven't let go, maybe you're right, maybe that's because of the way I was excluded from what happened at the time. I wasn't allowed to have my say or to listen to what was being said. I wasn't even allowed to go to her funeral for God's sake!' She falls silent for a moment, her shoulders rounded, eyes downcast in thought.

Margaret takes her chance, 'Katherine we were children. We weren't told things. Mum thought it best to protect you. There's no way Anne's death was your fault.'

'How do you know that?' Katherine turns round to her, frowning 'You don't know what I did.'

'Did? Honestly Katherine it was nothing *you* did...'

'Mummy, Mummy I need a drink, I'm thirsty.' Both women are startled by Sophie's sudden appearance. The little girl bursts into their conversation.

'Darling why don't you go back and play for a few more minutes and I'll get you a drink in a moment,' Margaret cajoles, eager to carry on her conversation.

'No. I'm thirsty, I really, really need a drink now.' Margaret looks at the defiant five-year-old in front of her. She's not budging. She sighs and throws a look to Katherine as if to say hold that thought.

'I'll get you one.' Katherine suddenly offers, jumping up off her seat and scooping up her handbag.

'Yay thanks Aunty Kath... Can I have a Panda pop… Please?'

'You come and show me what it is you want,' Katherine replies and the pair of them head off to the café, leaving Margaret to watch her sister disappear with her bouncing daughter in tow. Why has it taken so long for her to be able to watch this scene? She does regret some of the things she said last night, perhaps she's been a bit harsh, over reacted, but it's been a long time building. What really gets her is that Katherine thinks she's the one with the cross to bear. Her completely irrational guilt over

Anne's death drives Margaret nuts. Everybody knows what happened and it has nothing to do with Katherine. She's not the only one with regrets and a secret that eats at her soul.

24

1984/85, Jersey

After her miscarriage the weather seems to empathise with Katherine's mood for it rains solidly for days. She hides from the world for a week, but eventually has to return to work - steeling herself for the reactions of her colleagues. No-one says anything at first, there is an awkwardness in the atmosphere. She knows they've been told, the odd sympathetic smile or glance, or an extra show of politeness gives it away.

Her boss calls her in. 'Good to have you back Katherine,' he says. 'Sorry to hear your news, if you've any problems or you need more time off then just ask.' He looks awkward, embarrassed. People just don't seem to know what to say. Should they make a big thing of it, or try to cheer the afflicted person up? He goes for the latter, and smiling inanely adds, 'Well at least you've plenty of time to keep trying.' Then he half winks at her. The fact Katherine can see he's really not comfortable with the conversation at all is his saving grace. She half smiles, politely, and tries to calm herself down, telling herself not to be so angry at him for what he's just said. Before the day is out there will be plenty more awkward platitudes sent her way.

'Why don't people just keep quiet instead of making such stupid remarks?' She angrily asks John later. 'Do they really think they're helping when they say, *it was for the best*, or, *it's nature's way, there must have been something wrong*. Does that make it any less disappointing, any less upsetting for us? And what now? Does it mean there might be something wrong with the next one too?'

'You heard what the doctor said,' John replies, stroking her cheek. 'It's very common, nothing unusual, and we will be able to try again soon. You'll see, by next year we'll be knee deep in nappies and baby milk, and this will all be behind us.' Katherine says nothing. 'I know you're upset sweetheart,' he continues, 'we both are, but in a sense they are right, something was wrong and nature took over. We have to accept that.'

'What though, what was wrong?' She turns and looks at him beseechingly. 'If we knew why it might make things easier.' Katherine turns away again, she's struggling to get the words out, the back of her throat is so tight from holding back the tears she feels as if she might choke. 'And anyway, it doesn't ever bring that baby back does it? That baby, the person they could have been, has gone forever.'

Katherine's body quickly rediscovers its natural cycle and, around six weeks after their loss, baby-making resumes; and it is baby-making because instead of the relaxed love making they enjoyed before, their sex now has a defined purpose: to make a baby to replace the one they've lost. Timing becomes important, they're not just doing *it* because they feel like it. They're doing it because it's a couple of days since they last had sex, and for the best chance of conception another session is required. Katherine becomes desperate to get pregnant again, to get back that feeling, resume what has been so cruelly taken from her. She'd spent so long looking in the mirror, checking-out her growing belly, admiring the very slight convexity of her stomach - which nobody else would have even noticed - that now when she looks in the mirror her tummy, which is flat and trim, simply looks empty. She wants it filled again.

Life goes on around them. On the fifth of October the island celebrates the 25th anniversary of the opening of Gerald Durrell's Jersey Zoo with a visit from Princess Anne. Crowds of flag waving children greet her wherever she goes, but Katherine doesn't feel like joining in or celebrating. Instead she goes to the Odeon cinema with John and hides in the dark shadows trying to force out some laughs at 'Blame it on Rio'. Watching Michael Caine play a man who has an affair with his friend's seventeen-year-old daughter.

Autumn turns to winter, and it's a wet one. The yard is frequently filled with fast flowing channels of muddy water and the roads left slippery and dangerous from the mud pouring off the fields. Even the beaches develop slippery patches as the mud flows down the hills towards the sea, ending up layering the sand in brown or charcoal grey mucous smears. Katherine's birthday comes and goes. She's twenty-five now, although in the past year she feels she's aged far more than just the sum of twelve months.

Margaret is not only loving her new job as a post woman, getting up early every morning and cycling her round, but she's also declared her relationship with fellow postie Robert Phillips is serious. Katherine often wonders how two sisters can be so different. Margaret is a lark, relishing every new morning, always eager to get out of bed at first light. Katherine is, and always has been, an owl; lying-in as a teenager and staying up late. Where Margaret seems content with her island life, Katherine often found it suffocating, dreaming of escape from all that Margaret holds dear. John has anchored her, but it is the all-consuming desire to get pregnant which dominates Katherine's thoughts. Each month in the week before her period she will interpret every twinge, every change in her body as the possible forerunner to pregnancy; but each month her hopes have turned to disappointment at the sight of crimson.

Should she ever dare to try and wallow in her loss then something comes along to shame her. In October it's the horrific images from Ethiopia, the hundreds of thousands of starving people suffering in Africa's drought. Images of skeletal mothers with empty breasts and dying babies fill the television screen. The sunken faces of children, who have given up hope, linger in her mind. In December, Katherine buys a copy of Band Aid's 'Do they know it's Christmas', and shares in the nation's philanthropic unity along with Bob Geldof, Bono, Sting and the others.

When Christmas comes, for Katherine it's just another reminder of her loss. She'd dreamed of sitting with John by their tree, stroking her stomach and talking about how this would be their last festive season as just two, that next year the focus of Christmas would be the little person she is carrying.

The weeks slip by, one grey week after another. January arrives and John is busy with the planting of the Jersey Royals. This month she's determined not to calendar watch, not to count down the days until her period is due, and she nearly makes it. Only in the last two or three days does she start to get excited, dare to hope that this time they might have done it. She was due a few days ago and so Katherine goes to the chemist, handing over money in return for a stick which could change her life forever.

Now, here she is again, staring at the blue cross which tells her that her womb is no longer empty - hope has returned.

Katherine promises herself not to get too excited this time, to be realistic, not to get attached to her unborn child until she can be sure everything is OK. But that's so much easier said than done. Just knowing there's a baby inside of her is enough to make her want to rejoice again. Lightning won't strike twice, this time everything will be all right. Didn't the doctor say that it was an unlucky break and everything will be fine next time? Only, just to be sure, she doesn't want to tell anyone about it, only she and John will know the secret within her. It would worry her mother and she doesn't want to face the uncertainty of people not sure whether they should congratulate her after what happened last time. This is going to be their secret until they're absolutely one hundred percent sure, and then they'll share their joy. John's delight at the news is all she needs for now, and apart from a visit to the doctor to get back on the ante-natal treadmill, they will tell nobody else.

Before the twelve-week scan she doesn't even allow herself to pick up a book or magazine about babies. She's determined not to consider the possibility that everything will go according to plan so she doesn't have the plummet of disappointment again if it doesn't. Once there in the ante-natal clinic, lying on the couch, watching the image on screen of the same little jerky, twitchy human looking well and definitely alive, she can't help but feel attached. They leave with another grainy image of their baby which she places in her purse where the other one once sat. Katherine struggles to hold down her excitement, she stops herself from even mentioning possible names, and they wait, knowing that last time their twelve-week joy turned to sadness.

By the time the sixteen-week check-up is due she feels like she's been holding her breath forever. John has been treating her with kid gloves not letting her do anything, and Katherine's followed every rule in the book to ensure a successful pregnancy. When she walks into the midwife's room it's like facing judge and jury as they decide whether or not to sentence her child to the death penalty. She follows the same routine: urine test, blood test, blood pressure, and then the couch to listen...She can't believe her blood pressure tests normal. It feels like the midwife is taking forever to finish her paperwork. Find the listening monitor. Walk over to her.

Finally, she's on her way, six feet...three feet, a foot. 'Now just lie back and relax whilst I have a listen.' she says, poised above Katherine's belly. Relax! That's the last thing she's able to do. Katherine closes her eyes and feels the cool monitor touch her skin. Then she hears it, the fast sloshing pump of a little heartbeat from within. The baby is alive and well.

She would never have believed it's possible to physically feel lighter with relief, but she does. She walks out of the midwife's clinic a different person. Hope restored, excitement beginning to trickle through the cracks in the shell she's built up around her heart, swelling it like parched earth in a rainstorm. Katherine drives home straight away to find John. He's still in the yard fiddling with a tractor, although she has the suspicion he's been finding reasons not to go out into the fields until she's returned. The second he sees Katherine he knows, and a huge grin breaks across his face.

'The baby is fine,' she says, allowing herself to be enfolded into his big arms. It feels so good to be wrapped up in him like this.

He kisses the top of her head tenderly. 'Well done darling. I told you it would all be

OK didn't I?' Katherine doesn't reply, just sighs, not wanting to break his hug, feeling secure, loved and at last content again. 'Margaret's invited us round for a drink at five, says she's got some news, so perhaps we can tell your mum and her then. Why don't you go and have a lie down for a bit first?' John adds.

'Oh really? She looks up at his face now. 'I wonder what she's going to tell us. Sounds like a great plan. I've got the rest of the afternoon off and I'm feeling a bit tired.'

John has already broken their embrace and started to turn to walk away. 'You go and have a nice sleep sweetheart,' he says. She can see his mind has already switched back into farming mode, listing all the chores he's failed to do that morning, but must get done. She watches him climb onto his tractor, her heart and stomach buzzing at the sight of him. He fires it into life and disappears round the barn to the fields. Katherine takes herself, and baby, off for a sleep.

'Kath, we're engaged.' Margaret simply can't contain herself and her news bursts out the second Katherine walks into the kitchen. She's standing next to the Rayburn holding a glass of something fizzy in one hand, and her new fiancé Robert Philips in the other. They both have the slightly flushed excitement in their cheeks of the newly pledged, warm with love and years of endless possibilities.

'Oh wow. That is so fantastic. Congratulations both of you.' Katherine rushes around the big wooden table to give Margaret a huge hug. She means it, she's delighted to see her so happy. Their mother standing on the edge of their new life, is clearly happy for her too. Katherine gives Robert a hug and a kiss as well, she knows he'll take good care of her sister.

'Robert got down on one knee on the beach.' Margaret tells her, eyes shining.

'Thought it might be a bit softer on the sand,' he jokes. 'Still had my postie shorts on.'

'He's so romantic.' Margaret brushes away his flippancy and thrusts her left hand under Katherine's nose. A shiny, sparkly gold ring, encrusted with tiny diamonds, glitters on her wedding finger.

'So any idea of a date?' Katherine asks.

'Well we haven't properly discussed it yet...'Margaret tentatively replies, clearly not about to let that minor detail get in the way of planning her big day. 'Well need to save up, I want to do it properly. So maybe the summer after next.' Katherine catches her throw a glance in Robert's direction, there's no dissent. The talk dissolves into discussions about dates and who might come, churches and reception venues. In the excitement nobody notices that Katherine doesn't even sip at her glass of bubbly. By the time John arrives she's already decided now is not the time to tell them her baby news, it will take the shine away from Margaret and her announcement. They've already waited months to tell them, another couple of days won't make much difference. She manages to convey that thought to John by means of a few careful facial expressions and some hasty whispers, and their evening turns into an impromptu engagement celebration.

25

1985, Jersey

For the next couple of days Katherine is busy at work, and John is flat out with planting.

Before they know it the weekend is upon them and they still haven't shared the good news with their family. Katherine has, however, allowed herself to go to the newsagents and buy a pregnancy magazine. She's starting to relax into the idea that everything is going to be all right after all, and the baby name options start being thrown between them again. She's even started talking to the tiny baby which lies inside of her, filling her unborn child with dreams and hopes, a life of happy families and a shared future.

It's Sunday evening when their dream starts to crack.

Katherine has gone to bed early, conscious of the fact she has a busy week at work ahead of her. It's as she's lying still and quiet in bed, that time when your body and mind are just about to float into sleep, that she becomes aware of it: the feeling something isn't quite right. It's difficult to pinpoint what she notices. The baby is too small for her to feel any definite movements, it's more subtle than that. What comes to her mind is a feeling the ship's engine has stopped, that the chugging and throbbing from the life support machine inside of her has ceased. Fear clamps hold of her with a jolt causing her to lie still barely breathing, desperately trying to feel what her body is doing, to understand what is making her think this way.

It's dark, only a dim white light from the moon strains through the curtains illuminating the mirror on the dressing table and coating the room in a shadowy kind of light which creates soft, fuzzy edges around everything. From downstairs she can just hear the murmur of the television, intermittently spaced with the rattle of canned laughter. She's no idea how long she lies there listening, frozen in the face of what she's contemplating. Could it have happened again? Her body which should be nurturing and feeding her baby, keeping it safe, growing its tiny form, could it have let the baby down again? Is something terribly wrong? Are all their dreams, all their excitement about to be shattered? Have the last three months of hoping, waiting, being tired, feeling sick, and busting with the knowledge of their baby, all been in vain? Has her baby died again?

Finally, she hears the Ten O'clock News titles on the TV and she knows it will be time for John to come to bed. Katherine hears every movement he makes: picking up his empty plate, placing his mug on top and carrying it out into the kitchen. The click of the light switch, the thud as he places his plate down on the work surface near the sink. A cupboard door opens and shuts, the tap runs and she guesses he's filling a glass with water to bring to bed. There's the click of a light switch again, his feet treading their way through the living room and up the stairs. The bathroom light suddenly appears, squeezing through the crack at the bottom of the bedroom door. More water running, toothbrush on teeth. The toilet flushing, and then the doorway grows dark again. Only the moonlight is left to show John the way to where Katherine is lying, eyes open to the possibility of heart break.

'I think something's wrong.'

She hears John take a quick intake of breath, she's startled him.

'I didn't know you're awake love, I thought you'd gone to sleep ages ago. You gave me a turn.' He clambers into bed. 'What did you say?'

'I think something's wrong with the baby.'

'Why? Are you bleeding? Are you in pain?' John fumbles for the bedside lamp and switches it on making her turn away from him and shut her eyes tight against the glare. 'Katherine?'

'No. It's hard to explain.' She can feel him

watching her, and although her eyes could now open without any discomfort, she keeps them squeezed shut. She doesn't want to see the disappointment or worry on his face. 'I just know something's wrong.'

'Oh sweetheart you're worried because of what happened last time, it's perfectly understandable. But you had a check-up only a few days ago, you're not bleeding or anything. It's just a reaction to all the stress.' Katherine feels the touch of his hand on her head. 'Katherine turn over, everything will be fine love, don't worry. You need to get some sleep. You'll feel better in the morning. I expect you've just been lying here on your own in the dark getting yourself all wound up haven't you?'

She doesn't answer. Perhaps he's right, but she doesn't think so.

'Look if you're concerned why don't you pop into the hospital tomorrow morning before you go to work, put your mind at rest. I'm sure they'll understand after what happened last time.' John says reassuringly.

'Yes, I think I will.' Katherine replies, her voice is croaky but she opens her eyes to look into his. 'Goodnight darling.' She kisses him gently on the lips and rolls over onto her side, facing away from him.

John turns out the light and settles himself into bed silently. He's beside her, but not with her. Neither of them fall asleep quickly.

Here they are again, both of them. John was summoned as soon as she saw the results of the scan. They're both sitting together, his hand holding hers tightly. Katherine knows that like her he can't believe this can be happening all over again, that all their joy has evaporated a second time. A doctor is in front of them explaining the situation in a quiet professional manner. The pale blue characterless box of a consulting room is a blur around her. She's all but switched off, a balloon deflated and shrivelled. No tears yet, just numbness.

Then just as she thinks it can't get any worse, Katherine catches the doctor's words. He's telling them it won't be possible to remove the baby like last time, that she's too far gone, that they need to induce her for labour. She can't believe she can feel any worse, but now horror and fear are added to the trauma of loss. Now all she can think about is giving birth. Giving birth for the first time – to a dead baby. She knows it will feel like a dead baby, she doesn't need experience to tell her that she'll feel it slip from her lifeless. There'll be no vibrant little being to cry and be comforted at the end of all the pain. No celebration to erase the experience.

Katherine wants to be unconscious. She wants to be unconscious now. She wishes she could just close her eyes and wake up with everything over and done, or maybe not even have to wake up at all. She's frightened. Scared of the process, of the pain of pointless labour, and most of all scared of the emotional aftermath. She doesn't know if she's going to be able to cope with this, whether she can hold it together.

Katherine feels John with her, anchoring her, but it's going to be her body that will have that final heart wrenching feeling of loss as the midwife calls for one last push and she feels the limp body of their baby leave hers. The little body they'd dared to hope would be their first child, imagined holding and kissing. All those hopes, all that love reduced to this. Why?

A very nice midwife fills in all the paperwork for them. John answers most of the questions, and the midwife calls to see if there's a bed available.

'I'm sorry but the maternity unit is full at present. We'll book you in for the morning.' She tells Katherine.

They nod. What else can they do? So, almost silently, they leave and drive home, shutting the door of their cottage behind them, hoping to shut out the world and its realities.

When Katherine awakes the next morning it's from a hellish excuse of a sleep. Dark troubled jumbles of thoughts have been spinning around her head. Images of a tiny dead baby, a large headed foetus, fully formed but lifeless, kept flashing into her mind. She forces herself to get out of bed and get ready. She's on autopilot. Into the bag she'd bought for her maternity stay Katherine places some clean underwear and her hairbrush, some toiletries and a nightgown. All she wants is for this to be over, for the dead baby to be gone from inside of her, for the next 24 hours not to have to happen. One thing she knows for sure - she doesn't want to see it, and certainly can't even contemplate holding it. Katherine is detaching herself, distancing her mind from the broken dream she will soon expel.

At the maternity unit they are ushered quickly through the wards filled with the sounds of crying infants and chattering mothers, past a closed door where a groaning woman can be heard, giving Katherine a hint of what's to come. After more paperwork she's given some pills and medication, and then they wait. Wait for her body to react and for its muscles to contract and push the contents of her womb out. John makes idle chatter; she knows it's to take her mind off things: or maybe his mind. Katherine wishes he'd stop. She doesn't want to chatter back and she doesn't want the television on. The sound of other people carrying on as though everything is all right, as though nothing is happening, nothing has changed, seems invasive not comforting or distracting. John resorts to reading a magazine. Katherine just waits for it to start.

It begins with an aching in her lower belly and back like really bad period pains. The midwife gives her some strong painkillers, their existence yet more evidence to hammer home her reality: pills that would never be allowed in a normal birthing situation. No need to fear harming her baby now. Then she starts to shiver. At first Katherine thinks maybe it's because she's just sitting around and getting cold, so she gathers up the bedclothes around her, but the shiver takes hold shaking her body.

'I'm cold, really cold,' she tells John. He instantly jumps up to ask the midwife for more blankets.

She comes straight away bearing an armful. 'It's probably a bit of shock,' she tells her. 'I'll fetch you a hot water bottle.' In its absence Katherine huddles down under the blankets trying hard to control her shaking body and the urge to just hide her head under the bedclothes and wish herself someplace else, just like she'd done as a daydreaming child.

The contractions become more painful, more pronounced.

She tries to concentrate on something, anything...the waffle blankets on the bed, like giant sized versions of the ones she had as a baby. Only her mind can't help wandering and she starts thinking about how many women will have given birth in sight of them.

The pain heightens. Her head is fit to burst. If John hadn't been there she would have sat on the floor and banged her head against the wall. Bang...bang...bang...
Rhythmic...soothing...thuds... Anything to block out her thoughts...the pain...her emotions. Her dead baby.

Now the pain is so intense she can't help but cry out with the contractions. She squeezes John's hand with each one. She doesn't see him, but he's watching her. With each groan of pain, he cringes. Even in the private world of hell that's going on inside of Katherine, she knows he's hurting too.

She moans, deep moans of pain that resonate through her body, animal like sounds that she'd never have thought she was capable of. She remembers the cows at the Dairy, their mooing at calving time – and later the distressed sounds when the calves were taken from them.

More pain, faster, less breaks and the midwife is there with her now encouraging her to push. Katherine is crying, sobbing with the pain and with grief. She doesn't care who sees her, what she looks like or who knows it.

Finally, she feels it. A warm, slippery sliding object which leaves her body and is taken away quickly by the midwife. Katherine collapses into John's arms, both of them crying now. It's over.

They keep it between them, unable to bear sharing this grief, to face the prospect of talking about it, voicing it out loud. If they can keep it between themselves, keep the rest of the world, the rest of their family out of it, then perhaps it will be less real. A self-contained nightmare trapped inside of them, but unable to taint the rest of their lives.

John is kind and patient, fussing over her, protective; but his grief has limits. Hers has none. Even before she's stopped bleeding it seems to her he's already starting to bounce back. He doesn't have the hormones to contend with, it wasn't his body that went through the trauma of a pointless labour; it wasn't his soul temporarily entwined with another in one body. The results come back from the hospital, they can't find anything wrong with the baby.

'It must be me then.' Katherine pronounces. 'It's obviously me, my body must be doing something, or not doing something it's supposed to.' John doesn't know what to say, he shakes his head.

'Not necessarily love, we don't know what it is. As the doctor said, it could just be a fluke, a very unlucky fluke.'

It's Katherine's turn to shake her head. 'No. I don't think so.'

Silence, she can almost hear his thoughts.

'Don't worry,' he says, 'I'm not going to put any pressure on you. I understand if you don't want to go through this again. But if you do then I'm here to support you, it's completely your decision.' Only of course it's not. Katherine knows John wants a baby, just as badly as she does.

As the days move into weeks she finds herself withdrawing not just from the outside world but from John. She knows he's upset about their babies but for him they never really existed, they were just an idea whereas for her they were physical realities and a part of her died with each one. Katherine's emotional state is so fragile she doesn't even dare connect with John in case it opens up some floodgate of feeling that will drown her in its misery. Knowing they can find nothing wrong with the baby, that it could have been a healthy child, that's made things worse, not better.

The depression doesn't fall down on her like a big heavy weight dropping from on high. It is far more insipid and subtle than that. At first she begins to notice the odd day when she's feeling a bit down. Nothing she can properly put a finger on: just a bit over-sensitive, prone to crying at the silliest of things, generally not feeling happy with life.

Then as the days move on she starts to realise it's the odd day when she doesn't feel down that stands out. Her life has begun to look less appealing. She finds excuses to stay inside and not go out, not face people.

The weeks turn into months and still she struggles. Her body is no longer hers, it's a failed baby making device. Whereas John still treats her as the wife he loves and longs to have sex with, Katherine doesn't see herself as the individual she was before. She can only see a failed mother. Her desire for sex doesn't return, and John's interest in her becomes an annoyance not a pleasure. She's scared of having sex in case she becomes pregnant because if it fails again, she doesn't know how she is going to cope. Her mind, her emotions seem to have disconnected from her body.

Every criticism, no matter how small, or no matter if it's a joke, hurts. She's become porous, her hard protective shell compromised. She did try to explain to John one day her fear of failing again, but he simply replied that she shouldn't be negative. She can see no way of explaining to him how fearful she is for her state of mind. Most days Katherine simply exists, working on auto pilot, doing her job, her chores, playing the roles that are expected of her: wife, sister, daughter. Some days she finds it difficult to socialise at all. Anything outside of her comfort zone, which consists only of

John, her mother and Margaret, anything else can be daunting and overwhelming. It's all a struggle. She's not achieving anything. She doesn't know why she bothers, why any of them bother? What point is there to life? We exist: working, eating, struggling, and all for what? The inevitability of death.

Sitting watching the Live Aid pop concert she cries herself into exhaustion, partly for the starving people, and partly because it's the perfect excuse to allow her emotions to flow out without having to explain them. All Katherine wants to do is scream out to everybody to leave her alone so she can just curl up into a ball in the corner and hide.

She doesn't talk to John about it, what could she say? How could she explain what she's feeling? He's sure to tell her not to be so 'sensitive', not to 'dwell' on things, that he loves her and everything will be all right. After all people go through far worse don't they? Neither does she let on at all to Margaret or her mother; they would only worry, and their sympathy might increase her pain not diminish it.

Then there's the guilt. Not just the guilt for letting down her babies, but the guilt that she should feel like this. So self-indulgent in her grief. Millions of women have miscarriages: it's just something that happens, part of the process, a way to ensure that only the healthy babies are born. How much worse the grief of the mother who has lost a child? A baby she has held and nurtured, a child she has sung to, looked into its eyes and talked of dreams and possibilities. How much worse her loss?

When Katherine is in *that dark place*, the old guilt is there to nag her too: Anne. Maybe this is payback. Maybe not supporting Anne, being an accessory to her death, maybe that has cursed Katherine. Cursed her children. She shouldn't become a mother because she's proved herself unworthy even of a friendship. Anne's been on her mind a lot lately, not that she ever went away. Maybe this is what Katherine deserves - but not John. John is suffering now because of *her* past sins. Now she has that guilt on her conscience too.

26

1986, Jersey

Work is a welcome distraction from Katherine's personal grief. Here she seems to make a difference, achieve recognition for the things she does. Here she can work harder for promotion and lose herself in a world where babies, family and guilt just don't figure. This is a world of black and white common sense, of numbers and business principles – not emotion. Katherine sits at her neat desk, everything in its place. They all know to come straight to her if they need to track down a file or find some client information. Here she is in complete control. There's nothing left to chance or luck, no possibility for nature's seemingly random cruelty. This is a world of cold hard economics, and it's her sanctuary.

It's summer, but a rainy day. Everyone glad to be indoors out of the weather. At Katherine's office there's a waste bin full of dripping umbrellas by the front door. It looks like it's going to be another day much like the others that have gone before it, but then her boss calls her into his office.

Katherine's boss is a thin stick insect of a

man. Small features on a small head and skinny body; hair that's more downy and infant-like than a grown man's should be. Although he's married he's nervous around women. She hears some of the others in the office complaining about him failing to sort out disagreements. Conflicts, especially with a female, are just not his thing. Numbers are though, he's got a quick sharp mind for business which Katherine respects. She's witnessed numerous times when colleagues are having a problem with a job, they'll show it to him and you can almost see the processors in his brain working. His eyes flick over the information, page after page, turning back to check something he's read, and then coming up with a solution in what seems like mere minutes. He's not a Jersey man, the Head Office sent him over a few years ago, but he loves being here. If he'd stayed in London he probably would have gone a lot further, still could go further if he wanted, but he and his wife started a family a year after they arrived and have chosen lifestyle over money and career.

'Katherine come and sit down a minute,' he beckons her in.

As she walks towards his desk she searches on its surface for a clue as to what it is he wants to talk to her about.

He sits up, placing both hands palm down on the surface in front of him. 'Katherine your work has been consistently excellent. I know you're capable of far more, but we have a little problem.' She panics. Has her recent depression been noticed? Has she been foolishly thinking her torment is hidden, whereas in fact it's there for all to see? 'Your qualifications are the issue my dear. For me to be able to start pushing you and giving you the bigger jobs I need you to have some formal accountancy qualifications to your name.'

'Oh I see,' is all she can answer, relieved but at the same time disappointed she's not up to the job.

'You have a lot of potential, but obviously this is going to have implications for your husband as well as yourself so you need to consider what I'm going to say carefully.' He pauses, the possibilities hanging between them. 'I would like to propose you for the company's apprenticeship scheme. Are you familiar with it?'

'I've read about it. It's not something you can apply for though is it? I thought it was only offered to employees who are thought to have management potential...'

'Yes that's right, and I think you do have management potential. So do the assessors. I've already recommended you for it and you've been accepted.'

Katherine is shocked, she doesn't know what to say. 'Oh wow! Thank you. I'm really surprised I had no idea...' she stutters.

He smiles, then looks more serious. 'Yes, but the downside Katherine is it's going to mean some sacrifices. You would have to go to London for a while, train there. It's something which will have an impact not only on you, so you need to think carefully.' He looks at her now, scanning her face for information, his data processor mind trying to work out if he's come to the right conclusions.

A million different things run through Katherine's head. 'How long? How long is the training for?'

'Two years,' he replies.

'I see. OK.' What does she say? He wasn't joking when he said it has implications. Two years away from Jersey. Not such a bad idea if she were single but John is unlikely to want to leave the farm – that could mean two years away from John.

As if her myriad of indecisions are there to read on her face he quickly steps in to reassure. 'Look, there's no pressure at all. You've got plenty of time to think about this. I've got an information pack here which tells you about the scheme, what's expected of you and what you can hope to achieve at the end.' He holds out a large coloured cardboard brochure to her. It's covered in images of smiling professional types in suits with briefcases and the look of success. Is she really suitable for this? Could she really be one of them?

'So did you say I've definitely been accepted?' Perhaps she'd heard wrong.

'Yes. You've definitely been accepted.'

'When would I need to start?'

'Well it's fairly open, there are two start dates a year. The first one we could get you on would be next September, so you've plenty of time to think about it, and there's an option to hold over until the following spring. It's all explained in there,' he points to the brochure.

'OK, thank you. Thank you for putting me forward.' She gets up now wanting to escape his gaze and allow her face to dissolve into the shock and excitement that are trying to erupt from below. He believes in her, believes in her potential. This is something Katherine has always dreamed of. A ticket to bigger things, a new world, London and the stairway to management. A few years ago she would have jumped at the chance without a second thought, only now... Recently her mind has been consumed by other things but then perhaps this is what she needs. 'Is there any alternative? What I mean is, if I don't go, will I still be able to go further, to do some training here perhaps, or distance learning?'

He gives nothing away on his face so she guesses he'd been expecting this question. 'We can look at other options but, I'll be honest, they won't take you as far as this can. This course will make the most of your talent, give you all sorts of options and fast track you up the ladder. But I'll understand perfectly if it's not right for you, if you don't want to spend the time away. You'll do well whatever path you choose.' He smiles at her reassuringly, but she knows exactly what he's thinking.

How lucky Katherine is to have John, he's always so supportive.

'Of course I'll miss you if you go away,' he's saying to her.

She's sat him down at their little kitchen table at home, the scene of so many different announcements in their short time together. A small thin vase containing a drooping yellow rose is the only other thing on the table besides the colourful brochure of smiling professionals. The matured scent of the rose is in Katherine's nostrils and she's absentmindedly stroking the cool china of the vase with the fingers of her right hand.

'If it's what you want Kathy, if it's really what you want then we'll manage. We'll work something out. Maybe I could try and find somebody to look after the farm, come over with you for a year or so. Two years isn't that long in the grand scheme of things. We'll do it somehow.'

'Really? Would you really not mind?' she asks him, looking up from the table.

'Really. If it's what you want, then it's what I want too,' John smiles at her, but there's a sadness behind it.

She can feel the difference in their emotions: hers excited with possibility, his muted. She's asking a lot of him and she knows it. She also knows what else is on his mind - will it mean an end to their dream of a family? 'Look I don't know yet.' she adds. 'I'll have to read up on it, think about it carefully. It's a big step.'

He simply nods his head at her and gets up to leave the table. Katherine's eyes drop back down to the folder. Is she kidding herself? Could she really fit in with those slick suited professionals in London? Is she really management material? Or has her boss taken pity on her, maybe simply made a mistake? She's only got one suit. She'd have to buy a whole new wardrobe; her clothes are more personal assistant than manager. Then there's the whole prospect of living in a big strange city. She's visited London of course, but always with somebody else. To contemplate navigating the tube or the buses on her own, of being a single tiny grain of a person in those busy streets surrounded by strangers, is daunting.

Katherine isn't convinced John is all for it, he's just saying the words. She knows he'll do it for her, but in his heart she just doesn't think it's what he wants. She knows he wants her to be here with him, and preferably with a baby. She's asking a lot, but then again doesn't she deserve something positive at last? Besides it would be good for them in the long term.

'Just think of the money,' she says to him. His back is facing her as he fills up the kettle at the sink. 'We'd be able to buy our own farm. I could get you that tractor you were eyeing up at the Foire last year. We'd be able to afford proper holidays.'

He drops his head down before turning to her. 'I don't care about those things Kathy, I'm happy with what we have. Getting a bigger tractor isn't going to improve my life that much. I want you to be happy, fulfilled. If this is what it takes, if this is what you want to do - or you need - then go for it but not for money. Please don't do it just for money.'

'I wouldn't... I was just saying...' Katherine trails off, he's made her feel almost embarrassed by her avarice and his humbleness. If she's honest she doesn't really know what she wants anymore.

27

1987, Jersey

Christmas comes and goes and then while Spring wakes up the world around them, Katherine is too busy helping Margaret with her wedding plans to think too much about September and beyond. As the weather warms up, without realising it, she finds herself creeping out from the fog which enveloped her. It isn't until one fine spring day when she's standing on the beach; the sea a refreshing blue, Jersey's coastline curving away in front of her, it's only then, as she's thinking how beautiful it all is, that she realises her depression has given way to renewed hope.

They go to the new James Bond movie with Timothy Dalton in the role and John spends the next few days repeating catch phrases from The Living Daylights and calling her Kara while driving round in his tractor as though it's a Bond car. It makes her smile again.

By the time Margaret's wedding arrives she finds the old connections with John starting to buzz. She watches him dressing for the occasion and thinks how handsome he is: tall and well-toned from physical labour. She looks at him properly for the first time in what feels like ages. It's as though they've co-existed in two different time zones. Two people living in the same house but not really connecting. It's nearly five years since their own wedding, but it's been a tough time with the pregnancies. There was no long honeymoon period for them, life threw them straight in at the deep end. It's now she realises the old longing has come back: the longing to give him a child to complete their family.

Perhaps time has given her enough distance from the last experiences for her to have forgotten just how awful they were. Perhaps she just doesn't like to give in. Perhaps she's an optimist, or perhaps it's simply the deep rooted need within Katherine to be a mother that just can't be ignored. Whatever the reason, or reasons, helped by the joy of the wedding celebration, and the wine that goes with it, she and John make love that night and their third child is conceived.

Katherine wonders if other people stop to consider the wonder of creation. She's not talking Adam and Eve; she means everyday creation. How a man and woman create a little clump of cells that multiply and grow into a tiny person. What an incredible piece of natural engineering: that the cells know where to put the arms and the head, that the little human needs lungs and a heart, it will want eyes to look at the world, ears to hear music. That some can be born with beautiful voices, others with legs that run faster than anybody else, or a brain which can further the human race. Katherine appreciates the marvel of this creation, because she also knows how it can go terribly wrong. She no longer takes it as given that they're going to get a healthy baby. Her pregnancy becomes nine months of worry. Will it survive? If it does survive is it OK? Have the arms and legs been put in the right places? The internal organs fully formed? Some people worry about getting the nursery painted, Katherine just worries whether or not she will get a baby, or will they be mourning yet another lost soul.

Blood.

It's so black and white isn't it? There's no manoeuvring with blood. No confusion.

When Katherine sees it she knows exactly what it means. Life is a little less cruel to her this time round: the miscarriage comes earlier, heralded by bleeding. She loses the baby spontaneously at eight weeks. The onset of the bleeding, the stomach and back pains are traumatic but at least she's saved the artificial intervention of another operation, or worse still – labour.

She surprises herself with her resilience.

Maybe it's because she's hardening, or maybe it's because it seems a normal part of the pregnancy cycle to her; or maybe she just didn't get so attached to this baby. Didn't allow herself to dare imagine it in their lives. Katherine isn't sure if she's kidding herself, or if some emotional volcano is lying in wait buried beneath a granite wall of protection, but this time she doesn't get depressed. If anything she's more determined. She wants a baby.

Within three months they're trying again. She tells herself if it's a girl she will call her Anne. Perhaps that will appease the curse which is upon her. Even this promise gives her some hope, some kind of positive action in a process that until now appears to be completely beyond her control.

It's early autumn when she falls pregnant again. They've been spending long warm evenings sitting in the garden chatting to Margaret and Robert who have set up home in the main house. Their mother has retreated to a couple of rooms and given over the bulk of the house to Margaret and her husband. It's been a lovely summer, Katherine's never felt so close to Margaret as now. This evening the candle flames are barely moving in the heavy air. She and Margaret lie on the lawn, looking up at the flitting black shapes of bats swooping across the garden catching the midges which hang in small busy clouds.

The garden is walled in granite with the house on one side. All along the wall Jersey lilies grow tall and proud, their shadows elegantly etched on the moonlit night sky. There's the smell of freshly turned earth in the air, the men have been working late in the fields and Katherine is expecting John to join them at any time. She's just discovered she's pregnant again so she's only sipping water and her eyes feel heavy and dry with tiredness.

Turning her head to look at her sister she makes a discovery. Margaret is lying on her back next to her, contentment across her face, one hand protectively over her stomach.

'You're pregnant aren't you!' Katherine exclaims.

Margaret is jolted out of her dream and turns to look at her. 'Oh my God! How did you guess? Yes. I'm only nine weeks though, it's still early days. We thought that after... well you know after your miscarriage, it might be best to leave off telling everyone until a bit later. Is it that obvious?' Her face is consumed with joy. 'I've been dying to tell you, I'm so glad you've guessed.'

Katherine smiles back at her. She would so love to tell her sister that she's pregnant too, but that would involve telling the whole story. Margaret is happy, enjoying her expectant motherhood. She knows there can be problems but she's not aware of just how risky it can be. If Katherine tells her any of their story it could take away the joy of her first pregnancy.

'It's wonderful news, I'm really excited for you. I shan't tell anyone don't worry.'

'Thanks. Have you...you know, have you never thought about it again?' Margaret asks tentatively, 'It would be lovely for us to have little ones at the same time, cousins who could grow up together.'

A knife stabs into Katherine's heart and slashes a huge wide open slit all the way down to her belly. If only.

'Yes it would,' she simply replies. 'Maybe one day... but you know work is busy at the moment, so we'll see.' It's the best brush off she can manage right now without getting upset and giving the game away.

They fall silent for a while, Katherine can guess what Margaret is dreaming about, lying there a smile on her lips, thinking about nursing her baby as she herself has done so many times before. All Katherine can think about are the grainy grey scan photographs, her babies that were not to be, and the possibility she might be setting herself up for more heartache. Above them the two bats continue their silent diving dance, dipping and turning, first one way and then the next. So fast you could miss their swoop in a blink.

Katherine's need for a baby is heightened by Margaret's news. She'd never wish her misfortune on Margaret in a million years, but what if her own pregnancy fails again and Margaret's doesn't. How is she going to cope with watching her younger sister with a baby? Part of her will be happy for her, but part of her will be screaming, *why not me?* As for John? He'll no doubt be thinking he'd married the wrong sister, taken on the faulty one, the one who can't bear children; can't give him the son or daughter he longs for. The world is carrying on around her but Katherine's need for motherhood means she's stuck in a deep pit of desperation, a pit with slippery walls and an endless drop before she can see the bottom.

September is here and her boss needs an answer. It's no. She can't see anything else right now except her need for a baby. Katherine simply waits. Waits and prays that perhaps this time their perseverance, their past suffering will be rewarded. That pity will be taken on them.

Pity is taken on them, but not in the way Katherine hoped. At week-fourteen, when the doctor confirms yet again their baby is lost, he also promises extensive tests.

'I suspect that what might be happening is your placenta is failing,' he announces to them both. 'It's the baby's life support, if not enough hormones are being produced it will fail. We need to do some more blood tests, check how your hormone levels are progressing. I'm sorry this must be very hard for you both I know, but we will try to find out all we can. See if there's something we can do to help.'

Katherine nods, offers up her body to the medical instruments and needles, and then goes home to await the results.

Three weeks later Margaret announces to everybody that she is pregnant and everything is absolutely fine. Katherine rejoices with her, kissing and hugging her with relief, so glad her little sister won't have to go through what she's having to. Then when she gets back to their empty cottage, she sobs. Deep, body wrenching sobs that come from the pit of her stomach and take all her energy until she falls down onto the bathroom floor, hugging her empty womb, tugging at her hair and rocking backwards and forwards on her knees; until her eyes are so puffy with tears, they sting, and her jaw aches with the effort of her grief.

When she hears John return Katherine showers and washes away the evidence of her emotion, brushing off his comments that she looks 'wiped out,' with the excuse it's been a busy day at work. She doesn't want him to see her upset. She wants to show him she can be strong, that she's up to trying again. He's already begun to question the wisdom of continuing saying he's worried about her, but she doesn't want to stop now, the very thought that 'this could be it' panics her. Whatever their next move the doctor advises they wait, give her body a few months to recover, and the medical staff time to work out if there's something they can do to help.

Even the weather works against her. In mid-October a hurricane hits Jersey and the UK, devastating the countryside, ripping mature trees from the ground and tearing roofs from their walls. 134 miles per hour winds batter their tiny island which sits open to the raging of the weather gods with no shelter from the ferocious sea winds. It rips off barn doors, flings heavy slate tiles into the yard where they smash, and covers the fields in debris. It takes John weeks of long, back-breaking days to clear the fallen trees from the fields and repair the damage, and that's after he's helped his community using his tractor to clear fallen trees from roads. John is simply too exhausted to contemplate baby making in these weeks, leaving Katherine to wonder if the Universe is completely stacked against her.

28

February 1988, Jersey – Margaret

There's no doubt Sara's birth is the most wonderful day of Margaret's life so far - but it isn't one without sadness, for it's also the day she feels she loses her sister.

Nobody could have prepared her for the emotional volcano of motherhood. That first night lying in the hospital bed, completely exhausted after nearly twenty-four hours of labour, physically in shock from the pain and exertion of it all, but unable to take her eyes off the tiny pink bundle lying wrapped-up in the Perspex cot by her bedside. The only thing she can think about is to love her, protect her, nurture her and how vulnerable she looks expelled from the safety of her mother's body into a world where they could become separated. Ultimately will be separated.

In later years, after Margaret learns her own mother's 'secret', she will remember those first feelings, that first sight of her child and she will put herself in her mother's shoes. It will help her to understand how she felt, and Margaret will find comfort in that.

For now though that shadow doesn't exist

in her life, her only focus is the brand new baby who lies next to her. Eventually her exhausted body and mind succumb to a deep dark pool of sleep where even dreams struggle to follow, and only the squeaky cries of her daughter learning to call for her attention drag her back and wake her. She sits in the half darkness of the hospital ward feeding her baby, aware of the wind flinging the rain at the windows outside, hammering on the glass. Sometimes there's only a few big drops, at other times hundreds, thousands of little droplets hurtling down to hit the few square metres of glass standing between the early spring Jersey storm, and Margaret and baby Sara. She feels secure, safe, rooted onto their tiny island sitting defiantly surrounded by sea and open skies. Their independence is what shapes them, people as defiant as the rock they live on. Swearing allegiance to the British crown nearly a hundred miles away rather than the neighbouring land mass of France to which they were once connected. That history, Margaret's history will become Sara's.

It's dark outside except for the lights of the hospital and surrounds of St Helier. Most people are warm and dry, asleep in their beds leaving the storm to rage. The ward is half draped in grey shadows hiding the beds at the centre where neither the light from the corridor nor the faint glow from outside can reach.

Margaret and Sara are the only occupants of the ward tonight, with just the odd laugh or slice of conversation from the midwives managing to slide in with the light under the closed door.

This is a twilight world Margaret learns to inhabit over the coming weeks. The small hours of the morning, half asleep, half awake, feeding a hungry baby. A time when reality can become confused with the dream world as her tired human brain attempts to shut down for sleep but is constantly nudged awake by the needs of the precious baby cradled in her arms. Margaret's eyes are heavy, dry, blurring with the battle of consciousness. Her head hangs down, nodding as she struggles to keep her brain from falling into the abyss of sleep. She might be tired but she's certainly happy.

Robert arrives first thing the next morning bearing flowers and a handful of cards from colleagues at the post office, plus a gift they'd all clubbed together to buy. Margaret loves the new look in Robert's eyes. He's always loved her, she knows that, but now that love has strengthened and when he looks at her holding little Sara she can see no bottom to its depths. His gaze envelops her and their baby in a warm soft fuzz. Robert sits on the chair next to Margaret's bed and takes their sleeping child very gently in his arms while she opens the cards and presents. The sight of her big brawny husband gently holding their tiny daughter almost makes her shiver with the wave of contentment that breaks over her.

'I bet Carol got this didn't she?' Margaret says to him as she unwraps the present. She can see Carol at work collecting the contributions and revelling in choosing it. Carol, is in her fifties with five children, only one still left at home, and she's enjoyed Margaret's pregnancy almost as much as she did herself.

'Yeah, got it in one.' Robert smiles. 'She asked if she could pop in this afternoon after her shift.' Robert replies without taking his eyes off the sleeping Sara.

'Of course she can. That would be nice.'

'You're not too tired are you?' Robert looks up now, searching her face for any signs of stress or discomfort.

'No I'm fine. Tired yes, but not too tired to show off our new baby.'

'Your mum and Katherine should be here soon,' Robert adds, as Margaret continues to open her cards.

She can't wait to share her baby with them both.

Margaret has just finished changing Sara when her mother and Katherine arrive. The changing process took at least fifteen minutes, she's so unused to her baby's delicate little frame that Margaret does everything ultra-slowly for fear of breaking or hurting something. She'd just settled into the soft chair by the window when Margaret hears their voices coming through the door. Her mother's excitement fills the entire ward, her face exploding with pleasure and pride as she hugs and kisses Margaret and Sara one after the other, over and over.

Perhaps it's the enormity of her mother's joy, or simply that she's so focused on showing off her new baby, but it isn't until they've been there for around ten minutes that Margaret notices the muted reaction from Katherine. There's no doubt their mother has taken the lead, perhaps forced Katherine onto the side-lines; but once Marie has taken Sara and started walking around the ward, rocking and cooing softly to her, Margaret becomes aware of her sister standing a few feet away as though there's an invisible barrier between the two of them.

'It all went OK then?' Katherine asks.

Margaret nods, 'Yes apparently as smooth as they go, although it was bloody painful and seemed to go on forever. But at least there were no problems and I haven't even had to have any stitches.'

'That's good,' Katherine smiles at her now, but it's a cladding smile without foundations and Margaret isn't prompted to say anything more. She's waiting for some enthusiasm, some genuine show of interest and sisterly bonding. All she gets is, 'You must be tired then.'

'Yes but it doesn't matter, you know.' Margaret replies.

'I guess you're just going to have to get used to that anyway,' Katherine half jokes, but she looks awkward as though she really would rather not be there. Margaret wonders if the idea of babies and children can abhor her sister so much now, that she can't even bring herself to share in her happiness.

Their mother returns with the sleeping Sara and Margaret's attention is drawn to them, but when Marie suggests Katherine holds her little niece, Margaret seizes the opportunity to try and force some reaction from her sister.

'Yes Kath, you hold her for a minute, she won't bite.'

Katherine hesitates for a moment opening her mouth and taking a short breath as if to protest.

Their mother takes this to be concern at handling such a tiny baby. 'It's all right love, just support her here and here and you'll be fine. It'll be good practice for you, perhaps you and John might think about trying again for one of your own.' Subtlety has never been one of their mother's strong points. Before Katherine has the chance to say or do anything else little Sara is placed in her arms. Margaret watches her face, but their mother begins to ask a thousand questions about the birth. 'So did you have any pain relief? How many pounds is she? Has the doctor checked her over yet?' Distracted by their mother, Margaret's attention wavers from Katherine.

When Margaret looks again Katherine is standing at the window, her back to them both, motionless, staring out. There's not a view from the ward and Margaret strains to see the reflection of her sister's face in the glass, but it's too bright outside. Katherine bows her head over her niece, holding her close. Is she kissing Sara? Whispering something to her perhaps? For a moment it gives Margaret hope that her sister is after all taking an interest in her child, but it's short lived. As soon as the head rises again Katherine looks back outside briefly before turning round and bringing Sara back to her. Her face is stony, fixed, not soft and motherly like Margaret had hoped.

It's the one and only time Margaret will see her sister hold her child, and this indifference becomes a cancer in their relationship. No matter how hard Margaret tries to include her over the coming days, weeks, months and ultimately years, all the attempts are met with a cool polite rebuff. At first Katherine goes through the motions of showing interest, religiously remembering birthdays and Christmas but there's always something missing, a connection that has failed to fuse.

When Katherine announces she's leaving Jersey for London less than two months later, Margaret isn't surprised. It seems to her that this is all Katherine has ever wanted: to escape the confines of their island home, to concentrate on her career, to not be everything that Margaret is.

Margaret never felt as clever as Katherine, the older sister she worships. There'd been no rivalry between them - their needs were different. If there'd been any jealousy from Margaret at all it had been directed at Katherine and Anne's relationship. When the two of them were together it wasn't just one girl joining another, somehow they seemed much more. They'd known each other for so long it was as though they'd swelled and absorbed each other to become one greater whole: two small raw dumplings put on a stew, soaking up the gravy of life's experience and growing until the edges of each other were blurred and the pan covered by their presence.

When Anne died, Katherine shrivelled and shrank overnight. For months afterward she'd hidden away in her room, hanging around the house like the air-dried skeletons of the spiders in the barn - blowing with whatever breeze arrived that day. It was only John's arrival that seemed to bring her out of this hibernation from life, but she never did reclaim the carefree confidence of her teen years. Even now, years later, Margaret can still see the scar of Anne's death on her sister, its toxic roots sunk deep into Katherine's soul.

On Katherine's last weekend in Jersey they find themselves sitting in the heart of the family home drinking red wine, surrounded by photograph albums their mother had sought out to show Sara's resemblance to previous generations of the family. As they'd drunk the wine and listened to their mother's garrulous commentary on nose forms, ear shapes and chin dimples down the ages, they'd once again found mischievous common ground and kept swapping glances or mouthing comments to each other. When their mother finally talks herself off to bed the two of them sit for a while longer finishing off the wine.

Margaret becomes emboldened by the drink, the first she's had since getting pregnant. When Katherine grows quiet and reflective, she takes the opportunity to ask her the question she's been dying to ask for ages.

'I know you had the miscarriage, which must have been awful,' her first words seem to shock Katherine for she looks at her with such force it makes her falter slightly, 'but do you think you'd ever want to try again? Have a baby?' There she'd said it. Katherine seems to be studying her face, then she looks down.

'It's not as simple as you think,' she replies

and starts to fiddle with her wedding ring.

A thousand things go through Margaret's mind: work, John, Katherine's fertility... and then she makes a mistake, one she realises almost as soon as she has done it. Instead of letting Katherine find her own words, give her time to carry on with her train of thought, Margaret's eagerness takes over and she puts the words into her sister's mouth for her. 'You mean your job and this training scheme?'

Katherine looks up, her eyes settling on Margaret's. Then she drops them again looking at her glass of wine, a faint wistful smile on her face. 'Yes that's right. That's why.' The very second those words have left her lips Margaret knows she is lying, that she's taken *her* words, *her* reason as her own with some kind of disconsolate defeatism.

They stay chatting for another hour, but the bridge has been closed. Any further attempts to steer the conversation back onto the subject are adeptly deflected by Katherine.

Their conversation is soon forgotten once Katherine has left for the UK, and Margaret's thoughts turn to other matters. She wonders how John will cope. He stays moping around the farm for a while after she's gone, harvesting the valuable Jersey Royals. As soon as the earth has given up its last potato and he's found someone to manage things, he follows

Katherine across the sea.

Robert shakes his head and predicts doom.

'He's a man of the land, a Jersey lad. He's not going to take to the big city.'

29

1988, Jersey

Margaret's baby is born one fine crisp cold day in the middle of February. Katherine watches as Robert walks her around the house and yard for a while, allowing her contractions to build, before driving her into the hospital in St Helier.

Katherine had been in the same hospital just one day earlier, only she'd been getting an injection to see if she could retain her baby, whilst Margaret came to set hers free.

Katherine fell pregnant in early January, immediately they'd resumed their attempts for a baby. She at least feels lucky to be so fertile, only now she has another guilt to add to her list: Margaret. As Margaret's belly has swelled before her, she's struggled with the turmoil of being happy for her, but so jealous. Jealous of the fact she's been able to fill up with a child. A child Katherine wants so badly for herself. She always tries to appear enthusiastic when Margaret takes her hand and presses it onto her stomach to feel the thud of a foot, or fist against hers. So many times Katherine has nearly broken down in front of her, told her everything, told her how badly she wants to be in the same position: complaining about her back, about how heavy and slow she has become, sitting with swollen ankles up and taking something for the indigestion. She hasn't though. She knows how much it would upset Margaret to know that just by being pregnant she is causing Katherine torment. Although she is completely overjoyed for her sister, she's riddled with an aching pain that gnaws right at her core.

Katherine showers her niece with presents but holds her only once, sucking in the smell of her until her head is light. Touching her soft smooth hair with her lips, letting her wrap her tiny pink hand around her finger. Then she hands her back.

She starts to stay late at work so as to avoid being around them. John asks if maybe they should get away for a couple of weeks, pop across to France, get a change of scene. Katherine hopes Margaret hasn't noticed what John has. They don't go, further injections are required. They are all in vain.

Little Sara is just six weeks old when her cousin loses her fight for life.

John finds Katherine on the toilet sobbing. She's shivering with cold and she's no idea how long she's been there. He carries her to their bedroom, trying hard not to let her see the tears in his own eyes. She's engrossed in her loss, but not so engrossed as to miss her strong husband coming apart at the seams. He wraps her up in bed and gets some painkillers and water, sitting with her until the darkness settles on their grief. Neither of them talk, but they both know that this is the end.

It wasn't supposed to be like this. It's not how Katherine dreamed it would be. They are happy, they love each other, they married. They are supposed to have children next, confirm their love, establish a family, bring on the next generation. Katherine is supposed to have produced a tiny baby for them to love. A child they could nurture and nourish, be proud of and cherish. They should have the opportunity to watch their children grow and take on life as they slowdown in theirs. Only she doesn't seem to be able to. She can't provide John with the one thing he wants more than anything in the world. She's failed him. She wouldn't blame him for not wanting her, for resenting her. Why would he want to be around her, an empty vessel of a person sucked dry by grief and longing. Barren.

Nowadays they only ever seem to make love when the need is for conception. Sometimes Katherine catches him looking at her when he thinks she can't see. What's going through his mind? Regret? Regret that he's ended up with her, a woman who is just not quite woman enough to give him a child?

There comes a time when everyone has to accept their own reality, when Katherine has to accept *her* reality. A baby is simply not going to happen for them. No matter how hard she prays, no matter how long she crosses her fingers, or counts and waves at magpies; no matter how hard she stares at the photos of smiling healthy babies, she cannot suck one inside of her by some process of desperate osmosis. It's not her destiny to be a mother and never will be.

She longs for the little things which so many mothers take for granted. She longs to bury her face into the soft downy hair of a baby and walk down a street holding a tiny hand in her own, just chatting, shopping, or walking to the beach – it doesn't matter. She longs to come home from somewhere to be greeted by an excited cry of 'mummy' and be squeezed and hugged by small arms. She longs to be able to give her love to a child, to watch it grow, to help it through life. To go to the school sports days and music concerts, to help them with their homework. To put dinner on a table full of little faces, take snacks to them as they revise for exams. To be there to comfort them when life hits back and to watch them try out their wings, take flight and soar above life taking in all it has to give. She longs for all of these and more.

She wants to go up to mothers who are hot

and cross, shouting at their children in the supermarket, stressed by motherhood, desperate for a few minutes of 'me time', for a little peace and quiet and she wants to shout at them. She wants to say she would give anything to swap places with them, anything to have a child hanging onto her skirt all the way round the supermarket. That all she ever has is 'me time', all she has is deathly, empty, no way out quiet – and it doesn't bring peace.

She's never held any of her babies, never been able to look into their faces, or have them look into hers. She now knows that she never will.

There are some days when Katherine sees her children everywhere she looks. They're in the barn, laughing faces playing hide-n-seek amongst the tools of their father's trade; or splashing in the puddles in the yard wellington boots on, rain macs glistening in a shower. She hears their footsteps running across the wooden floors upstairs, catches a glimpse of their sleeping faces in the moonlight: soft, pale, peaceful. She sees herself hugging them tightly, walking through the fields with them to visit their father and sitting together eating a picnic lunch.

There is only one escape from this ghost world for Katherine - work. At work she is no longer Katherine the wife, the failed mother; at work she is simply Katherine the professional.

She's good at what she does and when her colleagues see her they see a businesswoman not a scarred soul. If she stays with them, sees the world through their eyes she can forget - for a while at least. Concentrate on the figures on the paper in front of her, and not on what's inside. Worse things happen right? She's got to get this all into perspective, to realise how lucky she is. She's not dying of a brain tumour. She hasn't given birth to a child with a terminal illness who every day will shatter her heart into a thousand tiny painful shards.

One morning Katherine leaves their bed and finds herself sitting at their kitchen table feeling like a stranger who has just walked in and sat down. The table seems too small, she doesn't want to live amid the sentimental clutter of previous generations, or the hand-me-down recipe books anymore. She needs to escape and live a new life. In front of her is last Saturday's JEP, 'It's a Bergerac Bonanza' it proclaims, a multitude of newspaper and magazine articles about Jersey featuring John Nettles from the Bergerac series has created an avalanche of holiday enquiries for Tourism. They're welcome to it, Kathy thinks. She wants to go in the opposite direction. All the tourists might want to flock here to see this beautiful, quaint island but she needs to get away from it.

Later that morning she goes into the office

and asks to speak to her boss. It's not too late for her to join this spring's apprenticeship scheme. She's ready to go now. Defeated. She can't stay in Jersey any longer. She has to get away from her pain. Perhaps she also needs to give John the opportunity to get away from his too; allow him an easy option to throw in the towel, find himself a woman that can make him happy and fulfil his fatherhood dreams. She knows he's too honourable to leave her, but with distance between them? Perhaps it will be the excuse he needs.

For Katherine the prospect of a strange city, with all its distractions, doesn't seem scary at all anymore. She wants to get lost, to lose herself and leave the old Katherine far behind.

30

March 2008, Jersey - John

After bumping into Katherine in the yard, John sits at the little kitchen table; the same table they'd sat at together so many times all those years before. He had intended to make a cup of tea, perhaps have a piece of toast or a snack, but his body's basic needs are swamped by the emotion of seeing her. Even after all these years of separation neither of them has filed for divorce, they are still man and wife. He is sure people must find that a little strange but he doesn't. From his point of view, he has never fallen out of love with Katherine, she's simply chosen to live her life away from Jersey whereas he has not. Why would he want to break a union with somebody he pledged his lifetime's love to?

John couldn't believe his luck when Katherine fell in love with him. From that first day she'd popped her head out of the bedroom window he'd wanted her. At first there'd been a definite melancholy about her, but as the weeks went on she seemed to blossom and her mother said it was he who was bringing her back to life in the wake of Anne's death.

There had been other girls but Katherine felt right in a way that none of the others had. Finding Katherine, the woman who is the love of his life, was like re-discovering the lost page torn from his favourite book; a forgotten key that is the only means of opening a lock. It's a feeling that it's just right somehow. Relief that the searching is over, happiness coming from the completion the other person brings to you. John's not a particularly romantic man but he came to view their love rather as a bee does its honeycomb. Working at it bit by bit, adding layer upon layer until they've created a beautiful sculpture, a wonderful creation that pays homage to their union. Only the trouble is honeycomb can be quite fragile.

They were happy, blissfully happy, and then they started trying for a baby. How can a man deal with miscarriage? It's not his body that's involved, not his hormones. He's on the outside of a very private tragedy. How does anyone cope with the stolen promise of a baby and a wife's distress? John did what he thought was the best thing to do - he stayed strong. He wanted to be there for Kathy, a solid rock for her to be anchored to. He wanted her to feel she could take her time to find her bearings again, that he would keep them both safely rooted.

He watched that first time as she endured the trauma of it over and over again: forced to explain to people what had happened, why she was no longer pregnant. All he could do was stand guard over her. He couldn't protect her from the pain within but he could try to prevent external hurt and that's why they decided not to tell anyone the next time - kept it between themselves to ease the pain.

Hindsight is a wonderful thing - or perhaps a curse - either way it's useless. He can see now that in not sharing their grief it made it more difficult to move on, to heal. A secret so big and consuming as the repeated loss of their hopes, their dreams, their family, served only to make Kathy withdraw. Her reality became her own private hell not the world around her. If only he had seen it sooner.

Watching her trying time after time, only for it to end in disaster, was soul destroying. It is the flaw of many men that talking is not one of their strengths. John simply didn't know how to comfort her, what to say. Most often he would simply hold her hoping she would feel his physical comfort, that words would not be needed.

Yet, even when she wasn't grieving, their relationship was different. Their sex life, which had been full and giving, became a function: a function of the means to conceive. They no longer made love, passion didn't enter the room. Their house and their relationship became as barren as their parenthood. Throughout it all John felt completely powerless, unable to help, unable to give her what she wanted most of all - a baby.

In all truth he would have stopped trying sooner. Katherine made him happy, her love would have been enough to fill his life. Of course there was disappointment at not becoming a father, but that was a background heat of an emotion compared to the roaring inferno created by Kathy's distress. The more they kept on trying, the harder it became to penetrate the wall she built up around herself. He wasn't her partner in this. He was an awkward passenger and it was she who took the battle on, allowing it to consume her, leaving him behind.

The last time if she hadn't said 'no more' he would have. It broke his heart to carry her to bed as if she were a broken sparrow. This was no longer the Kathy he'd married. The woman lying curled up sobbing on the bed was an eggshell of the person she had been; completely consumed with pain, with the need to complete a pregnancy and become a mother. He doubted her poor body could have finished the task now even if there wasn't a problem.

And what of them? He knew the link between them was becoming more fragile. When she announced she wanted to go to London it didn't surprise him. He placated himself by saying it would do her good to get away, and he knew it probably would. His fear was she might never want to return to him.

Others were more shocked at Kathy's news. Her sister Margaret was clearly upset, and seemed to take it almost as a personal snub having recently given birth to her daughter.

'Perhaps you should tell Margaret about our troubles,' John suggested one evening as they were having dinner.

Katherine was pushing her cold food around the plate but at the suggestion suddenly became animated. 'No. Definitely not. Not now. She's just had a baby, how's she going to feel if I tell her that we can't? It will pour cold water on her happiness. It's not the right time. I'll tell her one day.' So she'd withdrawn again into her shell, and that was the only time it was ever mentioned.

Then she was gone.

Her toothbrush was no longer in the glass, her wardrobe half empty, the bottles vanished from the top of the dressing table and her pillow stayed plump and pristine. Yet still John believed she needed him as he needed her, that she wanted him to fight for their union. Once the harvest was in he followed her to London.

31

1988, London – John

Abundance. If there is one word to describe London, then it's abundance. An abundance of people of cars and lorries, of noise and smells. An abundance of shops: big ones, small specialised ones, shops selling only buttons or handbags, shops offering to find you anything you want. An abundance of tastes and styles: the clothes people wear, their haircuts, the furniture in the shop windows. An abundance of nationalities: black, brown, yellow, white skins; and an abundance of all sorts of people. Serious young men just starting off in the world, flirty young girls aware of every pair of eyes that come their way. The eccentric singleton using his 'individuality' as the excuse for why he's never married. The dry brittle divorcee - her face a barometer of her coldness. The young couple plumped pink with expectation of the life they dream of together. The student emaciated by his first time away from his mother's cooking. Two businessmen lost in their conversation - oblivious to the thousands of other human beings who jostle for the restricted pavement space around them. A waitress scurrying to the restaurant where she will spend the evening enveloped in the noise of wine fuelled chatter - serving, taking orders and not being seen. The tourist couple wandering, taking it all in, looking up at places Londoners don't see - buildings looming overhead but never noticed. A young man walking out his daily routine, picking up his sandwich from his favourite deli and planning the night's entertainment with his drinking buddies. Abundance. So much choice. So much variety. So much of everything. That's how John found London.

He travels from the airport via train trapped in a window seat by a large man who looks respectable in his suit, but whose flatulence throughout the journey constantly assails John's nose with an unpleasant smell of stale peanuts. He's afraid the stench is going to seep into his nostrils and stay there like a stain; but he doesn't want to move. His seat is right by the luggage rack and from here he can keep an eye on his cases.

From the train to the underground with its huge long rickety old escalators, which are tricky enough at the best of times but even more of an assault course when you're trying to manage two heavy bags. Standing on the platform: the slightly oily, tar like smell, the tiny little mice scurrying under the tracks searching for tasty morsels amongst the commuters' rubbish, and the ever-filling platform as more people arrive. He's always hated crowded platforms where so many people jostle for the train, it would be easy for someone just to give a little shove and you'd be under the wheels.

When the train does finally arrive John's Channel Island politeness ensures he misses out on a seat as he stands back to allow others off and more seasoned commuters slip in through any gap they can find.

Seeing Katherine is his reward.

'John.'

Her voice reaches him through the throng of people milling around outside the tube station. He's a little bewildered by the crowds. She looks genuinely pleased to see him. They hug each other so tightly he thinks they might never come apart again, but how wrong he is. The separation has already begun.

'Isn't London just so exciting?' she asks him, 'It never stops, there's so much to see and do, you'll love it.'

It has certainly given her a new lease of life, but he's worried it won't do the same for him.

'Everything still going well with the course?' he questions on their walk back to her flat. They'd talked regularly on the phone and everything seems to be going well. He feels guilty for the question because a little part of him is hoping one day she might say things aren't fine, that she hates it and wants to return to Jersey; return to him and never leave again.

'Yes it's brill. They're really pleased with me. Oh I'm just so glad you're here with me now.' She genuinely seems to mean it, wrapping her arms around his and clinging on tight. 'I've booked us tickets for Les Miserables, you've always wanted to see that haven't you? Then we can go for dinner in China Town afterwards. There's also a rounders match in the park this weekend, we can take a picnic and you can meet some of the guys from work. Oh, and I must take you to the coffee shop near the flat, they do the most divine bacon sandwiches.'

John smiles down at his excited wife, it's good to see her so full of life again, to see the colour back in her face and some energy in her body. He wonders though how deep the glow goes, is it just superficial? Underneath this smiling exterior is she still red raw and hurting, or has the city really been a cure-all panacea? Would this city cure him and the rift in their marriage, or will it tear them apart forever?

They go to the theatre, try a range of different foods from around the world, visit museums and art galleries, play rounders in the park and walk along the Thames. They take in the history with visits to the Tower of London and a trip out to Windsor Castle. Kathy introduces him to her new friends, and they have people round to the flat for dinner; but all the time he feels like a shadow in the glare of Katherine's new found freedom. An impostor. Can she not see how he's struggling? Or does she not want to see?

John vows to give himself time, perhaps he too could come to see the excitement rather than the noise of the place. He applies for a job as a park keeper with one of the boroughs, and gets it. Day after day, week after week, he travels through the heaving streets to his green oasis where he can rub the earth between his fingers, create life amid the concrete, and make believe he could be happy here. But the earth doesn't smell rich and full of iron like at home, it is grey and dusty. His flowers are often vandalised, and the air is thick with exhaust fumes not fresh and salty, just blown in from across the seas.

He tries, Lord knows he does, because he wants to be with Katherine; but he just can't make himself enjoy living in the city. They have a pleasant enough flat in a modern block: functional, comfortable, seven floors above the teeming streets below. Floor after floor of people, all piled up on top of one another. Tiny windows to the outside world, each living in their private pen oblivious of those above, below or around them. There is no social contact, nowhere to stop and chat. No front yard or street to stand in and catch up with the neighbours. John wonders how children growing up in these concrete towers can be expected to become adults with social skills and consciences when they have no real idea what society is, let alone their place in it?

It's all about money. They work to get the things they want, as defined by the conduit that has access to almost everyone – the TV. Television is the one ubiquitous thing John hears when he walks past the other doors, not conversation or laughter, but the incessant sound of television voices playing to an audience choosing to watch drama or be a fly on the wall of somebody else's life rather than live their own. Yet he can't see how television can impart a sense of history, belonging, or value like conversations with grandparents or shared family meals. To him, television value is only defined in monetary terms.

Everything seems to be played out amid a frenetic pace of life. For an outsider, like John, people aren't people - they're a blur rushing from one place to another. The endless stream of cars. Never any peace. It's constant. Nothing except the buildings stand still to watch. Dirty, tired buildings, chewing gum splattered pavements, walls covered in graffiti: illegal and purposeful as buildings and signs. Life that needs a new lick of paint.

John has been in London around six months

when things come to a head. On the surface their relationship is fine, sex has started again, although Kathy is obviously taking contraceptives this time. They don't talk about what happened, she hushes him if he ever broaches the subject, as though to speak the words in her new life will somehow taint things. It's almost as though she wants to completely wipe her slate clean, deny her own past. John has begun to wonder if Katherine thinks of him as her past too. He doesn't feel able to keep up with her new way of life and friends, Katherine simply doesn't seem to need him anymore. Has he become a millstone around her neck? The man she's married by mistake? He imagines that if he suddenly disappears she probably won't even notice.

It's a Friday night and they are out for dinner in the West End, just the two of them. London is lit up with multi-coloured lights, it seems like a million eateries are vying for their attention. All the focus is on the streets, on the people, the shops still open for business and the Maître d' trying to tempt them into their restaurant. Nobody seems to notice the black sky with its beautiful full moon and sparkly stars - it might as well not have bothered.

They choose an Italian which looks traditional and fairly busy. Several of the customers are Italian themselves, 'You can trust a restaurant where their own nationality eats', has always been the advice John's father gave him.

They sit at a window seat and John orders some Lambrusco. Kathy is chatting about her day at work and John idly looks out of the window. Outside young people are spilling out of pubs onto the streets, smoking, drinking their pints. Inside the pub he can see a mass of heads like pins crammed tightly together on a board. The pub is packed, a people-stuffed sausage. Any movement to the bar or to the toilet requires a group ripple, a giant intestinal contraction to expel the object of irritation elbowing its way along. All around the street the lights are on, empty offices bleaching energy into the darkness.

The door springs open with a chime and a man with his basket of single wrapped roses comes in, targeting the couples. He walks up to their table with his salesman's smile proffering a flower to Katherine. John looks at it. A single lonely bloom, probably flown thousands of miles half frozen from some foreign country to end up here in a restaurant in London as a trite gift. The price is extortionate, his sales will get better as the evening wears on and suitors become more intoxicated.

John looks at Katherine; a single rose isn't what she needs. He waves the man away. The man doesn't hang around, he has a hundred other places to try and is quickly gone.

Four elderly people sit next to them chatting over old times, hair brittle and white, skin dry and transparent. Fading eyes in deep dark sockets that have seen a million things - but right now struggle to focus in the dim light.

At home - home! How could he have ever thought anywhere else but Jersey could be home? If he'd sat for an evening looking out a window in Jersey, watching people go by, he'd have seen at least one, if not several people he knows. Here he could sit for a lifetime and never see a friendly face just happen to walk past. Cast adrift in a sea of strangers he realises the experience makes him want to launch a distress flare, whereas Katherine is not only enjoying the sensation, she is positively seeking it out. She wants to be lost, to break her anchor and drift away from her rock. Sitting here it dawns on John that he has been watching her drift away from him.

He chews his food but he isn't tasting it. A gaping chasm has opened between them. Katherine could be sitting at the other end of one of those huge medieval dining tables for all the closeness he feels tonight.

He can't finish his meal. At another time he might have felt a little guilty, or embarrassed, in front of the waiter's question, 'Was everything all right sir?' but not tonight. He will never be here again, never see the waiter another time. He owes him nothing.

After the meal they walk home arm in arm, Katherine still chattering about work and what they can do at the weekend. He wants to hold her. Not to feel skin on skin, flesh on flesh, they do that – no, to *really* hold her. He wants to feel the true Katherine, the electricity of her body instead of the warm soft nothingness she has become. He wants to hold her, to envelop her so she's welded into him, protected, nourished and they become one again.

She's still chattering on. Now she's talking about the future.

'My boss says there'll definitely be a job for me here at the end of the course. He's really pleased with how I'm doing; says I'm going to do great... Perhaps we could start looking into buying a place, nothing too big but...John? Are you listening to me?'

'Yes sweetheart I'm listening. That's good. Well done. I knew you'd be brilliant.' There is a resigned weariness to his voice which Katherine can't fail to pick up. They are almost back to the flat now and John feels a storm brewing between them. Perhaps it is time. Time to have it all out and say what needs to be said.

Katherine rises to the atmosphere. 'You're not really interested are you? You just don't care about my career!'

'I do Katherine, honestly I do. If that's what you want, then I'm happy for you.'

'Happy for me. But you're not happy.

Right?'

There is a silence as she puts the key into the front door lock and opens it.

'Right,' he finally says with a sigh as they enter the flat.

For some reason she doesn't think to turn on the lights and the sitting room is illuminated only by the white glow of the city streaming through the windows.

'Why John? Is it me? Is it because we can't have children?' Her voice has risen, the all too familiar notes of distress creeping into her tone.

'No. God! No darling. I love you.' He spins her round to him holding onto her shoulders with both hands. 'I'm happy with just you and me.' But she's spoiling for a fight now, he can tell whatever he says she's going to twist it.

'I see. You love me, but only on your terms right? Admit it, you don't like the fact that I've got a career now, do you?' Her anger, or is it something else, is coming out in her physically. She flings his hands off her and starts to pace the room.

Still neither of them turn on the lights preferring instead to hide their emotions in the half light, like some strange black and white Hitchcock thriller.

'Of course I want to support you Katherine. If this is what you want to do then I'm a hundred percent behind you, I've told you that and I mean it. But are you sure this is you, are you sure that moving here away from all your family is right, that you're doing it for the right reasons?'

'The right reasons? I'm here because I want to be here. Because I'm fed up with being trapped on that tiny island. Here there's so much opportunity, I can be somebody, do something with my life.'

John looks at her shadowed face. He wants to say all he sees is a wounded deer shying away from the light, that she's still hurting, that she's running away. He wants to tell her in this city of millions the last thing she is likely to become is a 'somebody'. The most likely outcome is she'll end up a nobody in a crowd of strangers. Perhaps that is what she really wants, to lose herself, to escape everything she was before. He says none of this.

'OK. But I'm sorry Kathy I can't. I just can't do it - live here I mean. I have to go back. I miss the land, I miss home.'

'So that's it... just give up?' She's venomous now, 'Roll over, don't try. You've only been here a few months and you've hardly made any effort. Let's face it you never wanted to be here in the first place.'

He sighs, 'Maybe you're right, but I came didn't I? I came because I wanted to be with you. I came because you said it would be two years and I didn't want us to be apart that long. Now you're saying you want to stay on after the course as well.'

'You said you'd support me, that I should do what I really want to do...and what do you mean by wanted? You said you *wanted* me, so does that mean you don't want to be with me anymore is that it?'

'No Kathy, no, that's not it. I love you. I will always love you, but I'm accepting that right now you have to do this. It's what you want. Only I can't do it Kathy, I'm sorry but I can't. Please. You have to understand, it's just not me.'

'Sure, I understand all right.' She turns away now, her voice changing, the fight going out of her. In the semi darkness it's impossible to see if there are tears or not.

'I'll still be there for you Kathy, I'll come and visit, and you can come back and visit too. Other people manage long distance relationships, why can't we? I'll always be there for you...'

'Yeah sure.... Well don't hold your breath.' With that she walks into the bedroom and slams the door.

Is this it? Is this the end of their marriage? The complete destruction of the honeycomb?

John sits for a good hour on the brown leather sofa, his head in his hands. His stomach is hurting and he feels sick. They are at opposite ends of a spectrum. Katherine sees the big cosmopolitan city as freedom, John instead feels trapped. Trapped in a concrete maze where building after man-made building rises up around him. The little patches of green park where he works just aren't enough, they're tiny sticking plasters on a giant graze. He misses the sea, the big open skies that surround Jersey where he can see for miles, pick out the houses on the French coast, watch a storm roll across the horizon towards him. He can't breathe here sucking in the recycled air of a million others, his ears bombarded by a hundred discordant orchestras of daily life.

Freedom to him is being able to stride across an open field or walk for miles along the golden sands of St Ouen. For Katherine freedom is to escape who she is; and sitting on the sofa is when John realises freedom for her is also to escape him. His presence is like an open sore to her. Every time she looks at him she must be reminded of what they've been through, the childlessness of their situation. How can she be free with him hanging around her neck like an albatross? He must go home not just for his sake, but for hers as well.

32

1988-2008, Jersey – Margaret

Margaret's life with Robert and their new baby settled into a gentle cruising speed. Their marriage a comfortable holding pattern interspersed with the birth of James and then Sophie. As Robert predicted, John returned to the farm from London; picking up his tools from where he'd left them. They watched as he drove his tractor in and out of the yard in silence. There was barely a word from Katherine. She called occasionally: birthdays, Christmas, but she didn't come back to her husband. Her training course developed into a new career path.

Cocooned in Jersey, Margaret's family travel together through a succession of Bonfire nights and Christmases, first days at school, sports days and noisy children's birthday parties. Her life is rich from loving them all. She never takes for granted their wide-eyed wonder as she reads them a bedtime story, or the squeals of happiness at the first warm spring day when they can walk on the beach without their boots and socks; allowing the return of sand between their toes. Most days she finds another 'special moment' to add to her family's treasure store, just like the jar of seashells and sea glass which shine on her kitchen windowsill.

Of course not everything is perfect in their family life - what family ever is. Sara starts smoking at thirteen and there are terrible rows as they try to get her to stop. They bully her, grounding her for weeks, but it simply makes her more determined to rebel against their authority. They bribe her, but she's sneaky and it's months before they realise she's kept up the habit using breath fresheners. There is no end of tears and tantrums. In the end it's Sara herself who makes the decision to give up when her first proper boyfriend says she tastes awful, 'Just like an ashtray.'

Then there are the current troubles with James, who at times makes unwise choices for friends. It means days when Margaret has questioned her mothering skills. She loves her children with every molecule of her body, but there have been occasions when she's felt completely unappreciated; when she has questioned why she didn't spend a little more time on herself. Perhaps had a career like Katherine's, something to show she's a separate entity to her family and their needs. The next day, when the storm of emotions created by their adolescent hormones has subsided, leaving a calm clear time, then she can see just how rich her life is for all its downs as well as ups. Guiding your children through the pitfalls of growing up and the struggles of containing hormonal surges, well that's just all part and parcel of being a good parent - even if it is hard work at times. The little bubble of dissatisfaction pops and is gone.

There have been times when the fragility of motherhood has depressed her. The worrying beginning the second each child has left her body. A few years ago they'd lost James on a busy beach in France. It was the worst feeling in her life. He'd gone down to the water's edge with Robert and Sara while Margaret stayed looking after the bags and reading a book. A few minutes later she'd looked up, but couldn't see James. She stood up and waved at Robert asking through sign language where James was. He didn't know. It was instant - a buzzing in her head and ears as her blood pressure shot up and she went into panic mode. Every possible scenario went through her mind. He could have been taken off the beach by somebody and be long gone. He could be drowned in the sea. There were hundreds of people scattered all over the beach, how on earth was she going to be able to find a little lost boy.

They started to shout at first, looking left and right, desperate to see his little brown head and Thomas the Tank Engine swimming trunks. Nothing. Margaret started walking to the left, Robert to the right. Searching... Calling... In the end it was Robert's big voice that found him wandering lost, tears in his eyes. He'd been walking back to Margaret but been distracted by another child's sandcastle and then become completely disorientated. At moments like that motherhood seemed like a curse, the realisation something so precious and fragile can be taken from her in seconds.

Margaret doesn't judge people their life choices, a career versus having children. She'd like to think she's never judged Katherine for her choice. It's not the fact her sister chose not to create new life with a family of her own, it's more that she's turned her back on her existing family which annoys her. Katherine's visits, when they come, are brief to the extreme. She usually says she can only stay a long weekend at maximum due to work commitments. It's not even just her lack of contact with their mother and her own family that annoys Margaret, but there's also John. He never talks about it. She tried to get him to open up in the early days when she had naively thought perhaps she could broker some kind of reconciliation, but John has always been tight lipped and loyal to his wife. Not once has she ever heard him say a bad word about her sister. Not once has he ever complained about his lot; and in Margaret's knowledge not once has he strayed in his love for Katherine by finding sanctuary with another woman, saving himself from the solitary purgatory she has condemned him to.

Year in, year out, Margaret has watched him quietly getting on with his life - but he's only half a jigsaw. He floats in formaldehyde asphyxiated by his love and loyalty, never moving on, unable to break free.

As the years go by Margaret's feelings harden against Katherine, and John becomes more like a sibling than her own sister. She can't forgive Katherine her treatment of her husband. If she doesn't love him then why hasn't she set him free? Filed for divorce? Allowed him some kind of closure instead of the film reel endlessly looping with no final scene to bring it to a conclusion. The way Katherine's treated John has not just been selfish but downright cruel, as though she's punishing him for something. Margaret wondered at first if perhaps she was. Maybe he'd had an affair, done something to hurt her deeply? As the years stretched on and John never wavered in his devotion, she's long since discounted that theory. In Margaret's eyes John has become a martyr and her sister the persecutor.

33

1988-2008, Jersey - John

It is December 21st when John returns home without his Katherine - the hardest thing he's ever had to do. He keeps telling himself that it isn't going to be forever, that she has to chase her dream, heal her pain, and then she'll be back. Only he's not sure he believes it. He knows she doesn't understand why he's gone, but he's sure he's done the right thing for them both. The problem is he worries that away in the big cosmopolitan city her life will change. She'll change. She won't want him - the farmer with the dirty hands from the tiny island.

The fact he flies home the same day as 270 people lose their lives in the Pan Am flight 103 bombing over Lockerbie, gives him at least some sense of perspective; but it doesn't help him feel any better about 'abandoning' Katherine in London. In fact, that makes it worse thinking of her watching the horrific news on TV, alone and vulnerable.

He is grateful Margaret doesn't question him when he returns, just seems to accept that he is home and that is that. She can't possibly understand what is going on because she knows nothing of the miscarriages, but he senses she empathises with his feelings about home and city life at least. He is tempted to tell all, to sit down with her and just let it all spill out; feel the huge burden he carries slip from his shoulders in the telling - but he doesn't. He knows Katherine doesn't want anyone else to know and it is more her secret than his. Hide it all away, don't tell anybody, and then they can both pretend none of it has ever happened. With the potato planting season starting in the new year - work, thankfully, demands more than his full attention.

He and Katherine parted amicably. There were no more arguments. She accepted he was leaving and saw him off at the airport. He wasn't quite sure why she made the journey to Gatwick to say goodbye instead of staying behind in London. Perhaps she was finding it harder than she let on. He hoped that was the reason. He hoped that seeing him go might make her change her mind. His hopes were never realised.

At first they call each other a couple of times a week but as the months move along it is usually him who tries to call. When they do talk, when she is in, she sounds bored with his stories of the farm and Jersey life. So eventually he decides to run a test - he doesn't call her. He waits for her to ring. She doesn't. He waits.

By the following December, a year after he's returned, he hasn't spoken to her for three weeks. Eventually the phone rings but it isn't because she's missed him. She calls to say she isn't coming back home, they're short staffed over the festive season and she's volunteered to work - so those with children can be at home. When John puts the phone down he puts it down on their relationship. For the next few years they still visit each other but gradually the contact becomes more minimal and formal. She never forgets his birthday and every Christmas there is a little parcel and a card but they become penfriends: not a married couple. The visits dry up. Until now. Now she has returned home.

It's so difficult to understand what it is he's feeling. Seeing her again, hearing her voice. He had an urge to embrace her, to take in her scent like he used to, but he didn't. He'd dreamed about this moment for years, but how much of his Katherine is left? The woman that just stood before him might only be a facsimile of the girl he once loved. All the memories that were theirs replaced with ones they don't share. Does she still like the same things? Would they still laugh at the same jokes? Or is the Katherine he married gone? Was she so worn out when she left that she simply disappeared into the hypnotic fire of London life, reborn a stranger.

To him the fact she never asked for a divorce, and he'd never heard from Margaret of any other men, means there has always been some hope - however faint. People can live apart and still love each other. Not every marriage conforms to the accepted norm. All those years he's clung onto a dream. Now though, now she's back and as reality hits him he finds himself on the defensive. He can't seriously think she might want him back, not after twenty years? They are like strangers. If she'd really loved him she would have come home before now. If anything she probably despises him, his small island ways. Perhaps she wants to meet up and talk so they can discuss a divorce. Draw a line through this long, sad affair.

Twenty years away have changed her. Her body and face aren't just rounded from middle age, but from the wealth of experiences she's gathered over that time. Him? He's stayed in the same house, doing the same, albeit slightly altered, job and barely left this island of just nine by five miles - unless it was to visit her. No, he's not fool enough to think she will find him attractive anymore. She outgrew the little corner of the world they'd created together decades ago - branching out over the wall; spreading her tendrils into new flowerbeds. He simply embedded his roots, pushing them deeper and deeper into the ground, burrowing

them in the soil, establishing the corner as his
own solitary patch.

34

March 5th 2008 – Margaret

An awkward truce settles over Katherine and Margaret following their trip to Fort Regent. They haven't really had any more time on their own to carry on their conversation, or work through some of the issues Margaret raised on Monday, but they've learned to be civil to each other. Sophie seems to have decided that as she's only just found this new aunty she's not going to let her out of her sight, and wants to do absolutely everything with Aunty Kathy.

The two women have lunch in the kitchen served by a short but very serious waitress called Sophia. She reads out a beautiful long menu to them, that includes such delights as 'lobster biscuit' and 'spaghetti bolog-knees', only to discover that everything is 'off' or 'all gone', apart from the egg mayonnaise sandwiches Margaret made earlier.

After lunch they go to the Co-op for some supplies and are driving back into the yard when they see Margaret's friend Carol chatting to John. She waves at them, peering into the car. Margaret knows why she's here, not just for the coffee she'll claim she's after, but to check out the long lost sister. John disappears as quickly as a hermit crab.

'I just can't believe it,' Carol plonks herself down at the kitchen table. She's one of those women their mother might have called, "blousey", a tad too much makeup for her age, clothes a little too provocative and a distinct lack of inhibition; but an honest and loyal friend. 'I mean I know when we were kids we used to say we didn't want to get sent to that place, it was known for being tough. Lots of children's homes were in those days. But I never would have thought kids were being murdered there. Here on our island.' She's back on the major topic of island conversation, Haut de la Garenne, after warmly welcoming Katherine. 'I told you about my sister didn't I?' she continues, not waiting for a reply, 'Got a knock on the door yesterday, it was one of them newspaper reporters. Offered good money for stories too. She told him where to go.' Carol shakes her head.

Katherine watches her quietly.

Margaret is busy with the kettle pouring water in the cafetiére. 'Good for her,' Margaret replies, not turning round.

'Yeah but listen to this - this really annoys me,' Carol has the day's Jersey Evening Post spread out in front of her on the kitchen table. 'It's from an A. Sowman from Preston in Lancashire, right. He or she says that *'as a regular visitor to the island of Jersey'*, so a tourist, not somebody who lives or been brought up here, *'it's my recollection that rumours have abounded about the goings on at Haut de la Garenne for many years, with nothing being done about it.'* I mean how much crap is that? I've never heard anything, you never heard anything and we've lived here all our lives. Yet some bloody tourist who visits for a week or two a year now reckons there's been some great open secret about the place.' Carol shakes her head and carries on looking at the paper. 'Don't get me wrong,' she adds, looking up at them both, 'I'm not saying that nothing happened. God knows you've got to feel sorry for those poor sods who are coming forward now telling their stories n'all, but to make out as though we all knew something was happening, as though it was acceptable to us, well that's just bloody ignorant, that is.'

Katherine and Margaret both nod in agreement.

'You know the police have dismissed the rumours the body they found is Neolithic don't you?' Carol says to Margaret.

'No I didn't,' Margaret replies walking over to look at the paper herself.

'Yep, it's in here today.'

'So bang goes the theory that it was from one of the Dolmen burial chambers,' Margaret adds.

'Yes. It's just terrible it is, terrible...those poor children,' Carol shakes her head at the paper for the umpteenth time. 'And they say there are still calls coming in from victims.'

Every time she thinks about it Margaret feels sick. Sick for the victims. Sick with the fear that somebody she knows might have realiscd it was going on. Sick for the fact the people who had done it must still be walking around, possibly in Jersey, and possibly still hurting children. It feels like having a plaster ripped off a gaping wound. The island has lain quietly for years and now suddenly the plaster has been pulled back and, underneath, the soft naivety of the community is in agony from the onslaught of outside scrutiny.

It's made Margaret look at her world in a different way. 'Something like this makes you think more carefully about the adults your children are in contact with, or have been in contact with,' she says. More to Carol than to Katherine, but they both murmur in agreement.

She can remember the day the story first broke: the shock of it. Robert parked himself in front of the television, shouting updates to her from the sitting room to the kitchen. By the Monday the reality was starting to sink in. She'd been sitting reading the Jersey Evening Post when Robert called.

'You seen the Post?' He asked.

'I'm reading it now,' she sighed back.

'Telegraph are reporting the bodies of at least seven children could be buried there. They're quoting the copper in charge, Harper, as saying "There could be six or more, but it could be higher than that..." I just can't believe this is happening. How could so many children have gone missing and nobody notice?'

Margaret sighed again, 'I know, and the JEP says the police want to talk to decorators who discovered bones at the site in 2003. It says they're seriously concerned about the way that discovery was handled. If that's true, if they found remains of children then, that means it's people in charge now who have been hushing it all up.'

'Doesn't bear thinking about does it?' Robert's depressed tone came back to her. Their world was changing colour, growing darker and there was nothing they could do about it.

Afterward, when Robert had rung off, Margaret carried on reading the JEP. On page two she found further information about the dogs being used in the search, 'One of the dogs, a springer spaniel called Eddie, which was used in the hunt for missing toddler Madeleine McCann in Portugal, detected the remains found on Saturday through two inches of concrete.' Finally, she read a quote from Lenny Harper the man in charge of the investigation, 'We just do not know how many kids may have disappeared.' That was enough for Margaret. She had to get out the house, get some fresh air. So she went for a drive, travelling around her island 'looking' at it with different eyes.

She saw the granite cliffs, the foundation of everything that Jersey is, standing firmly, unmoving, as the surrounding sea ebbs and flows bringing all manner of things to its shores. The beauty of the slightly wilder west side, the huge long sandy expanse of St Ouen's beach stretching for miles; and then up away from the flat west to the north end of the island where beaches give way to cliff top walks and dark caves.

In the east is the low tide moonscape of rocky beach stretching out to sea for what seems like miles, to be replaced within hours by waves that leave at most a golden sandy fringe spattered with the green of seaweed. This eastern run of beaches is interspersed with pretty little harbours: La Rocque, Gorey, and the long arm of St Catherine's breakwater; and dotted with solid grey Martello towers. Evidence of an island once in need of defence from more than just tabloid reporters.

In the south is the busy built up harbour and town of St Helier, tipped with the magnificent outcrop of Elizabeth Castle and skirted by a long curving sandy bay stretching all the way to St Aubin Fort. This is her island. Small, yes, but upon it a wealth of varying landscape. Layer upon layer of history has been foisted upon it. The ancient burial chambers, the Dolmens, which once littered the island. Some now gone completely, some broken and smashed but others like the mound at Hougue Bie positively steeped in the generations that have made their mark upon it. From the first Pagan worshippers of the sun, who toiled to move giant lumps of granite to build it, the Medieval Catholics who added the ancient chapel above and most recently the scar of German occupation gouged into its side by wartime slave workers.

Of course there are more recent superficial things to have altered the island, like the human planning abhorrence that is the Le Squez social housing flats, blighting the landscape all around them. They rise up from the St Clement plateau - symbols of grey concrete ignorance. An attempt to help society, to house people who need homes, but at a price which offends the eye and does little to offer its residents a home that makes the most of their environment. Margaret can never forget the words of a teacher who worked at a school near the estate. Her pupils were in the reception year, around about Sophie's age, and she told her how some of them only ever went to the beach when they were on school outings. A beach which is just a few hundred yards from their doorsteps, a ready-made playground and garden, and yet their parents don't take the time to show it to them. For someone like Margaret who positively revels in the joy of taking her children to the beach most days of the year, whatever the weather, it's an anathema - a travesty for childhood. What more though this revelation from Haut de la Garenne, what more a travesty can there be than this?

The conversation in the kitchen has moved on, Carol is quizzing Katherine about her life in London. It's quite interesting for Margaret to just listen, get an outsider's perspective.

'So where do you live?' Carol starts by asking Katherine.

'Not far from Tottenham Court Road.'

'Ooh that's busy isn't it?' Carol replies, 'Don't you get sick of all the traffic? It would do my head in.'

Katherine smiles wryly, 'Well, I think you just get used to it, I don't really notice it to be honest.'

Carol is quick to come back with more questions. 'So why have you come now, in March? You should have come back in the summer when you can go on the beach and enjoy some sunshine.'

'I'm not really here as a tourist...' Katherine hesitates, Margaret is purposely not looking, but she's sure she feels her sister's eyes on her.

'I came to see my family and sort out a few things.'

Perhaps Carol senses the tension in the air for she switches tack, turning the conversation to talk about Sophie. Katherine makes her excuses and goes upstairs.

When Carol leaves shortly afterward Margaret is glad of the peace; so many things are whirring around her head. She sits quietly in her kitchen - her place - and tries to figure out just how she is feeling about everything.

This time of year isn't depressing for Margaret, although of course weather has a lot to do with it, a month of cold hard rain can make anyone feel fed up. Already the fields around them are coming alive, bringing the promise of warm sunshine just around the corner.

It starts in the early hours of the morning, before the office commuters have gobbled their cereals and organised their children for the school run, usually around the time Margaret is waking up. In the darkness she will hear the big powerful engines flat out coming down the road, the clang of trailers bouncing along; and see the orange flashing lights that sit on top of the cab warning anybody out at that time of the morning that a wide vehicle is heading their way. Where all the tractors suddenly appear from has always been a mystery to her because the roads are suddenly full of them, and if you don't see one you'll certainly not fail to notice where they've been from the muddy tyre tracks they leave behind.

The tractors bring trailers full of wooden trays stacked high and carrying the valuable Royal Jersey seed potatoes, all sitting neatly like little princes waiting to put their purple and white root buds into the soil to grow. Other tractors will take the portable blue toilets around from field to field for the workers who arrive and leave in dirty minibuses. Seasonal migrants from Eastern Europe mostly, who spend the day with their backs bent double placing each potato into its allotted bed by hand. The planting field will be filled with the colour and the noise of them for a couple of hours and then they'll move on. Behind them a smaller team will begin to unroll the huge polythene sheeting which will bathe the entire field in a silvery shimmer and defend the fledgling potatoes until the weather warms and they thanklessly tear and split their plastic protection, breaking out to freedom and sunshine.

By now, fields all around the island lie shimmering in their spring overcoats, mirroring the flinty white sky as though panels of cloud have fallen to the ground and now lie there. The planting season marks Margaret's new year, the start of things to come, only this year even that has failed to raise her spirits. The potato fields are irrelevant frivolities, costume jewellery on an island which appears to have turned ugly and unpleasant, in the face of the revelations from Haut de la Garenne.

This introspective searching causes Margaret to feel her age and mortality. She once wandered through the streets of Jersey as a small child looking up at looming adults who cooed and smiled down at her, until she grew to their height and gained children of her own to lead around by the hand. Everywhere she goes on the island she sees familiar faces: someone she went to school with, an old family friend, another mother from one of the children's schools. Lately though she also sees familiarities where there are none. Faces she thinks she recognises, only to realise they instead merely contain characteristics of somebody she used to know. Somebody who was part of her world but has since died. Another flake of human life shed and come to rest on Jersey's shores.

Margaret wonders what their parents would have thought of the stories coming out of Haut de la Garenne. She tries to see her father in her mind, but these days it seems to always be the same short clip - a snatch of his voice, a flicker of his presence. No matter how hard she tries to hold onto him time is slowly erasing him. Not his love or her love for him, but his physical memory. It's cruel enough that loved ones get taken away but even a clear memory is denied her and she's left with just fuzzy feelings and vague recollections of days spent together.

There are times when Margaret wonders if her father's spirit and her memories of him stay away because of the secret she now carries - her mother's secret. Yet somehow she never feels he stopped loving them despite it. A couple of years ago she had a dream in which her father was as real to her as Robert was when she woke up next to him. She'd hugged her father; he'd talked to her. She'd seen him as clear as day and the feeling of comfort and love from that dream lingered long after she'd woken up. It's been times like that she's glanced twice at the church and its graveyard. Margaret's had little time for religion and its cruel God, but sometimes she's wondered if maybe there is something in it. Did her father come to comfort her, or was it simply the chemicals in her mind reaching into the depths of her memory banks and taking old film, splicing it and creating a new storyline?

She knows their father would have been horrified by the current news. She remembers enough of him to realise he had been an honourable man, with the best interests of his patients and others in the forefront of everything he did. In the national media they talk about a 'closed society' in Jersey, about an island where the establishment rules. Margaret wonders what they mean by *establishment*. Do they mean the traditions and foundations of their society or the men and women who currently, but temporarily govern it? She is starting to question what price they've paid for their lifestyle, for the low crime rate and wonderful schools, for the fact that if somebody has their car scratched the police still issue an appeal for witnesses and it makes the Jersey Evening Post. Isn't all that a product of Jersey's traditional society? Its Honorary Police system? Its sense of community? Or has she been completely blind to another parallel universe, one where the vast majority are hoodwinked by an evil minority ruling with subversive subtlety, taking what they want from those around them like leeches?

Who was the young child the papers say was murdered at the children's home? What was their name? Where did they come from? How many more little bodies will they find? Try as she might Margaret cannot see the Jersey being portrayed in the newspaper articles. She scans faces in the street, a subconscious cowboy movie trait searching for the black hat that will give the bad person away. She doesn't see it, of course, life isn't that simple. Colours aren't on the outside they are hidden away in people's hearts.

She's even found herself studying her children's faces when the story is mentioned on radio or TV. Thankfully there have been no adverse reactions from them, no flicker of a buried memory related to the revelations. Like everyone else she knows Margaret hopes that anybody who committed crimes like these is caught, that they receive a fitting punishment for the tormented lives they've left behind. Also like others she's been hurt by the tarring everyone in Jersey has got from the brush of the tabloids and television reporters who scenting a flaw in the image of the island, have gone for the jugular.

The newspapers and radio brought this unwanted news into Margaret's kitchen. Her kitchen which has soaked up her family life as it has done for generations before theirs. It's been a warm safe womb around her. From the chip in the stone floor by the door, to the pictures created by the children stuck on a board by the fridge; and the huge granite lintel above the range which has been cloaked in the steam and aroma of thousands of dinners. If, as they say, the fabric of a building soaks up the energy around it then the lintel must contain a very happy, fat ghost. Now this evil from Haut de la Garenne has gained access to her sanctuary and worms into Margaret with its disturbing threat of more disclosures to come.

All through this time the only voice she listens to and believes is that of the investigating police officer. He will hopefully uncover the truth. She knows whatever she's feeling is nothing compared to what the victims have gone through, and must be going through now as they recount the trauma of their childhoods; but nonetheless it has affected everyone. It's turned Margaret's mood black - dejected. When people question everything you have believed and lived with your whole life there can be no other outcome.

35

March 5th 2008 – Margaret

What would old Vi from across the road have made of all the Haut de la Garenne news? She always seems to have been there in their lives, old, a widow longer than she'd been married. She lived in the cottage just across the road. Nowadays she is still across the road from them, only a little further down, lying in the double plot she'd reserved when her Jack died all those decades ago. Not for her the freshly landscaped newcomers' section at the top of the graveyard, where in January and February it seems every week the boards go up and a new resting hole is dug. Vi probably would have enjoyed the company of the mourners. At times big groups of all ages crowd around to say goodbye to their loved one. On other days just a handful of sombre elegiac faces stand by the grave, talking over their memories, dressed in their smartest black clothing; the women's heels click-clacking down the path to where the hearse and cars await.

Vi always wanted to know all the gossip. There wasn't much that went on in the Parish which she hadn't heard. It was Vi who'd told

Margaret her mother's secret; a secret only she had known. There are days when Margaret despises the old woman for her honesty. Why couldn't she have taken it with her, left things as they seemingly were?

Old Vi let go her secret one day when Margaret went round with a plate of dinner for her. She was virtually bedridden and failing fast. Her skin hung off her bones as life ebbed away. She shared her knowledge in the little bedroom with faded rose pink curtains, the one at the front of the house where the new couple have placed cream blinds. Margaret received the news amid the smell of a decaying body and damp house; the aroma of her homemade cooking - which sat on the old woman's lap - mingling with the scent of impending death. She'd stared at Vi's blue and white bony fingers holding onto the plate which came from a service her family has used since she was a child. The gravy congealing in a brown pool around the roast potato, its sticky substance holding fast to the bright green peas she knows Vi enjoys.

Just before she leaves Vi grips her arm with an energy Margaret hadn't thought she'd be capable of. 'I'm sorry,' she said, 'I didn't want you to find out one day when I'm gone, and think ill of your mother. What she did, she did to protect your dad and you.'

When Margaret returned home, back to her

family sitting around the kitchen table enjoying their lunch, she'd been unable to eat. The smell of her own food kept the shock of Vi's words vivid in her mind, and eventually she'd excused herself and been sick.

Margaret never saw Vi again. The dilemma of whether to avoid her for fear of further secrets coming out, or check to see if she was all right, wasn't there for long. Two days later the Health Visitor arrived to find Vi stiff in her bed, Margaret's plate of half eaten roast dinner by her side. She'd passed on her burden and was free to go.

That had been nearly four years ago. Margaret never mentioned it to anyone, not even Robert. She couldn't bring herself to speak it aloud. Speaking it would have changed everything, given the shadow permanence in her life. Instead she pretended she'd never heard it, that it wasn't true, just a bad dream to gradually be forgotten. Only secrets like that, a secret which runs to the very core of your being, those kind of secrets aren't so easily forgotten.

36

March 5ᵀᴴ 2008, Jersey – Katherine

Perhaps the talk of Haut de la Garenne and its consequences makes Margaret get things into perspective, but when Katherine comes down a little later she finds her sister more relaxed than she has been since her arrival.

'Do you want a glass of wine?' Margaret asks her, smiling warmly.

'Yes thanks, I will,' Katherine replies, 'Is there anything I can do to help with dinner?'

'No, no you're fine,' Margaret answers, 'it's all under control.'

Katherine sits down at the kitchen table with her glass.

'I'm sorry for having a go at you the other night. I went a bit over the top. Too much vino I think,' Margaret begins. She is at the sink peeling potatoes and has her back to her sister. 'But it's just... it's just I missed having you around all these years. I was angry at you, angry that you left us all: me, John, mum… and you just didn't seem to care.'

Katherine looks at her sister's shoulders and sighs. 'I know, and I'm sorry too. I did care though,' replies Katherine, 'honestly I did –

and I still do, it's just...'

Margaret turns round from the sink to look at her sister.

Katherine's face is contorted with some inner battle. 'I'm sorry I went away for so long,' Katherine begins, 'but I had to get away.'

'I'm not blaming you for going, Katherine,' Margaret encourages, still a little defensive about her verbal onslaught of Monday night. 'I know you wanted a career and you were fed up with Jersey, and I don't think choosing not to have a family is bad, it's personal choice.'

Katherine looks at the glass of wine she's cradling in her hands. Margaret in turn looks at her and listens to the silence, waiting; but there's too much rushing around inside Katherine's head to even contemplate opening up that can of worms.

There's no opportunity to carry on the conversation as the kitchen soon fills up with the rest of the family. First James appears for food, followed shortly after by Robert and Sophie. The meal is pleasant and Katherine finds herself relaxing for the first time, but she's tired, really tired and shortly after dinner excuses herself to go to bed. She's not sure if it's the sudden exposure to the sea air, or the feeling of security on returning to her childhood home; or perhaps it's just the emotional strain she's been under. She hasn't felt as tired as this in a long time and as soon as her head hits the pillow she is asleep.

Finally, alone, Margaret sits in her kitchen, a book on her lap unopened. Their unfinished conversation preying on her mind. It's like prising crab meat out of a claw. She can see Katherine is full of something, but as usual her sister is refusing to give up her inner thoughts. Just like that night before she'd left all those years ago.

Sometime later, Katherine is woken by raised voices downstairs. It's dark in her room, only a faint glow of street lamps finds its way in. For a few moments she lies still, hardly breathing; at first unsure of where she is and then listening to what is being said. There's shouting and a note of distress in her sister's voice, so she gets out of bed, slips on her dressing gown and goes to investigate. At first she hesitates in case she's intruding on a domestic, straining to hear the thread of conversation. There are three voices: Robert's, Margaret's and James's. She's about to go back to bed assuming it's a family row when she catches the unmistakable sound of somebody retching and vomiting, followed by a shriek from her sister. Katherine quickly switches on the stairway light and hurries down to see if she can help.

'I'm telling you this is the last straw,'

Robert's voice is raised and angry, Katherine has never heard him like this; he's the type to let the world wash over him and not get riled by things.

She hesitates again afraid she's intruding, but then she hears her sister say, 'Look at this mess, I can't believe you can be so selfish,' and decides to ask if she can help - despite the fact the prospect of clearing up vomit isn't at all appealing to her.

All the lights downstairs are blazing and the commotion is taking place in the doorway from the hall to the kitchen. Robert appears supporting a slumped James who has vomit all down his front. His head is lolling and he's clearly very drunk. Robert doesn't even acknowledge Katherine. His face is set, eyes fixed forward with anger and his jaw white with tension. The pair proceed awkwardly up the stairs towards the bathroom, Robert dragging the not insubstantial weight of his son upwards.

Katherine peers around the doorway looking for her sister. Margaret is still dressed; she must have been waiting up for her son. She is leaning on the table with one hand, the other scrubbing at her face and hair in exasperation. In front of her a splashed pool of alcoholic smelling vomit is congealing on the kitchen floor.

'Margaret...are you OK? Can I do

something to help?'

Her sister looks up, tears brimming her eyes. 'Do you know what Katherine? Sometimes I think maybe you had the right idea after all – I really do wonder why we have children when this is all the thanks we get.'

Katherine lets Margaret's words dissolve in the air. She doesn't answer straight away, then quietly she says, 'You don't mean that.'

Margaret looks up at her, 'Don't I?' She answers defiantly.

Katherine is about to say more, but her nostrils remind her of the congealing vomit. 'Come on, where's the bucket and mop kept?'

'Oh no, I'll do that,' Margaret sighs, switching back into practical mother mode.

'Well, I'll make you a cup of tea then.' Katherine gratefully offers and heads towards the kettle as her sister disappears into a cupboard retrieving Dettol, a mop and bucket.

Margaret's comment, 'I think you had the right idea,' keeps circling around Katherine's head. She almost feels as though she's betraying her sister by not telling her the truth - perhaps she has the right to know. It would certainly be better if she did, if it was all out in the open and Katherine didn't have to tip toe around the subject anymore. The cracks are appearing in her impenetrable shell.

It surprises her but she starts to feel the need to talk, to empty out all her festering baggage. By the time the tea is made and on the table, Margaret has adeptly cleared up the remains of James' night out.

'That's the third time he's come home like this. Not just drunk but completely paralytic. Why do they have to drink so much?'

'Pressure from his friends?' Katherine suggests.

'Friends!' Margaret says disdainfully, 'They're not friends. Ever since he started hanging out with this current group it's been nothing but grief. You try and guide them in the right direction, give them a good start in life and then they just throw it all in your face. Sometimes I really do wonder why we bother.'

'You bother because you love them, because hopefully this will only be a short term blip. You bother because you care about what they're doing, who they're seeing and what kind of future they're mapping out for themselves. You bother because you want to. You bother because you're a good mother, Margaret and because, no matter what, you'll always be there for them: and they'll eventually be there for you too.' Katherine delivers her lines earnestly and honestly - a barrier fallen.

Margaret looks up at her surprised by this sudden pro-children speech from her sister, the sister who didn't want a family. 'OH come on, don't tell me you've not enjoyed doing your own thing, never having to be beholden to anyone?' she replies, 'I never have time to do my nails like you, I don't even have time to sit down and read the Sunday papers. If I'd tried to have a career, I would forever be feeling guilty because I'd think it's taking me away from the children. Not to mention all the money they cost. Think of the clothes and holidays we could have gone on instead.'

'Yes, but do those things really matter?' Katherine calmly asks.

'Yes... Well... No... I suppose, not really. Of course I wouldn't change it for the world.' Margaret replies, her thought process reflected in her face. 'OK you win,' she smiles at her sister. 'Although coming from you, that's quite ripe.'

Katherine is silent.

Margaret tries to look her in the eyes, but she's looking down at the table. 'Kath, I'm only joking,' she says tentatively, concerned now at her sister's silence.

'I know, don't worry,' Katherine replies. 'I think it's time I put the record straight about something though,' she continues, her voice soft and calm. When she looks up Margaret sees tears brimming in her eyes.

'Are you OK?' Margaret asks her, taken aback.

'Yes. I'm fine. But you're wrong you know, Margaret. I didn't choose my career over a family,' she swallows hard. She can't help it.

Despite the years, or perhaps because she's bottled it up for so long, her face starts to quiver; her chin crumpling into creases as she struggles to prevent tears. When she does manage to talk her voice is small and weak. 'I didn't choose a career instead of a family – I needed it, I had to concentrate on work because there were some things John and I never told you or mum, never told anyone actually.'

Her sister is holding her breath now.

'You know I had a miscarriage?' Margaret nods slowly, 'Well that wasn't the only one. We had five. Five times I got pregnant and five times I lost the babies. One after the other. It devastated me Margaret...'

'Oh my God Kath,' Margaret's face registers the shock, and she reaches out across the table to hold her sister's hands. 'Why didn't you tell us...talk to us? You should have said something...'

'I couldn't. At first I didn't want to worry you both, and then I think we started to believe that if maybe we could keep it between us and not let anyone else know, then maybe it wouldn't be so bad.'

'That's ridiculous Kath, ridiculous. We would have wanted to help, to support you, dear God it must have been awful going through that time after time.'

'Yes,' is all Katherine replies.

'Is that why you left?'

'Yes. You'd just had Sara, I didn't want to ruin your joy, I'm sorry I just couldn't cope with not being able to have a baby of my own. It sounds really selfish, I know, but I had to get away. I was scared Margaret. Scared if we tried again, and failed, it might tip me over the edge. It was only real to me, to anyone else it was just some kind of concept. Even to John. I couldn't face seeing him every day, watching him with Sara and knowing I could never make him a father.'

'Kath, that's just awful. Couldn't the doctors help you? Did you ever find out why? Why you had so many miscarriages?' Margaret gently asks.

'Not really, they did think that perhaps it was the placenta not working properly, but that was never confirmed. Of course if I'd been a little older, more mature, I might have pushed for some answers, demanded to know why we'd failed time after time. I think I was just too young and too much in pain to be honest.'

Margaret nods and sighs, 'I so wish you'd told me. Given me some credit whether I was pregnant or not. You needed our support.'

'I know but I honestly thought that if I allowed even the tiniest bit of emotion to escape it would have let the floodgates open and I wouldn't have been able to stop it – and that scared me.'

'I've often wondered what happened

between you and John. Why you left him. You'd seemed so happy the pair of you I just couldn't understand it,' Margaret says softly.

Katherine nods and wipes away a tear. 'I thought that at least if I wasn't around, he had the chance to try with somebody else. I didn't intend to leave him, I just needed some time away. Somehow... Somehow that time just got longer and longer.'

'But John came to London.'

'Yes and he hated every second of it. He just didn't understand why I needed to be there – I guess he couldn't... He'd never held any of the babies or had any kind of physical relationship with them – but every one of them had been a part of me, inside of me...' She looks at Margaret, 'You know what I mean?'

Margaret nods. 'Yes I do,' she replies softly and squeezes Katherine's hand.

'It's so difficult for other people to understand how hard each loss was for me, how desperate I was for each pregnancy to work, how much I mourned all our lost children. I knew that if I stayed I would be tempted to try again, and then what if I lost another one? I felt like I was a failure and I didn't want to be seen as some sympathy case that everyone pitied because we'd spent years trying to have children and couldn't. I wanted people to see me as a success, so I turned to my career. At least in my job I could succeed, get some sense of self-worth, feel like people would look at me and think wow she's done something with her life instead of shrivelling up like a dried, infertile fruit.'

'Oh Kath...' It's Margaret's turn to cry now. 'That's so stupid, we wouldn't ever have thought you were a failure...God it must have been awful for you I can't imagine...come here.' Margaret stands up and walks round to her sister's side of the table, her arms open wide. Katherine can't remember the last time they'd hugged. There had been a brief kind of back patting at their mother's funeral, but not this kind of a hug, the kind where you feel enveloped by love.

Robert found them like that, wrapped in each other, two sister's sharing - both of them crying. He'd finished putting James to bed and was ready for a rant about his son, only to walk in and find the two women sobbing.

'Are you two OK?' he asks. 'James is in bed now, he's all right.'

'Yes we're fine,' his wife replies and waves him away. Robert raises his eyes to the ceiling and wonders if he's the only sane one in the house, before taking himself off to bed.

'Poor John,' Margaret mutters. 'He's not said anything about it all these years.'

'Yes, I know,' Kathy sighs and looks at the bank of photographs on the dresser, finding John with a young Sara and James sitting on his tractor; all of them with beaming smiles.

'I don't blame him for coming back to Jersey, London was suffocating him, he's happy when he's in the fields.'

'He never stopped loving you. You know that don't you?' Margaret adds, 'Never found anyone else.'

'I know and believe it or not I didn't either. I did try once but it just didn't seem right. I've always considered myself married you know, strange as it might seem. I guess it's been an odd sort of a marriage but I never thought about divorce.'

'Have you ever told John that?'

'No,' Katherine replies quietly.

Margaret says nothing further; she knows she doesn't need to. She stands holding her sister and secretly wishing their mother could be here now to hear what Katherine has said. All these years Marie never understood Katherine's reasons for upping and leaving her husband and her island, and it had driven the two of them apart. Now it's too late for explanations.

37

1982, Jersey – Katherine

Katherine had never been as close to her mother as Margaret was. On the beach Margaret would want to walk in the sand shapes of her mother's footsteps. Katherine would run ahead and create her own track. In her teen years there was always the friction of Marie's disapproval of her relationship with Anne without there ever being any good reason for it. Sure she realised Katherine saw Anne at school, Marie tolerated that - she had to - but outside of school she frowned upon their close friendship. Katherine was convinced it hadn't always been like that. She and Anne had been friends since nursery and back then her mother would have had it in her power to determine who Katherine mixed with. So what changed it all?

After Anne died, Marie seemed to sympathise; but Katherine's anger at not being allowed to go to the funeral became a festering boil in their relationship. On the night before her wedding to John, it burst.

Margaret, Marie, Katherine and her friend from work, Trisha, went out for dinner to celebrate Katherine's last night as a single woman. It was an evening of girlie laughter and fun oiled by wine and the excitement of the wedding to come. When they got home, Margaret went to bed while Marie sat with her eldest daughter checking through her dress and accessories for the big day.

'I'm so pleased for you,' she said, rubbing Katherine's arm tenderly. 'I wish your father was here to see this.' Marie had perhaps drunk one too many glasses of wine, or perhaps it was the emotion of the event, for she allowed herself to cry.

Katherine didn't know quite what to do at first, her mother had always seemed so strong, even after their father's death she'd barely seen her crying. Now here she was sobbing.

'Come on mum don't cry.' Katherine tried, putting her arm around her slightly awkwardly. She wished Margaret was still up, her sister is always so much more forthright with her hugs and physical contact. 'I know Dad will be with me anyway, with us all.'

'Yes, of course he will love, of course he will.' Marie struggles to hold back her tears and manages a smile. 'I'm sorry I don't mean to upset you it's just... well it's just I wish he was here that's all. I still miss him you know.'

Katherine rubs her mother's back. 'I know mum, I know. I wish Anne could be here too.'

Her mother doesn't look up from her lap.

'Anne! No I don't, she's better off where she is believe me.'

Katherine takes her hands away. Her mother looks up. 'What do you mean *better off where she is*? Are you glad she's dead?' Katherine's voice has risen, her whole demeanour suddenly defensive.

Marie's face registers the realisation she's just said something she would have been better off keeping to herself. 'No. I'm sorry I didn't mean it like that. I just meant that she's at peace now, that's all...'

Katherine isn't convinced. 'What do you mean? She's better off dead? How can you say that?'

'I know, I didn't mean it to come out like that, just forget about it darling. Forget I said it.'

'I can't believe you said that mum, I really can't.'

Her mother closes her eyes and sighs, shaking her head. 'Sorry Katherine. Please don't let's argue about Anne, not now, not today.' In the space of just half a minute her mother seems to have aged. Suddenly she looks weary, drained. Katherine holds her tongue, confused.

'I think we'd better get to bed now, you've an exciting day ahead,' Marie continues, eager to move on. 'I'll wake you in the morning darling. Get a good night's sleep. I love you.'

She tenderly kisses Katherine on the cheek and then with a sorrowful backwards glance leaves her.

'Goodnight mum,' Katherine returns.

Later as she waits for sleep, Katherine goes over her mother's words. What could she have meant? Why did she say that? Did she really hate Anne that much?

It was a slip she never forgave her mother. Not then, not years later. She knew her mum loved her. She remembered a happy childhood but that comment was never again discussed, or explained, and it niggled her. When her mother suddenly died of a brain haemorrhage in 2002, Katherine buried her with regrets. They never sorted it out; never mentioned it again. She'd loved her mother, of course she had, but she couldn't work out her motivation, her dislike of Anne.

Now her mother isn't here and Katherine's questions will remain unanswered.

38

March 6th 2008, Jersey

The next morning James comes down to breakfast expecting a tongue lashing from his mother. Sometimes it's difficult to tell who will be the angriest. His dad can be more physical but his mother has a different kind of punishment, more emotional and, at times, crueller. Trouble is, he's got the post-drinking munchies and has to get food a.s.a.p. He decides he might as well face the music with his mother and hope the presence of his aunt might embarrass her into not going over the top.

He can't be more surprised when he walks into the kitchen to find her chatting and laughing with his aunt - like two girlfriends. His mother ten years younger and his aunt without her sharp edges - as though overnight she's become softer, more pleasant.

'I'll talk to *you* later.' His mum tells him, knitting her eyebrows but he knows her well enough to realise that's more for show than carrying any real threat. 'Now what do you want for breakfast? Bacon and egg?' James isn't going to miss the opportunity. He doesn't care what has happened since last night. His mother and aunt could have been abducted by aliens and morphed into these two friendly, chilled out clones for all he cares. What he does know is he's going to take the chance to have a big slap-up breakfast to soak up his hangover.

To say Katherine feels relieved from telling Margaret about the miscarriages is an understatement. She feels almost foolish for having waited so long, and why? Why she'd never told her she doesn't know. It had been a lot easier than she thought and by sharing, she's rebuilt a bridge with her sister. The atmosphere between them has cleared, the storm passed over - no more tiptoeing around on eggshells. The whole experience makes her more confident, more positive about why she's come back. It's also served to remind her of the catalyst for her return: Anne's mother's letter. When Margaret says she's going out for some shopping Katherine excuses herself from the trip and instead goes upstairs to where the letter sits waiting - a loaded revolver in her suitcase.

It still says exactly the same as it had when she was in London. Only now she is back in Jersey the words seem to stand out from the paper, urging her on. Katherine doesn't even know if the woman is still alive - the whole thing could be completely irrelevant by now. She does know she will regret it if she doesn't find out. She's spent too long not dealing with things. Buoyed by the relief she feels from sharing with Margaret, she decides there's no time like the present, she'll go round to the house now and see if she's still there.

When Katherine walks downstairs to leave, Margaret is still out at the local Co-op. James is lolling at the kitchen table mopping up the egg on his plate with the last piece of bread in the house.

'James, could you tell your mother I've gone out for a walk please? I've got to go and see someone.'

'Sure,' he replies, 'have a good one.'

Katherine smiles at his indifferent teenageness and heads out the door.

Anne's house is a brisk twenty to thirty-minute walk from their home. As she walks, Katherine's mind struggles back into the past searching for memories. She can't remember going round Anne's house when she'd been alive. Of course her own mother hadn't approved of Anne as a friend but Anne never particularly encouraged her round either. As for what Anne's parents looked like, they are vague blurs in her head from the last time she'd seen them. She remembers Anne's house though, the front of it. The street. She'd driven past it many times after her death and she wonders if it will have changed much. Will she see the ghost of Anne at the window or peering round a door in the house?

As she approaches the street Kathy begins to feel butterflies in her stomach and instead of going straight there she deviates to the beach. She's a little distance from Havre des Pas where the sea pool still dominates the tiny bay. On this winter's day it looks tired and battered, the pier strewn with seaweed. To the right of it, the new reclaimed land juts out, and to her left the beach stretches all the way to Green Island. The tide is out, so far away she can barely see its blue line. There are a few people on the beach walking dogs but the March weather doesn't encourage a casual stroll. It's hard to imagine that hot summer's day in 1976 when she and Anne had strolled along this beach with their ice creams. The last time she had seen Anne alive.

39

1976, Jersey

It's a couple of weeks since they'd picked up their exam results, and Katherine hasn't seen Anne once. In fact, she's been positively avoiding her. Katherine has been working most days at Dorothy Perkins due to staff holidays and she uses the excuse of being tired in the evenings. Every time the phone rings she expects it to be Anne ranting because she's just bumped into Mark or Darren and they've had a go at her for what Katherine said. So far so good - but she can't rely on Anne not meeting them forever - Jersey is a small island. She knows she's going to have to clear the air, come clean about what she'd said to Darren before Anne finds out for herself.

She arranges to meet Anne outside the ice cream shop at Havre de Pas.

'We can cool off after the walk there with one of the parlour's specials, my treat and then go for a paddle in the sea,' Katherine tells her friend. Anne is eager to meet up, her enthusiasm pricking Katherine's guilt with its innocence.

Katherine gets there first; it's really busy

which isn't surprising considering the weather is still relentless sunshine. The coolest place to be is by the sea and half of Jersey, plus a great number of tourists, seem to be doing just that. All around Havre de Pas, people in shorts and swimming costumes are spilling out of hotel entrances, towels under their arms, flip flops on their feet; or they're returning from the beach with red shoulders and sandy feet, to seek shelter from the heat. A multitude of brightly coloured floppy sun hats pass her by as she stands under the shop's awning. An endless stream of ice cream-licking people exit the doorway, only to be replaced by more eager customers. Katherine keeps one eye out for Anne while checking every young man who walks by.

Anne's face erupts with a smile when she spots her. She's so clearly pleased to see Katherine it makes her feel even more guilty about why she hasn't been in touch, and what she's about to tell her. She convinces herself it will be OK; Anne will be a bit annoyed but she'll forgive her. She decides to soften her up a bit first with an ice cream, encouraging Anne to choose the most expensive and biggest.

They leave the shop and walk down the steps to the beach, meandering through the sunbathing bodies and sandcastles with their dry moats, heading straight for the incoming sea and its refreshing coolness for their feet.

They walk away from the Havre de Pas sea pool, full of bobbing heads and splashing children wearing a variety of blow up creatures around their waists.

At first there isn't much chance for conversation, their ice creams are melting so fast it's a job to keep licking the dripping sides. Eventually Katherine decides she might as well just get it over and done with.

'I bumped into Darren Le Brocq the other day.'

'Oh yeah,' Anne responds, no sign of the tension Katherine expected in her voice. She's a little taken aback.

'Do you still fancy him? Did he say anything about why he didn't phone?' Anne asks, oblivious to Katherine's inner thoughts and guilt.

'No. No I don't, and he didn't, but I did have a go at him for what Mark did to you.' There. She'd said it. Katherine watches Anne's face intently, holding her breath, waiting for the onslaught. It comes.

'What? What do you mean? You promised me. You promised me you wouldn't say anything to anyone,' Anne spins round, stopping in her tracks and glaring at Katherine with anger in her eyes.

'Yes I know, but Darren was there so it wasn't like he didn't know, and besides I think what Mark did was wrong...he really upset you, I...'

'You had no right,' Anne vehemently interrupts. 'You should have left it alone. It's done. Over.'

'Yes, but it's not though is it? You still get upset about it.'

Anne tightens her jaw, pulling her mouth into a grimace and staring off up the beach.

'What's wrong Anne? Why won't you talk to me? Why won't you tell me what's upsetting you? We've always shared everything.'

'You've no idea Katherine, no idea at all and I obviously can't trust you. Leave me alone and stop meddling in things you don't understand.' Her voice grows quieter, more intense.

'What do you mean things I don't understand. I was there remember? You told me Mark attacked you. That he did things to you which you didn't like and wouldn't stop. Ever since then you've been grumpy. So, is it true or not?'

The fire returns to Anne's eyes. 'So you're saying you don't believe me now is that it? Is that what your precious boyfriend Darren said, that I was lying, and you believe him rather than me?' Anne throws the rest of her ice cream onto the sand. 'Well thanks a bloody lot. Some friend you are Katherine. You're a self-centred bitch sometimes, do you know that?'

She marches off along the beach to where the crowds thin.

Katherine stands for a few moments staring at the remains of Anne's ice cream pooling on the sand, mixing with the grains; a little white stream running round a pebble and to oblivion. She might as well be looking at their friendship. Anne's words screech round and round her head like an angry bird. She doesn't attempt to go after her. Their conversation couldn't have gone any worse. It's like all of a sudden they're reading the same passage of a book in different languages where once they'd read aloud, together, as one voice. Katherine just can't understand Anne's anger. She's been a different person ever since that night at Sands.

Before Katherine turns back to walk up the beach the way she'd come, she looks up at Anne's disappearing back – and that's when she sees him. A young man stands up from a group camped near the sea wall. It doesn't register at first but then she recognises his stride. It's Mark Vibert and he's very obviously seen Anne because he's walking purposefully towards her - only in her anger she is very clearly oblivious. Katherine can't do anything, Anne has gone too far away for her to shout and even if she runs at full pelt Mark will reach Anne before she can. She can only watch as Anne suddenly looks up and sees the danger ahead. He starts to shout and waves his arms around. Anne runs towards some steps, but even from where Katherine stands she can see him being cheered on by his group of friends and he isn't going to let her get away that easily.

Anne manages to reach the steps before him. She runs up them, almost free, but he takes them two at a time and at the top he grabs her arm. He is obviously shouting, playing up to the baying crowd beneath him who have stood up to get a better view. Katherine can't hear what's being said but she can see Anne as she backs away. She's getting perilously close to the steps. She nearly falls. Then she hits him. He steps back, shocked, and releases her arm. Anne's head turns and disappears from view over the top of the sea wall.

It is the last time Katherine sees Anne alive.

40

March 2008, Jersey

It's only a short walk from where Katherine stands at Havre de Pas to the steps Anne climbed that last day of her life. The beach was packed then, the heat of the summer stifling. Now the cold wind flings itself at her face, biting into her skin and spraying her with sand that threatens to blind her. She won't be driven from the beach though, instead she pulls her coat collar up and marches straight into the wind, preparing for the real challenge ahead.

She stays on the beach for at least half an hour just thinking. Kathy has been doing a lot of thinking lately, perhaps it's a mid-life crisis, all this soul searching and need to come to terms with her past. Or perhaps it's just a process long overdue.

Without noticing, she eventually finds herself in the same spot she'd stood in all those years ago, where she'd watched Anne's ice cream pooling on the sand, her friend marching off in anger. They were so young, so naïve; soft spring buds waiting to grow and blossom - only Anne never did.

Behind Katherine, the buildings may have

changed, new flats where once there was a hotel but the seascape is just the same. Timeless despite its constantly changing tides. How like the sea we all are. The sea may carry different burdens, treasures or rubbish. Some days it may seem angry and fearful, others sad and grey and then perhaps sparkling blue and inviting. Whatever its demeanour it's still the same sea washing over the same rocks, year after year after year. Life has thrown many things Katherine's way, leaving her soul pitted with regrets and loss, but if she tries really hard she can still remember being that teenage girl, standing on the beach all those years ago watching her friend disappear off to her death.

The screech of a seagull brings Katherine back to the present and she shivers, not sure if it's the cold or the memories. Enough of this reminiscing, she tells herself, she came here for a reason. Katherine turns and retraces those steps Anne took all those years ago, returning to the street where she once lived.

The one and only time she came to Anne's house, was after a worsening in the relationship with her mother. Katherine knew Marie never 'approved' of Anne, that she would have preferred they'd not been friends - but when she announced there was no way she was allowing Katherine to go to the funeral, that was the final straw. They'd had a blazing row.

A row they never fully recovered from. It created a crack between them which couldn't be healed. They papered over it but it was always there underneath, threatening and unexplained all through the years.

41

1976, Jersey

'I'm sorry Katherine,' Marie announces, the day before Anne is to be buried, 'I'm putting my foot down. It's not going to do you any good to go to that funeral.'

Katherine is shocked. 'She was my friend mum, my best friend.'

'I know, but it's better that you remember her in your own way. We can go and visit her grave another time.' Marie tries to take her hand but she pulls away.

'You just don't understand do you? My best friend is dead. Don't you care?'

Marie sighs. 'Yes Katherine, I do care and I'm truly sorry, but...'

'No mum, there's no *but*. I can't believe you won't even let me go to her funeral. What is it with you? Why have you never liked her?'

'Katherine, calm down, I've never said I don't *like* Anne, life just isn't simply black and white you know.' Her mother moves forward attempting to reach out to her again, but she's having none of it.

Katherine leaves, running out of the house and slamming the door. It is unbelievable, truly unbelievable. Her mother can be so heartless and cruel.

She marches down the road, fuming. She hasn't dared to tell anyone what happened, that it's her fault Anne is dead. Katherine doesn't know who to turn to for advice, and then it dawns on her what she has to do. She carries on walking until she reaches Anne's front door.

It is strange standing in front of her house, she's never been allowed to come round here before. Now Anne is dead and here she is, only her friend isn't going to be there. She doesn't even know if Anne's parents are in. Katherine hesitates at the gate. Admitting to her guilt could bring all sorts of trouble but it doesn't matter, she has to tell them; say sorry, explain what happened. They have a right to know why Anne was moody and upset before she died and maybe, just maybe, there could be some kind of repercussions for Mark. He deserves everything he might get.

Katherine glances along the road and sees the family Volvo parked a little further up. She opens the gate. It's now or never.

Anne's mother opens the door, her face pale and drained, more akin to the corpse of her daughter than to someone alive.

'Katherine!' she exclaims, looking uncomfortable.

'Mrs West, I'm sorry to disturb you...it's just...it's just I think I should tell you something.' Elizabeth West's face registers surprise and something else, if Katherine isn't mistaken, almost a little fear.

'I see. Do you want to come in?'

'Yes please.' Katherine replies and walks through the opened doorway into her friend's home.

Right in front of her, hanging on the hall stand, is Anne's coat. Its familiarity slaps her in the face, making her head spin and her stomach hurt. It looks so normal. So every day, in a situation that is anything but usual. Katherine shies away from it as though expecting Anne's ghost to jump out and shout at her.

Just a few steps away is the bottom of the stairs. Up those steps, above her, is where they found Anne. Swinging from the attic hatch. Katherine shivers, her emotions threatening to overwhelm her as the image of her friend, hanging, fills her mind.

'Through here.' Anne's mother guides her into a sitting room.

Katherine walks in, her knees beginning to feel wobbly. At the far end is Anne's father sitting in an armchair. He isn't reading, he isn't watching television, he's just sitting. He looks up when Katherine walks in. The surprise that registers on his features is more subtle than his wife's.

'I'm sorry to disturb you both...' Katherine can't wait any longer, she has to get this out now before she bottles it. 'I want you to know why Anne died. It was my fault. Well, actually it started with a boy called Mark Vibert who nearly raped her on St Ouen's beach. After that she was never the same, only I made it worse because I told his friend and then he had a go at Anne that day... and...'

Elizabeth West holds up her hand. 'Thank you Katherine. Thank you for coming but it's not necessary. We know all the circumstances surrounding her death.'

'You do?'

'Yes.' Anne's mother throws a glance at her father, who doesn't say a word. 'We know.'

'I'm so sorry. I'm just so sorry.' Katherine blurts out. Tears are coming down her face now and the room starts closing in on her.

On the wall is a photograph of Anne taken a few years earlier. In the cabinet is the trophy she'd won on school sports day last year. Even the smell of the house is familiar. Her parents knew all along.

'Sorry.' Katherine blurts out one last time and then she flees, running out past Anne's coat to the street. She doesn't wait to be shown to the door. She just leaves them both sitting there in their misery.

Knowing somebody else knows the truth helps in some way but it doesn't ease the guilt. Her mother keeps trying to mend the bridges, taking her up to the grave after Anne is buried, helping her to make a scrapbook of memories; but she wants Katherine's grief to be contained. At first Katherine thinks she is just trying to protect her, until the day before her wedding day that is. Then her mother shows her true colours, lets slip her real feelings about Anne and her death. After that Katherine can never bring herself to forgive her.

42

March 6th 2008, Jersey

Now, here she is again. Thirty-two years later. Katherine has returned to Anne's house and to the last remaining link with her friend and the events of 1976.

In some ways the street looks very different, in other ways it hasn't changed. There are a lot more cars nowadays of course, which changes the look of the road. The houses are painted different colours; some newly refurbished, others tired and run down. Anne's house is number fourteen and Katherine walks towards it with huge trepidation.

The house looks like it hasn't changed at all - apart from ageing. It's in desperate need of some attention. The gate is rusted and squeaks as it opens. The front garden is completely overgrown, weeds rising up from every paving-stone crack, and the pale green paint on the window frames is peeling. Even the front door looks like it has baked in the sun one too many years. Katherine sighs at its appearance, no doubt a reflection of what lies within. The curtains in the downstairs living room are open, a hopeful sign Anne's mother, Elizabeth West, is still there.

Katherine stands for a few seconds, building up her courage, and then walks up the path and knocks on the door. As she knocks her mobile phone starts ringing, making her jump. She fumbles in her handbag for it, one eye on the door. Margaret's name is on the screen. She doesn't want to talk to her sister right now, her mind is set on the task at hand, so she cancels the call. She'll talk to her after.

Katherine knocks on the front door for a second time, trying to peer through the frosted glass.

Her mobile rings again - Margaret. She might as well answer; looks like nobody is home.

'Hi,' she quickly says.

'Katherine where are you?'

'I'm at Anne's mother's.'

'Oh shit. Have you spoken to her?'

'No, I've literally just knocked on the door. I'm not sure if she's in.'

'Kath, I told you we need to talk.'

Katherine hears some movement from inside the house. 'Hang on, I think she's here… Look I've got to go Margaret, we'll talk later.'

'Kath. No. Stop. Listen to me now. There's something you don't know, something we weren't told at the time.'

'What? What do you mean?' Through the door's frosted glass Katherine can see a dark shape beginning to appear.

'Kath...oh God. Look I told you it wasn't your fault. It wasn't honestly...' The dark shape grows to person size. 'It was her dad. It was what he was doing to her, that's what all the rumours are about.'

'What? Rumours? What do you mean?' Katherine's voice is hushed, urgent.

'I'm pretty sure he was abusing her.'

Her sister's words crash into her ear just as there comes the clinking of a chain being drawn back on the door.

'Pretty sure?' Katherine questions in shock.

'Well, I'm sure Kath, I'm certain he was.' Katherine can tell by the earnestness of Margaret's voice she means it.

'I've got to go,' is all she can say and she ends the phone call, switching it off as the front door slowly opens. Shock pulses through Katherine's body making her legs feel weak. Her mind has gone completely blank.

'Mrs West?' She manages to say in a voice that doesn't seem to be her own. In front of her is what can only be described as a shrivelled woman. Her hair is thin and white and she looks incongruous in a pink paisley dress that sings of the first blush of youth, not the dying old lady within. It's hard for Katherine to recognise this dried-up person as the animated blur of her memories, but there is just enough familiarity about her to know this is indeed

Anne's mother.

'Yes?' She replies.

'Hello Mrs West, it's Katherine, Katherine Gaudin, Anne's friend.' Immediately her face flickers and she nods.

'Oh Katherine, yes, yes of course. I thought I recognised your face. You got my letter.'

'Yes, I hope you don't mind me just turning up like this, I should have called.'

'Mind? No of course not dear. Of course not, I don't mind anything nowadays. Not enough time for minding. Come in, come in. I can't stand long, so come along inside and sit down.'

Katherine walks in almost as though she's having an out of body experience. The shock of Margaret's words. The shock of seeing Anne's mother after all this time and the shock of walking into the home of her friend for the first time in over thirty years, gives the whole experience a sense of the surreal.

'I've got cancer,' Anne's mother is saying as she leads Katherine into the stuffy sitting room. 'Riddled with it. Doctor says it won't be long.' Katherine doesn't detect any sadness in her voice, on the contrary it's almost a tone of looking forward to the final outcome.

They walk into a room that hasn't changed since the seventies. Gaudy sofas and tired, faded wallpaper. A fake wood burning gas fire, almost childish in appearance, takes centre stage. Anne's mother flops into an armchair right beside it, which in turn sits directly in front of an old television. 'Just give me a moment, will you?' She says breathlessly and leans back closing her eyes, her whole body heaving with the effort of breathing.

Katherine sits down on a small green sofa, moving a pile of old Jersey Evening Posts to make room. The arms of the sofa are adorned with dirty white linen lace covers, yellowed with age and with the smoking Kathy remembers Elizabeth West being a slave to. Its nicotine residue coating everything in the room.

She no longer knows what to say, not now, not after what Margaret just told her. Anne's mother sits, eyes still closed, trying to catch what little breath she has left. Kathy looks at her hands clenching the arms of the chair, like the clawed feet of a bird-of-prey, all bone. Her skin is baking paper that's spent too long in the oven: thin, brittle, no flesh beneath and yellowed: mottled with black, purple and red bruising, lined by dry river beds of wrinkles. A thin, almost transparent skin - all that's keeping in her insides from the rest of the world. Katherine can easily imagine behind her shoulder, watching, waiting, growing impatient, stands Death.

There's a smell to failing flesh. Not the odour of gastric juices or the lapsing of personal hygiene, it's something else. Something like the dusty, damp smell that clings to an old house. The musty scent of inner decay.

Sitting here Anne's mother is simply waiting for death to come. The only sounds are the heavy ticking of the wooden mantelpiece clock, counting down her last hours, keeping time with her laboured rasping breath. Katherine imagines that if she were to step out the door a strong sea breeze would pick her up and toss her around the street, swirling, tapping her against walls like an autumn leaf to be finally crunched underfoot. Brittle, dried, life forsaken and done. Katherine wishes she could be outside in that breeze now, smelling the fresh air of the living, far away from this decay and the awkwardness of the situation.

The heavy ticking of the clock slows down all sense of time. Within minutes Katherine can tell, without looking, where the second hand is on its face. The tick, tick sounds louder towards the half past, quieter, more dainty on the hour. It marks time slowly. Elizabeth West's wheezing breath rattles in and out of her chest. She's not much more than a rattling bag of bones.

After what seems like forever, she opens her eyes again. 'I'm sorry,' she says, 'everything requires a lot of effort these days. It must be about twenty-five years since we saw you last.'

'Yes, over thirty actually. I've been in the UK.' Katherine finds herself saying on auto-pilot. The big speech she'd planned for so long has evaporated, completely annihilated by Margaret's revelation. Why the hell hadn't she told her before?

Mrs West is talking again, rasping out her words. 'I've often wondered what Anne would have done, I expect she'd have left the island too…' she trails off. 'I've some photographs here somewhere…' She leans forward and reaches under her chair, in a well-practiced act. She doesn't have photographs there "somewhere" thinks Katherine, she knows exactly where they are because her hand goes straight to them.

Despite years of pitying this woman, feeling guilty for her loss, Katherine has instantly come to despise her. Did she know? She must have, maybe not everything, but she must have suspected something. Her own daughter and husband. How did she rationalise that in her mind and conscience?

Katherine is almost surprised to find herself standing up, bending over looking at a well-used photograph album. They skip through the first few pages, images coloured by age, of people in old fashioned clothes: grandparents, great grandparents. Then there is one of Anne's parents on their wedding day. Two people smiling, happy, slightly awkward in their youth; their whole lives together ahead of them. So difficult to relate that to the wizened old woman in front of her. Does she think of the day she met her husband? Does she regret their life together? The lies. Does she ever think of what else could have been? Or does she just completely blinker herself against the truth; find her own reality? How do you come to terms with the fact your only child took her own life? Took her own life because her father, the one man she should have been able to trust more than any other in her life, was abusing her. What went through Elizabeth West's mind at the time? Did she just convince herself it wasn't true? Has she brushed it away under the carpet in her mind hoping it will go away? She stayed married to him after Anne's death, nursed him on his own death bed. If she hadn't forgiven, then she certainly condoned.

Katherine looks at photographs of the dead; all of them long since turned to dust: Anne, her father, and even her mother who is closer to the dead than the living. Katherine wonders if she contemplates her own end; the slow, painful, undignified failure of her body as one by one each of her vital functions betrays the soul they sustain. The messy, embarrassing failure of bowel and stomach. The wheezing pain of breath fighting a losing battle with nature. As the body gets weaker, so the mind can start to play tricks: hallucinations, failing eyesight, the wish to see Death at your bedside table.

She wonders what will happen to these photographs There are no other children to inherit them. Perhaps a relative will come and clear the house, pick their way through the accumulations of a lifetime, tossing aside personal memories and once loved mementos in favour of those with a monetary value. The photos on the wall, in nice frames, might find their way to an auction or car boot sale where new hands will claim them. Then the faces of the dead will be removed from their resting place and replaced with others. What will happen to the photographs of Anne? Will they end up in the bin to be burnt at the island's incinerator, scooped up from the piles of unwanted rubbish where they'd fluttered, trying to escape the flames. Ash. Just like the person they portray.

In the album there are black and white pictures of a beautiful plump little baby girl, smiling, held by a proud Mrs West. As the pictures turn to colour Katherine can see the awkwardness of teenagehood in Anne's face. This is the girl she remembers. Here she is at a family gathering. What of her aunts and uncles, did they suspect something? Had they, like her mother, simply turned and looked the other way?

Katherine wishes she had never come.

She'd hoped to find some kind of peace, to lay Anne's ghost to rest. Instead it has stirred a thousand other ghosts and they are now swirling around her in a cloud of grey, suffocating frenzy. Anne's father and all of those who knew her - who knew what was going on, or even suspected it might be going on. Of those still living, are they haunted by that knowledge? By their own inaction? Or did Anne, conveniently removing herself from the nightmare of her life, allow them to simply say, 'It's all over, there's nothing we could have done?' At what point does anyone say I've tried to do something but nobody will listen? At what point do those who suspect turn the other cheek and give up on a helpless child? At what point do they cross that line and condone the abuse by walking away from it?

Finally, Mrs West turns a page and there's one last photograph, Anne with both her parents. Gone is the proud mother cuddling her only child. Mrs West stands arms straight down next to her daughter, looking at the camera with a forced smile. There's no mistaking her face looks drawn, strained. Anne's arms are folded over her body. No smile. No enthusiasm; nothing but defensiveness. She could almost be a ghost herself by the look in her eyes. Only her father is smiling. Smug, confident, in control.

'When was this one taken?' Katherine asks

in a small voice.

'The week before she died.' Mrs West replies.

Katherine looks at it. Yes, she can see it now. See how the life had been drained from her friend long before she could take it herself. It's a horrible photograph, so clearly not a picture of a happy family. Yet Mrs West is staring at it wistfully, one of her bony fingers moving across the page as though caressing it.

For the first time in her life Kathy understands Anne hadn't taken her life because of some teenage misunderstanding about boys. She hadn't done it because her best friend made her life unbearable, she'd done it because of what lay waiting for her at home in the darkness of her bedroom. The click-click of the opening door, soft footsteps and then the rustle of her blankets. All at once the sickness of it all overcomes Katherine and she stands up and backs away.

Anne's mother looks up at her and at that moment they both know what isn't being said, what wasn't said at the time, and Katherine feels her stomach turn. Behind the failing eyes of Anne's mother is nothing but the rot and maggots of her own inaction.

'I think I'd better go now,' is all Katherine manages to say as her throat tightens.

'Yes perhaps.' Mrs West replies, sighing and returning her gaze to the photograph. 'I just wanted you to know that's all. You know, that it hadn't been your fault. All those years ago when you came here, I never said, we never said, to you that it wasn't your fault. Perhaps it doesn't matter to you now, but I just wanted it said.'

Katherine can find no words to reply. The years she's carried her guilt stretch out before her.

'You don't mind if I don't see you out, do you?' Elizabeth West asks, the breath now almost gone from her. Her confession done.

'No...' Katherine whispers.

'Goodbye Katherine Gaudin.' Kathy hears just before she closes the front door.

Kathy almost runs out of the house, just as she had done over thirty years ago, bursting from it into the fresh air as though her life depends on it. She gulps in the scent of salt on the sea breeze and feels it sting her skin where tiny tears escape her eyes. "I'm so sorry Anne," she says to herself. "I'm so, so sorry." She remembers her friend becoming more withdrawn, her school work worsening, the smiles rarely appearing on her face. As a child in a loving home she had no comprehension of the hell her friend found herself in, why her behaviour was a symptom of something so wrong. Now, as an adult, the jigsaw pieces fall into place.

So what of her own mother, had she known? Is that why Marie would never allow her to visit Anne's house, discouraged their friendship? How did Margaret find out? How many people must have known for it to be an open secret, rumoured and suggested? Surely their mother couldn't have known the truth because if she did she would have told somebody, done something. Wouldn't she?

Her personal torment of guilt is replaced now by a million other questions and fears. She is cut adrift in a stormy sea, thrashing around, looking for something to grab hold of and help her keep afloat. Now, more than at any time in her life, Katherine feels alone.

She walks down to the coast road and starts heading back towards home, oblivious to the sea wind which tries to distract her: whipping at her hair, pushing her, tugging at her coat. Amid the storm in her head she is surprised to find it's John who comes to mind first. Solid and dependable, unmoving. She has the urge to call him, to smash down the dammed up emotion, and let loose the torrent of words stored up inside of her.

Katherine retrieves her phone from her bag and turns it back on. There is a text message from Margaret simply saying "Call me". She hesitates for a few moments. The shock has started to make her feel shaky and so she takes the easy route, calling her sister.

'Where are you?' Margaret asks.

'Walking back along the coast road. I've seen her.'

'I'll come and get you.' Her sister says. She isn't asking, she's telling and Katherine doesn't complain. She sits on a bench near to the Rice Bowl Chinese, grateful to sit down, staring blankly at the cars queuing to turn into the road to Georgetown and making no sense of the questions and possibilities in her head. She simply can't contemplate being able to keep quiet if she knew a child was in that kind of trouble. If she found out her own mother had known...

As far as she's concerned Mrs West will rot in Hell. Her slow painful death from cancer is what she deserves and confessing to Katherine will not earn her a place at the Pearly Gates. Anne was just sixteen when she died - hung by her own tights from the attic rafters. Katherine only found that detail out when she heard it from some other school friends. It was almost as if her own mother wanted to wipe the slate clean, pretend like Anne and everything before her suicide had never happened. Was that the actions of a woman trying to protect her own daughter from the pain of loss? Or was it the nagging of a guilty conscience?

43

March 6th 2008, Jersey

'Are you OK?' Margaret leans across the passenger seat and pushes the door open for Katherine to get in.

'Not really. No.' Katherine replies. The barriers of her self-control pulled down by the shock of the last hour. 'Why didn't you tell me about Anne's father before, why leave it to the last minute?'

Margaret is silent for a moment. 'Sorry, I did try to at Fort Regent. There's a lot I've wanted to tell you.'

Katherine looks at her sister, properly looks at her; searching her face for signs of the emotions within. She is staring straight ahead and it's obvious she's struggling to hold something in. Her face is like a fat woman's corset, bulging and trembling in places as she strains to keep what lies beneath under control.

Margaret clears her throat but her voice still comes out slightly strangled as she fights to hold back tears. 'I thought you might feel guilty about it, that you hadn't realised. What did she say?'

'Nothing much really, just that it wasn't my

fault.' Katherine replies.

'Is that all? She didn't say anything else?' Margaret questions.

'No, to be honest she didn't say much at all. Didn't need to. Why?'

'I…' Margaret hesitates, 'Let's just get home, I can't talk while I'm driving.' She pulls herself together.

Katherine reaches for her seat belt and straps herself in as they pull out into the traffic. This emotional response from her sister has taken her by surprise. She'd been expecting Margaret to be the comforter, after all it is her who's just had the shock, just been to face her dead friend's mother - but she says nothing. Her sister is clearly upset and instead Katherine waits and dreads what further revelations might lay in store. Is it their mother? Does Margaret know something? A thousand questions fly around her head.

They drive back to their childhood home. The house in which they were both born, raised and had their wedding receptions. Neither of them say a word for the rest of the journey, each leaking enough emotion into the atmosphere of the car for it to be unnecessary to speak.

By the time they reach home Katherine's shock is transforming into anger. They get out of the car in silence but before Margaret even has the key in the front door lock, Katherine has exploded.

'I can't believe you never told me he was abusing Anne.'

Her sister says nothing as she pushes open the door.

'Margaret, why the hell didn't you tell me all this before? You know I felt responsible that she'd killed herself.' Katherine follows her into the kitchen.

'I know you *felt* responsible Katherine, but I never knew why.' Margaret turns to face her. She feels tired, really deep down tired. Years of holding in her own secret, the emotional exhaustion that it invokes. 'I've barely seen you over the last twenty years Katherine, how was I supposed to know you still felt guilty?'

That question silences them both. Katherine is about to retort she's sick of hearing that old chestnut, but then realises Margaret is right. She hasn't *talked* to her much over the years, not really talked, just recounted events and happenings.

Margaret switches into auto-pilot comfort mode and reaches for the kettle, filling it and turning it on as Katherine drags back one of the kitchen chairs and drops heavily into it. She rests both elbows on the wooden table and holds her head in her hands. Margaret busies herself getting mugs out of the cupboard, finding tea bags and milk. She doesn't even bother asking Katherine if she wants one.

Making tea is a requirement in such situations, one of her coping mechanisms.

'So when exactly were you going to tell me then? Or weren't you? At which point were you going to put me out of my misery?' Katherine lifts her head back up now, the anger bubbling to the surface again. 'I mean, Jesus Margaret, didn't you think about it with all that's been going on at Haut de la Garenne. Didn't it cross your mind?'

'No, not really. I'd heard it years ago...' Margaret says meekly, 'and it's not connected.'

'Years ago! Great this just gets better.' Katherine is on a roll now.

'I was going to talk to you about it today...this evening maybe...' Margaret counters.

'Maybe!' Katherine shakes her head.

Margaret bites her lip as she pours the boiling water into the mugs, reaching into a small drawer just to her right to find a teaspoon with which to extract the bags. 'It's not as simple as you think Kath.'

'Not as simple! Well I'm sorry for having expected you to tell me that my best friend, my friend who killed herself, did so because she'd been abused by her father. Which everyone in the island appears to know about - except for me! You knew I'd got the letter from her mother, that she'd asked me to visit.' Katherine's voice is raised now, her muscles tense throughout her body. She's rigid with indignation. Her younger sister remains quiet and meek. Katherine takes this to mean she feels guilty, perhaps embarrassed, and this only angers her more. 'When, exactly, did you find out?' She continues, her voice rising as she fires questions at her sister. 'Who told you and who else knows? Why did he get away with it? Why didn't anybody try to prosecute him?'

'He was arrested years after Anne's death. A fourteen-year-old girl accused him of abuse. They sent him to prison for three years. At the time there was talk, talk she hadn't been his only victim and Anne had been one. But there wasn't enough evidence, no witnesses, it was too long ago.'

'Did mum tell you? Did she know all along?' Katherine's anger is a runaway train. All the questions in her head needing immediate answers. 'Did mum know that Anne was being abused, is that why she didn't like me seeing her? Was that her grotesque idea of protecting me?'

Margaret doesn't answer at first, but the mention of their mother creates a flicker of tension in her cheeks. Katherine's voice is rising in pitch as Margaret's falls. She places the mug of tea in front of her sister, not failing to notice the irony of the brightly coloured image and verse on it which reads "Always look on the bright side of life." Finally, she whispers, 'I don't think so. I hope not.'

'Well you know she once said to me that Anne would be better off dead'

'Really?' Margaret is surprised by this, 'I hope she didn't know…' she trails off.

'Well why wouldn't she have, apparently you've known for years, along with...'

'Stop. Just stop.' Margaret's emotional damn bursts and she stands firmly in front of her sister. 'Why don't you just stop and give *me* a chance to talk.'

'OK, please fire away.' Katherine is surprised by Margaret's change of tack but is keen to hear what she has to say.

'Kath…' Margaret begins quietly, pulling back a chair next to her sister and placing her own mug on the table. Katherine waits. 'I'm sorry you found out like you did.' Katherine rolls her eyes to the ceiling, Margaret ignores her and continues, 'But you know what, I really meant it when I said it isn't as simple as you think…'

'What! That nobody thought to bother telling me, her best friend what had been going on?' Katherine retorts, unable to control herself.

Margaret sighs again and frowns looking straight at her, boring into her eyes. 'You know what Katherine; it isn't always just about you.'

'She was my best friend Margaret, *my* best friend.'

'Yes...' Margaret nods and looks down into her lap, 'but she was also my half-sister.' Margaret's eyes fill with tears which within seconds are spilling out and pouring down her face, the volcano she's been holding within erupting.

Kathy is dumbstruck. She sits looking at her sister's trembling face in shock. A hundred emotions and images crashing into her mind: her mother's face, Anne, Margaret as a child, that last day on the beach, their own father, Anne's father...all of them whirling round her head like a hurricane.

'What? What do you mean? What are you talking about?'

Margaret crumbles before her eyes into the little girl Katherine remembers from all those years ago. She makes small sobbing noises like a child. 'Jesus Margaret. Tell me. What are you talking about? Are you saying mum had an affair?'

Margaret looks up and shakes her head violently, as yet, unable to speak.

Katherine's eyes dart around the kitchen, the photographs of their parents on the wall, their grandparents. She's looking for clues but for what she doesn't yet know. Then she leans forward, putting her hand on her sister's arm, 'Margaret, please. What is it, tell me?' she speaks softer this time, her face quizzical, not angry and it helps.

'Sorry... it's just...it's just I've not told anybody about this and I've known for years.' Margaret looks up quickly and then back down again. 'Since just after mum died,' she adds rubbing at her eyes with her hands. She takes a few deep breaths which seem to tremble out of her, gets up and takes a tissue from the box on the shelf near the Rayburn. Katherine knows she must let her tell the story in her own time. Margaret blows her nose, composes herself and turns round to face her sister.

'It was Vi who told me,' she starts. 'You remember old Vi from across the road?' Katherine nods vigorously, eager for her sister to continue. 'I don't know if she'd gone over to have a gossip with mum, or perhaps she'd noticed the car arrive and not leave. I don't know. She might even have disturbed him, not so early as to have prevented what happened, but perhaps he wasn't finished. We'll never know. She knocked and when she got no answer, she came into the house. You know mum never used to lock the front door and if she did she'd leave the key under a stone.

'Vi called out to mum expecting her to be in the kitchen, but she wasn't. Then she heard heavy footsteps run down the hallway and out, followed by a car driving off in a hurry. Vi thought perhaps she'd walked in on something she shouldn't have. She was about to leave when she heard her. She heard mum crying,

314

sobbing.

'She found her, found our mother huddled and hysterical in a corner of the sitting room.' Margaret looks up at her sister. 'He'd raped her. Anne's father, John West had raped her. The sitting room was a mess. She'd fought back.'

Katherine's hand goes to her mouth, she docsn't say a word, just watches and listens to her sister intently.

'Vi said she wanted to call Dad straight away, and the police, but Mum begged her not to. She was ashamed, frightened of the consequences, afraid he'd say it was her fault, that it would destroy Dad. He'd threatened her, told her nobody would believe her, that he was well respected in the community. Vi tried to reason with mum but she wouldn't change her mind. Instead, Vi helped her upstairs to the bathroom, made her some strong tea with a splash of whisky. She stayed with mum, fetching you from nursery, tidying up the sitting room. Stayed comforting her until Dad was due to arrive home.'

Margaret's voice is filled with the emotions of the story, she clears her throat, taking a sip of tea before continuing. Katherine doesn't interrupt. 'Vi may have been a gossip, Kath, but she was also a woman of her word and Mum made her swear she wouldn't tell anyone. She didn't: until me that is. Like mum, she knew the truth. She saw in me what I was, and, more importantly what I wasn't. I wasn't our father's daughter Kath. Nine months after the rape I was born.' Her voice cracks and her eyes drop to the floor. Katherine can see the shame shrouding her and is about to speak but Margaret begins again.

'The one thing I don't know is if Dad ever found out, ever guessed. I don't think she ever told him. Vi says mum kept quiet for fear of the public humiliation, and once she'd found out she was pregnant, for fear of what might have become of me. She carried that with her all the rest of her life Katherine. So yes, Mum did know what kind of a man John West was, what he was capable of, why she didn't want you near him. I'd like to think she didn't know Anne was being abused, but once it came out she can't have been surprised. Did she feel guilty? Probably. But do you know what? I think the reason why she never did or said anything was because of me. If she'd spoken out about him then, told anyone what he'd done, or how she knew what he could do, then the secret of my birth would have been out and I don't think Mum wanted that kind of public shame for me. For any of us. So you see it isn't as simple as you think. If anyone is to blame then it's me, isn't it? I'm the reason mum didn't speak out and stop him sooner.' Margaret takes a deep breath and looks up. 'So now you know. I'm not really the sister you thought I was.'

Katherine shakes her head, not in answer to the question, but in complete shock and disbelief at what she's just heard.

'No.' Katherine replies, at first from a distance, then she pulls herself together, her thoughts turning to her sister. 'No. That's a ridiculous thing to say, of course it's not your fault. You are completely innocent in this. This doesn't change anything.'

'It changed a lot for me, 'Margaret replies.

'No, I mean us, our family. You are one hundred percent my sister and you always will be. It's ridiculous to even think you're in any way to blame for anything!' Katherine takes her sister in her arms, holding on to the sobbing Margaret just like she had when she'd been a little girl who'd fallen over in the yard and her big sister had come running to pick her up.

More jigsaw pieces falling into place. She understands now her sister and Anne's dark hair and olive complexion compared to her own fairness. Their mother's attitude to Anne and her family. Most importantly, the final missing piece of jigsaw in the relationship with her sister is replaced. No more secrets. Once more they stand connected in their family kitchen, hugging each other until their arms ache.

Margaret is back momentarily in that bedroom of Vi's with the faded rose pink curtains and the smell of decaying body, damp house and roast dinner; listening to the story Vi has just recounted. When she died a couple of days later Margaret felt guilty because she was almost grateful - it meant nobody else would ever know the secret. She and Robert went to Vi's funeral and she'd wept, body wracking sobs groaning from deep inside; her body involuntarily forced to squeeze out all the emotion to seek a release. She wasn't so much crying for Vi as for herself. It was the first and only time she'd showed emotion after being told the story. She never shared it, or allowed it to come out in any way. She simply carried on life as though nothing had happened. Just like her mother must have done. Only everything wasn't normal, everything had changed, all that she believed she was had suddenly been taken from her.

Robert was bemused by her grief at the funeral.

'I never realised you were quite so attached to the old dear,' he said later, putting his arm around her and squeezing her for support. Margaret said nothing. She wasn't ready to tell him, and she wasn't even sure if she ever could, but neither would she lie to him. What she didn't realise then is just how badly secrets can fester inside. Perhaps that's why old Vi shared it on her deathbed, unable to carry the burden with her any longer.

44

March to May 2008, Jersey

As if the weather is in tune with Katherine and Margaret's emotional turmoil, on March 10th, Jersey is hit by a storm. The force of the storm and the high tide causes flooding and damage to many parts of the sea wall. Victoria Avenue is particularly badly hit, the sea encroaching up into the town of St Helier and damaging buildings including the Opera House.

Katherine listens to the wind and rain thrashing the sash windows, making them rattle and bang. She hasn't witnessed a storm like this for many years and in the spirit of her new found rebelliousness she ventures out and down the road on the Monday evening to view the power of the sea for herself - despite Margaret and Robert telling her she is crazy. She knows John will be on duty with the Honorary Police as many of the coast roads are closed, too dangerous to drive along with the ferocious sea flinging huge boulders of granite at the land. She finds the anger of the storm magnificent, from a safe distance. Wild, unyielding and oblivious to mankind. Katherine has missed the sea, blue and calm or black and wild, it doesn't matter, she's missed it.

In the JEP the next day are photographs of the storm damage alongside the latest on the abuse investigation. The Chief investigating officer, Lenny Harper, says police received an eye-witness account of an alleged 'indirect act of violence' on a little girl at Haut de la Garenne in the 1970s. An account which is causing them concern. Mr Harper said if the account was accurate there was no doubt that serious injury could have been caused to the child at that time. Could that little girl be the one whose remains have been found? Katherine finds herself wondering what she would have looked like, who her parents could have been, why nobody missed her? Each time the face of Anne joins the questions in her mind.

The enquiry team continue to find teeth and bone fragments at the former children's home, every new revelation paraded to the media, each news story creating more fear and questions in the island community - but by April 27th the focus of the world's media has transferred to Amstetten in Austria. There, another community is shaking its head in disbelief. Questions are being asked how could people not have known about Elisabeth Fritzl, kept captive by her father Josef in the basement of their home for twenty-four years? How could his wife Rosemarie not have realised what was going on, not have wondered where three of the seven children he fathered with daughter, Elisabeth, suddenly appeared from to be cared for by her and Josef. Amstetten leads the headlines now, helping the papers to fly off the newsstands. While its community holds a candlelit vigil in solidarity and outrage, the readers of the newspaper headlines tut and gossip about the story in the pubs and on the bus.

In Jersey the abuse investigation doesn't go away, even though the world's media attention has. The police still dig at Haut de la Garenne. So far two men have been arrested and charged.

Katherine and Margaret are consumed by each other in the weeks that follow the sharing of their secrets, working hard to rebuild their relationship and support one another. Margaret's revelation makes up Katherine's mind for her. It is time she does what a big sister should. She returns to London briefly to resign from her job and arrange for the sale of her house. Her sister needs her, and she is not going to let her down this time.

As the dust begins to settle, Katherine knows she must sit down and talk to John. It's like some burning abscess inside of her needing to be lanced. She's seen him around the place, but they've successfully managed to avoid each other. For Katherine it isn't too hard, it's a skill she's been practicing for the last twenty-one years.

She isn't foolish enough to think there can be some magic reconciliation, she just feels it's time he has a full explanation, perhaps an apology...she's not sure yet. Not sure what she feels, or what she wants. It's another reason why she hasn't rushed to speak to him, but she can't put it off forever.

Standing at the kitchen window, she sees John walk into the barn. The afternoon is beginning to merge into evening and the sun is starting its slow descent into the sea. When she walks out into the yard a gaggle of sparrows argue noisily on the roof. Coming home and talking to Margaret has brought back many early memories, happy times she'd somehow blocked in an effort to erase the bad ones. Sorting out the 'bad stuff' she now realises has helped her to appreciate all the good things too. John is her last big blockage, the plug that is stopping the lava from flowing and her life from moving on.

'John?...John?' she calls into the darkness of the barn, her eyes struggling to adjust. As her pupils expand she sees him, right in front of her, watching.

'Hello Kathy. What can I do for you?' It does it again. Her heart starts to beat faster, betraying the emotion of her thoughts to the rest of her body.

'I didn't see you, sorry. Hello. I was just catching up with you...thought we could set a date and time for that chat we talked about?' She stammers slightly, the rehearsed lines forgotten.

He gives nothing away. 'Yes. Of course. Well I'm pretty flexible, any evening this week is fine by me.' John replies.

Might as well strike while the iron is hot then thinks Katherine, or is he calling her bluff.

'Great. How about tomorrow night? We can pop out for something to eat.'

'Tomorrow night is just fine,' he answers, betraying no emotion in his voice.

'I'll pop round about seven then if that's OK?'

'That's just fine.' he says again. He's being decidedly cool towards her, but then how can she blame him?

'I'll see you tomorrow then. Bye,' she replies and returns to the yard and the squabbling sparrows, who suddenly launch into the air in a riotous screeching as a couple of magpies fly in to see if they can take advantage of all the fuss.

What is it you say to the husband you've barely spoken to for fifteen years? She isn't even sure there's anything to be said, when they've had all this time to discuss what happened – but haven't. Perhaps some things are better left unsaid, except... why does the prickly hard knot inside of her burn every time she comes face to face with him? Surely this alone is her reason to at least attempt a conversation - and not just a conversation about the weather either. If she is really honest with herself, what she wants is to broach the things she'd been unable to say when she closed the bedroom door on him in their London flat all those years ago. Stuff which was too raw to say then but now, with the scabs of time, has healed sufficiently for her to be able to talk openly and honestly.

45

1988-1989, London

Katherine knows she over-reacted but she hadn't been able to help it. She's felt like a bubbling volcano ever since John joined her in London and this evening his attitude and long face just wound her up. There have been so many things she's wanted to say to him, to apologise, to hug him and be held like they used to when him putting his arms around her was enough to make her feel secure and protected. Only he can't protect her from the pain they've been through for the past four years and, although it wasn't his fault at all, she can't help but blame him for the fact every time she looks at him it reminds her of what's missing.

Added to that, she now has to watch as day after day he traipses off to work, through the bustle of the city to his little green patch of relief. Then back again. She watches as his complexion pales and his spirit flags. She knows he is only there for her but guilt is an emotion she has no room for anymore. She's had enough of guilt.

She ends up going to the airport with him.

Taking every second she can to try and find the words she needs to say, the words she knows he needs to hear. Only she can't. How do you tell the husband you love that you can't let him near you, you can't bear his touch, his kiss; because if you let him in, allow just one leak of emotion, you know you will crumble and collapse as sure as a sandcastle in the path of the tide.

It is easier when he leaves. It is even easier when she takes her wedding ring off because the questions stop. 'Have you got kids?', 'So I suppose you're thinking about starting a family?', 'Do you not want children? Not want grandkids, something to look forward to in your old age?' Inside, she wants to scream at them to mind their own business, to say, 'Don't you think people without children are childless for a reason?' Either they're suffering because they can't, or simply exercising their own free will and choosing not to: so butt out! She doesn't. Without John the questions tail off and without her wedding ring on, they cease. The solitude means she can have her chance to heal.

After he's gone and she's cried herself dry, she gets angry. Angry that he's just abandoned her, hasn't been prepared to live life on her terms - after all her sacrifice, after all she's been through to try and bear them a child. She persuades herself it is he who is selfish, not her.

Those long dark days and evenings in

London during 1989 pass in a blur. She knows John will be thinking she is going out every evening, having fun, socialising; and part of her wants him to think that, to perhaps get jealous and come back and get her. Truth is, there are many evenings she can't face anybody or anything, when coping at work is the sum total of her strength. So she turns off the phone and just sits in the shadows.

Towards the end of 1989 Katherine watches the demonstrations in East Germany growing until the overwhelmed border guards throw open the gates and hundreds and thousands of people unite the two Germanys. When the crowds begin to chip away at the Berlin Wall - chipping away at oppression and imprisonment, Katherine watches the news programmes and listens to the stories of re-united families, of those who never made it through. She cries along with the cheering, clapping, jubilant crowds until her head pounds. She cries, really properly cries for a whole day, until her body is dry and her emotions wrung out.

As Christmas looms she knows she is too raw to return home, and so she volunteers to work, afraid of how she will cope if she goes back to John and her family. She isn't sure she'll have the strength to return to London if she goes back to the warm, safe cocoon of Jersey. After that things just become easier. It's easier to avoid returning, easier to forget about who she had once been, and easier to ignore her husband and family who still wait for her.

46

May 5th 2008, Jersey

Katherine sits in the living room of her old family home sipping on some Dutch courage and psyching herself up for the evening ahead. The furniture in here has mostly changed with new sofas dominating the space, but the sideboard and nest of occasional tables are still there from her childhood. Her sister and Robert have decorated too. Plain buttercream walls stare back from where she can vaguely remember red flocked wallpaper once hung. She can't quite conjure up the pattern in her head, but she can still feel the soft velveteen of its design on her fingers. There is also a new wide-screen television in place of their old set; and fresh young family faces have joined the older generations in photo frames around the room. Yet even with her eyes shut, even if she couldn't see the old granite fireplace at the heart of the room, she will always know where she is for the smell of the old house never changes. It might entertain the aroma of a roast dinner or hold onto the scent of a perfume or aftershave for a while, but underneath it all is the unmistakable smell of home - slightly musty with age, the legacy of the granite shell and oak beams, but with a distinct smell you won't find in another old house; the scent of her family. Thousands of childhood memories playing in every corner of every room. She shied away from this for so long, resisting the temptation to come back to her nest, to feel swaddled by its security. Why? Had it been simple pig-headedness, or did she really need all this time to gather enough distance between herself and her pain.

In all honesty she's dreading this evening. She's been avoiding it for years, not because she is worried about how she'll feel or that it will end in an argument, it's because she's scared they'll no longer have anything in common.

John. Quiet, dependable John. A man who just couldn't get on in cosmopolitan London. They'd shared a Jersey upbringing but when Katherine went to London she knew she was leaving him behind in more ways than one. He's spent another twenty years living on this tiny island of just 9 miles by 12, doing pretty much the same thing, while she's been forging a career and living in the capital city. She's had conversations with her friends in London that John would feel completely out of his depth with. So what is she scared of? That she's moved on and left him completely behind? That they no longer have anything in common?

That the memory of a relationship she still holds dear in her head and heart will become yet another untruth in her life because she won't be able to understand what she ever saw in him? Those happy memories of their early years together would instead then become some sad story of a young naïve woman who settled for somebody who just happened to be there, rather than truly falling in love.

All those years of trying to make themselves a family, all the pain, would have been completely pointless.

So she finds herself trying to think of some general chat topics they can talk about when they first meet up. She's going to ask him about his business, how it's doing – apparently quite well; how his mother is – apparently not quite so well, about a couple of his old friends she remembers, and they can talk about Haut de la Garenne and what's going on there. Or perhaps not.

Half an hour later they walk down the road and along the coast to the Le Hocq pub where they'd spent their very first date. Katherine doesn't miss the irony. There are no longer any other pubs within walking distance, The Priory Inn was turned into houses many years before. She wonders if John has chosen it purposely? They could have taken his car and gone somewhere else. On the walk she runs through her list of chit chat topics, but it's hard to concentrate. He still wears the same aftershave and scents like songs can take Katherine back to another moment in time in a flash.

'How's your mum?' she asks.

'Oh not so good now. She's moved into the cottage attached to my brother's place in St Marys. Finding it difficult to get around, never been the same since Dad died. She's just kind of existed since really.'

'I'm sorry. Do you think perhaps she would mind if I popped up to see her?'

John turns and looks at her now, studying her eyes. Up until this point he's been keeping his gaze firmly fixed ahead. 'No of course not, I'm sure she'd like that,' he replies. Then there's silence between them, nothing except the sound of their footsteps.

'How long have those houses been there?' Katherine, eager to fill the conversational void, nods over to some new homes off to their left.

'A couple of years now. They wanted to build on the glass houses too but the Parish said no.'

'Don't they grow tomatoes there anymore?'

'No. Barely any tomato growers left, too expensive. The supermarkets just keep beating the prices down and the costs keep going up. Makes it all pointless really.' John sighs, Katherine murmurs in agreement. By now they have reached the coast road and without a footpath they are forced to walk single file, making it difficult to hold a conversation.

The pub has changed quite a bit since Katherine was last there. It's now a gastro pub rather than the old fashioned drinking hole it used to be. A young girl, New Zealander by her accent, shows them to a table. It's in the middle of the room, John points over to one in the far corner.

'Would you mind if we took that one instead?' He says to the girl and to Katherine at the same time.

'No of course not, no problem, come this way,' the girl answers, checking Kathy to ensure there's no disagreement. Kathy merely nods and smiles. John always did like his privacy, and if they're going to have a big talk then he's not going to want other people around him.

They sit down and John starts to look through the wine list. 'Red or white?' He asks.

'Red please.' Kathy replies, and nervously chattering adds, 'I love white in the summer, chilled, but in the winter I have to have red.' There's no reaction.

'How about number fourteen?' John asks proffering the wine list. Katherine doesn't take it, he always liked to choose the wine.

'I'm sure it will be nice,' she replies.

He nods and snaps the wine list shut. 'Do you still love scallops?' John asks looking up at her.

'Yes I do.' Kathy smiles, pleased he remembers. 'Pâté for your starter, followed by steak?' It's his turn to allow a small smile now.

'Maybe,' he says nodding. 'Was toying with the sea bass, but I do love my steak.' The waitress arrives hovering over their table with her notepad, and they order. Afterward without their menus as props they are temporarily at a loss.

John gets the first question in. 'So, what's prompted you to come back?' He's trying to make his voice sound as normal as possible, but there's a defensiveness to his tone.

Katherine, in turn, tries to keep her answer as light as possible, mindful of the invisible wall that splits their table. 'Well, it was a combination of things really. I've been thinking about coming back for a while, all the publicity over Haut de la Garenne kind of brought things home to me, and then I got a letter from Elizabeth West, Anne's mother.'

'I see. What did she want?' There is no warmth in his voice.

'She wanted to talk to me, I think to ease her own conscience really. Did you know about Anne's father?'

John furrows his brow, thinking. 'Not really had any dealings with the family, but didn't he get put away for being a paedophile?' He replies.

'Yes and apparently everyone thinks that he

was also abusing Anne. Margaret told me.'

'Oh God! Really? Poor girl.' John's face softens.

'Looking back now there were some signs, but when you're sixteen and completely naive you just don't notice these things do you?'

'No of course not, it's not something we'd have been aware of at that age. It wasn't talked about like now - there wasn't the education,' replies John, 'But what about her mother?'

'Yes, what about her mother! She must have known...I know she knew. I could see it in her eyes.'

'So you still went to see her then?' John sounds surprised.

'Yes I didn't know about the abuse before I went. She's like some dried up black widow spider just sitting there waiting to die. She knew, and she didn't do anything to help her daughter. I hope the guilt has been nagging at her all these years.'

John nods. 'Mmmh, but I'm not so sure those kind of people do feel it you know. If she didn't help at the time, then I doubt she's going to develop a conscience later on.'

It's Katherine's turn to nod and sigh. 'Yeah, maybe you're right. Well then I hope there's a Hell so she can rot in it.'

'Has it helped?' John asks, Katherine looks up a little confused. 'Has finding all this out and going to see Anne's mother helped you with accepting Anne's death? I remember whenever something bad happened you used to say you were cursed. Cursed because you'd driven her to suicide.'

Katherine sighs again. 'I know. I guess I was a bit self-obsessed about all that. Yes, it has helped actually. I know the truth now at last and although it's no better for Anne, in fact it's worse for her, at least I can understand *why* now. Why she took her own life.'

'Good. Then it was worthwhile.' John says smiling gently at her. His smile is the first warmth he's shown towards her.

It prompts Katherine to give him something in return, 'It's not the only reason I came back,' she adds.

The waitress reappears bearing their starters. Katherine waits until she's gone before taking a gulp of her wine. It's time to tell John about her conversation with Margaret. He needs to know her sister is aware of what happened. 'I had a big chat with Margaret the other day. I told her about the miscarriages.'

John stops chewing and looks up at her, his knife and fork frozen, 'Good,' he says surprising her, 'that's good. I think we should have told her a long time ago. Did you ever talk to anyone else in London about what happened?' he presses.

Katherine shakes her head. 'I didn't want people to know, I didn't want their pity, or to feel like a victim...'

John nods his head at this.

'I know… I know it's hard to understand,' Katherine continues, 'but I wasn't really thinking rationally. You pray to God, you cross your fingers and try old wives' tale fertility spells, and you search for some reason as to why it could be happening to you...' Katherine pauses, John doesn't interrupt relieved at last she is talking honestly; and then the words seem to tumble from her like a crate of spilt apples. 'I'm sorry John, I'm sorry we never had the baby we wanted. I'm sorry I left and didn't come back. I'm sorry for being a coward and for not allowing you to be a part of my life, or for me to support you.' John puts down his knife and fork. 'I know I kind of abandoned you, but at the time it was self-preservation, I had to get away. I realise the mistake I made was staying away for so long, thinking I could hide from myself. I might have achieved quite a lot in my career, but hiding from myself is one thing I just could never do.'

John stays silent watching every twitch on her face, the pulse in her temple, the flare of a nostril.

She looks up at him, staring straight into his eyes. 'September 18th, April 26th, September 3rd, December 14th, March 25th.'

At first a quizzical look shoots across his face, but as she goes on with each date he realises what she's reciting. It's the dates of each miscarriage, each day when their hopes were dashed and their hearts shrivelled just a little bit more. He'd never have been able to recall the list like that, he remembers rough dates; the April because it coincided with the potato harvest, one in September because it was close to his mother's birthday, but for Katherine these dates are etched not just on her memory but on her soul. He thought he'd understood how much harder it had been for her, but the truth is he just couldn't understand.

He sighs.

Katherine is looking down at the table again, her eyes watery. He knows she won't have missed that first look of puzzlement on his face.

'I also thought you'd be better off without me,' she adds quietly, her voice little more than a whisper. 'I couldn't give you what you wanted, what we wanted. I thought perhaps you'd have a chance to find that with somebody else.'

'That's ridiculous Kathy,' John answers quickly, frowning. 'I said at the time I'd be happy with just us if that's the way it had to be. I'd far rather have been with you, than without you.'

She looks up at him, there is years of frustration in his voice, tinged with a little anger. The raw emotion between them is too much for her and she drops her gaze again.

'I'm sorry too,' he says quietly after a moment's silence, a weariness in his voice which takes him by surprise. 'I'm sorry I couldn't give you the support you needed, that you had to go away. I should have been able to help you do that. You shouldn't have had to face it on your own.' It's John's turn to look down now, words don't come easy for him, she knows that. 'I didn't want people's sympathy either,' he adds quietly.

She looks into his face, recognising the pain etched on to it. It's what she's looked at in the mirror a million times before.

'I didn't want a repeat of all those awkward looks people gave us the first time,' John continues, 'You know when they don't know what to say, can't properly look you in the eye because they feel awkward. I just wanted us to deal with it together, keep it between us – just you and me. But that wasn't such a great idea was it? We should at least have told our family, had some support – especially for you.'

'It was hard for both of us.' Katherine simply replies by way of acceptance and absolution.

He nods sadly and they sit for a while allowing the words to hang between them like stepping stones.

After that, the air calms around them, a

spark of an old connection reignited. Albeit, a connection of shared pain and grief. John asks Katherine about her life in London and she gets to ask him her ready prepared questions about his life.

'You know I don't farm as such anymore, don't you?' He starts explaining.

'Yep sort of, Margaret told me you grow plants and sell them now instead.'

'Yes,' he nods 'but not just any plants, specialist vegetables and flowers. You know stuff you can't get in the garden centres. I've got my own website – a basic one, but it does the job.'

'So why did you start that?'

'Difficult to make money in farming nowadays, unless you're mass producing Jersey Royals for the UK supermarkets. Tomatoes are all but finished on the island. I just came across a little niche in the market and decided to go for it. I sell as much as I can produce. It's satisfying. More rewarding than growing a field full of veg that I'll be paid a tuppence h'appenny for by the supermarkets.'

'So are you expanding? If you think your website needs revamping, I've got a great contact in London who could help you. They owe me a favour so it wouldn't cost anything. You could...' Katherine stops mid-sentence.

John is simply looking at her and there's no enthusiasm on his face. 'Thanks,' he replies taking advantage of her pause, 'but to be honest I like it just the way it is, just me and my plants. I don't have to worry about staff and running a big business, I just get on with what I enjoy doing. I know you'll think me a boring island boy for that, no ambition and all that stuff, but do you know what? It makes me happy. I don't need to earn loads more money, I have plenty for what I need.'

'Sorry.' Katherine answers hanging her head.

'Don't be sorry,' he reassures her. 'I appreciate it, it's great you want to help, but I'm OK thanks. I'm just where I want to be.'

For the first time in twenty years, Katherine envies her husband. All this time she's been feeling sorry for him, for all the things he's missed out on, for all the experiences she's gathered whilst living off island: the shows, the people, the culture. In this moment she sees and recognises true contentment, something she's never been able to achieve. In her career there has always been something else to chase, to achieve. Every time she's moved up another rung or closed the deal she'd thought unobtainable, she was after a new one. She's never had the time to stop dashing from one experience to the next, to stop and savour. To study a tiny plant and wonder at its existence, nurturing it, giving it life. John has found his happiness without ever having to leave.

Katherine could have searched the world and she wouldn't have found that look of peace on his face. He doesn't need to expand his business, build up his website, he has nothing to prove to anyone - most especially himself.

Katherine looks at him differently, her eyes open, and finds herself wondering what happened to that love she'd felt for him? To that need to drink each other in, to fuse to each other, swap souls. She remembers that feeling. Where has it gone? Did it completely wither and die in the face of all their pain, or is it buried, deep down in the dark someplace, like a bulb waiting for spring?

47

September 2008, Jersey

It's one of the last good days of the year, good enough for swimming and sunbathing at the beach. Margaret and Robert take Sophie to Anne Port, Katherine goes too. They drive through Gorey and past the Castle.

Behind the houses on the hill the investigation at Haut de la Garenne is all but over. In May the Mail on Sunday revealed 'the remains of a child' found back in February, was in fact nothing more than a small piece of coconut shell. Lenny Harper, the Chief investigating officer, offered up other bone fragments and children's teeth to any media still willing to listen but most people, including Katherine and Margaret, grew wary of his finds. He retired at the end of August and the national newspaper buying public appear to have grown tired of the story now none of the lurid promises of 'mass graves' have materialised. Only the local media keep on top of the story and listen to the real victims - those still living and hoping for justice.

Life in Jersey has found a new rhythm for Katherine. Last night she'd found herself looking around the dinner table and feeling content. John had joined them all and they'd chatted and gossiped about old family stories, or the latest news from friends, laughing as James repeated all the jokes he'd heard about murdered coconuts.

Katherine wondered what kind of person Anne would have been if she'd been at the table with them. Would their friendship have survived her terrible secret? Would she ever have been able to stand up to her father and seek retribution?

At Anne Port, Margaret, Robert and Sophie head off into the water to swim but Katherine declines, instead sitting on a blanket on the beach just taking it all in. There are children playing in the water and digging holes in the sand; a canoeist who has been fishing carrying his boat up onto the slip. She sees somebody water skiing further out, several people wind surfing, two little boys rowing in an inflatable dinghy held safe to shore by their father at the end of a long rope. There are swimmers including Margaret, Robert and Sophie and a tiny sailing boat. It's the perfect day, bright hot sun and a sea breeze carrying the scent of seaweed and salt.

Small motor boats and white gulls bob together on the waves. The birds occasionally fly a few feet before settling back down again, too content to go far. The green topped granite sides of the bay curve their protective arms around them all and in the distance the coast of France, coffee brown, topped with dark chocolate icing and the white candles of a wind farm.

The sky is blue except for a few frothy milk clouds: a cappuccino sort of day. The gentle breeze carries the sounds of boat engines and children's squeals and giggles to her and all the time there is the gentle, rhythmic swoosh of waves on a beach. It could have been her childhood forty years ago, the endless joy of sea and beach. Katherine closes her eyes for a few moments grateful for the good memories. She can almost feel those worry-free days of childhood and the warm love of her family.

Katherine has thought a lot about her mother in the last few months. The grudge she'd held against her since the eve of her wedding has been brought into sharp context now. The pain she must have felt each time Katherine mentioned Anne, why she didn't want to go to the funeral, why she never wanted Katherine to associate with the family - all of it now makes sense. She can explain most of her mother's attitude as a result of the rape but that comment, 'She's better off dead?' still rings in Katherine's ears. Did she know about Anne's abuse? But how could she? Unless others also suspected and she'd been told. That thought makes her shudder and she opens her eyes again to take in the warm day.

There's no one left to seek retribution for Anne's death. Like many of the Haut de la Garenne abusers, time has either given them a lifetime without justice, or it's clouded evidence so convictions are difficult to attain. Anne and Marie have gone. Anne's father is dead and Elizabeth West is dying an agonising death alone. Time has played its card and the living have no need to stir up its rancid secrets.

Katherine knows her mother didn't have it easy, she lost the man she loved too early, forced to bring up her two daughters alone - and she got no thanks for it from Katherine. She took some flowers to her grave yesterday. Margaret came with her and the pair of them swapped stories from their childhood as they paid their respects. There's nothing Katherine can do now to make up for those lost years but there's plenty she can do for Margaret and her family. She's not going to walk out on them again. Talking has healed their relationship and they're both determined never to let the cracks return.

The sale of Katherine's London house is almost finished and although still living with Margaret and Robert, she is starting to think about what's next. To finally be able to talk about her miscarriages has been uplifting, invigorating even. They're no longer like some dirty guilty secret she's ashamed of, now she can stand up for them in public, talk about them. She has so often imagined her lost children as a little gaggle of babies and toddlers, now of course they would have been young adults ready to fly the nest. Kathy knows she needs to set them free.

She gets up to stretch her legs, sitting on blankets isn't as comfortable now in her late forties as it had been as a child, and wanders along the small beach. There's a mother with a young boy and their dog. The boy and his pet are playing in a rock pool together. He's happily chattering away in his own little world, the dog chasing reflections and bubbles in the pool. The mother is just sitting, watching, smiling. A serenity on her face that can only come from one human watching the happiness of someone they completely and utterly love; the kind of love where the joy of one creates happiness for the other. Katherine has long ago accepted this world will always be closed to her, but it doesn't hurt like it used to. Perhaps she can share in it a little now, enjoy the remains of Sophie's childhood. She knows Margaret is eager for her to become part of her nieces and nephew's lives.

Katherine wanders further along the beach and finds some blue and white pottery pieces. She places them in her pocket to take home to put into Margaret's jar - and she does feel like she is home, really home, for the first time in twenty years.

48

Not long after their trip to the beach the days turn shorter and the evenings longer and colder. Katherine has been over to the UK one final time to tie up all the loose ends. It's a relief walking out of her mews house for the last time, closing the door on its empty shell.

In Jersey the JEP headlines are all about another door closing. Katherine returns to the island and to Margaret's home to find her sister and Carol ranting over their coffee.

'A major review of the Haut de la Garenne enquiry evidence says there's no bodies, no skull, no cellars, no blood and no instruments of torture.' Margaret reads from the JEP.

Carol is sitting shaking her head, 'All those national newspaper reporters aren't here now are they?'

Margaret continues, 'The new officer in charge of the investigation says information given out in police statements had been incorrect.'

'Incorrect!' interrupts Carol, 'We trusted him, him and his coconut shell.'

'It's not just about that though is it?'

Katherine joins in, 'There was abuse.'

'Yes,' continues Margaret, reading from the JEP, 'The police say they're going to turn their full focus on getting justice for the abuse victims.'

Carol purses her lips. 'Shame they didn't concentrate on that in the first place instead of all this crap about murdered kids and the big conspiracy theory that we were all in on it!'

'People must have known about the abuse though,' Katherine adds, 'Not the whole island, but some people must have known.'

Margaret nods her head, agreeing with her sister, 'Kids in homes like that were easy pickings for paedophiles in those days. Just hope some good comes out of all this. You watch the victims on TV, telling their stories and you can see what it's done to them. How what happened all those years ago is still affecting them. You can destroy lives in lots of ways.'

Margaret's words stay with Katherine. A few nights later she stays up late after everyone else has gone to bed, sitting staring into the autumn fire; the roaring of the wind in the chimney like thunder rumbling in the distance. Tomorrow evening John has invited her round for dinner in the cottage. She's looking forward to seeing her old home again and reminiscing some good memories.

Tonight though, Katherine is enjoying being alone with just her thoughts for company. She opens the black notebook she's always kept in her bedside drawer. Inside are some small grainy images. One, two, three, four in total, showing almost identical little bodies. The faded grey print-outs of scans, of curled up babies waiting for a life that would never come. She'd waited for her life that never came too, and then mourned all of their loss.

Katherine picks up each picture, faded and worn. Max, Emily, Charlotte, Harry, Jack or Sarah, that's not what matters now. She loved them, she still loves them and always will. They say a small amount of a baby's DNA stays in the mother's body somewhere, even long after the baby has gone. Katherine's babies are a part of her. She never had the chance to hold them and to tell them, but just as they would have one day flown the nest for University, gone travelling, or fallen in love, so she must now let them go. In front of her the wood on the fire glows bright orange - its flickering promise to cleanse and erase.

One by one she places the pictures in the flames of the open fire. They curl and vanish in a split second to black paper ash.

From out of her notebook falls a piece of tissue paper. Katherine opens it carefully. Inside is a tiny flower, dried and brittle. Its colour once a pink, or perhaps lilac, is now brown. She can't remember when she picked the flower, why she decided to keep it. That day in 1976 is long lost to her. She picks it up and a petal falls from its fragile head. It no longer holds any of the sunshine, or the promises of the day it grew in the field outside their farm. The years have taken its energy leaving it merely a hint of a summer's day gone by.

Katherine lets it too float into the fire. Outside there are plenty of its descendants seeding themselves ready for the next spring. Perhaps one day soon Sophie will potter into one of the fields, spot the tiny flowers and pick some for her mother, or maybe for her Aunt Katherine once her vases have arrived from the UK and found familiar windowsills. Perhaps then.

Fact or Fiction?

All the characters in this book are completely fictional: Katherine, Margaret, John, Marie and Anne do not exist and bear no resemblance to anyone who ever has. All the facts about the way in which the Haut de la Garenne enquiry was undertaken and subsequently reported by the media are fact, as is the way it shocked the island of Jersey. Not all that was said and reported is true and there have since been inquiries into the handling of the investigation as well as how Jersey's care system can be improved.

There were no murders, no bodies or 'remains' ever found at Haut de la Garenne, but there had been sexual, emotional and physical abuse there and at other children's homes in the island. What went on in Jersey may pale into insignificance with the scale of the revelations which followed about Jimmy Saville and Operation Yewtree, but every single individual case leaves a victim.

HAUT DE LA GARENNE: AN ENQUIRY TIMESCALE

9.30am Saturday 23rd February, 2008
Jersey Police's Deputy Police Chief Lenny

Harper issues a statement saying, 'Today, what appears to be potential remains of a child have been recovered.'

Monday 25th February: Lenny Harper reveals police have uncovered a bricked-up cellar. Local newspaper the **JEP** reports: 'Police do not yet know the age or sex of the child whose bones were discovered, but say the remains had lain under the floorboards at the rear of the building for some time.'

They quote Lenny Harper: 'We just do not know how many kids may have disappeared.'

The Daily Telegraph headlines: Seven children 'could be buried at hostel' and reports: 'The bodies of at least seven children may be buried at a former care home in what police fear is one of the worst instances of child abuse in Britain.' The report continues: 'Scientists will take several days to identify the gender and DNA evidence may be too decomposed. However, the body is thought to be of a child, aged 11 to 15, dating from the 1980s.'

The **Daily Mail** headlines: Bodies of six children may be buried at the home of horrors. In its report it says: 'The discovery of the skeleton of a girl...' and reports that it asked Deputy Chief Officer Lenny Harper '...if he expected to find more bodies, he said: 'There could be six or more. It could be higher than that.'

Wednesday 27th February: Lenny Harper

gives a media briefing. He says sniffer dogs have had a strong reaction after going into 'the cellar'.

One of the dogs being used is a Springer spaniel called Eddie which was used in the hunt for missing Madeleine McCann in Portugal, and which was reported to have picked up traces of Madeleine in the back of her parents' car.

The Independent headlines: 'Secrets and Lies the Dark Side of Jersey, the report goes on to say 'The team mounting a painstaking forensic excavation of the Haut de la Garenne former children's home have pinpointed six more places where they think corpses are buried, in addition to the one set of child's remains they have already found.'

Thursday 28th February: Police say they've uncovered a feature, which some of the abuse victims had claimed was there. A journalist takes a photograph of it, it's a large concrete bath. Police say traces of blood were found in the bath after another sniffer dog Keela had identified places of interest there.

The Daily Telegraph headlines: 'Police 'on verge' of discovering more child remains'. The paper reports: 'Police feared they were about to uncover more human remains at a children's care home last night after breaking into a cellar and discovering another secret chamber.' It continues, '(The breakthrough) looks likely to confirm the worst fears of police, who indicated earlier in the week that the remains of up to seven children could be found.'

29th February: **The Guardian** headlines: 'Police discover shackles in Jersey abuse case home: Sources say find tallies with victims' accounts: Second underground 'punishment room' sought.'

1st March: The Daily Telegraph headlines 'Island of Secrets and Terror Was an establishment cover-up behind a child abuse scandal that went on for decades? In the report: 'The "deep, dark place" described by many of the 160-plus alleged victims who have now contacted police was exactly as they had last seen it more than 20 years ago and, as police prepare to break into two more cellars, the belief is that they will soon discover the remains of more children who "went missing" from the home. Outside, in the swirling fog that has shrouded parts of the island this week, officers are digging up nearby fields where it is feared yet more remains may have been buried.'

'...Jersey must ultimately answer two questions: how many of its 90,000 population knew what was going on, and why did none of them do anything about it?'

Monday 3rd March Media Briefing notes from the States of Jersey Police. In these the 'writing on the wall' of the cellar which has widely been reported by the media is mentioned, as too is the concrete bath which it's said, 'appears to link with accounts from witnesses.' This briefing also covered rumours on the island that infill for the building had come from elsewhere. It says, 'Infill to some of the building did come from elsewhere.' It announces that specialist military personnel are coming over to use ground radar equipment.

This press release also says, 'Callers to local radio are suggesting the presence of the media may be stirring things up out of proportion but the consensus is that the media reporting has been of benefit to the investigation – encouraging witnesses in coming forward and explaining to the people of Jersey why the enquiries have to be patient and methodical.'

The Daily Telegraph headlines: 'Revealed: the feared torture chamber at heart of Jersey abuse probe. The report goes on to talk about the 'cellar' and the 'bath' and says: 'On a vertical wooden beam rising up from the bath the words "Iv been bad 4 years & years" have been written in black marker pen.'

Tuesday 4th March: A Police press release makes mention of the previous use of Haut de la Garenne by the 'Bergerac' production team. 'The search teams are aware of this issue and the disturbance that may have been made to the grounds when TV sets were established temporarily.'

Tuesday 4th March. The Wiltshire Constabulary report into the handling of the enquiry later finds that Chief Officer Graham Power met with Jersey's Attorney General on this day, during which the AG raised several concerns that 'the media reporting to date would result in abuse of process arguments, on the basis that a fair trial would be prejudiced.' Already there were concerns from politicians and legal experts into how the media were being handled during this investigation.

Friday 7th March: A Police press release confirms that a 'specialist blood dog' was put into the cellar and indicated two different spots within the bath. 'Presumptive tests for blood have given a positive result.'

Monday 10th March: Work begins on a second cellar.

Tuesday 11th March: Lenny Harper says police had received an eye-witness account of an alleged 'indirect act of violence' on a little girl at Haut de la Garenne in the 1970s – an account which was causing them concern. Mr Harper said that if the account was accurate there was no doubt that serious injury could have been caused to the child at that time.

He said: 'Added to that, the witness claims that the child was not seen or heard from again after that incident – though, of course, there could have been an innocent explanation to her disappearance from the home.'

Wednesday 12ᵗʰ March: Lenny Harper says 'We cannot rule the possibility out that this could be a murder enquiry.' In response to media queries about a 'missing child'.

March. BBC television personality Jimmy Saville starts legal proceedings against the Sun newspaper after he claimed it had linked him to the child abuse scandal at Haut de la Garenne. Saville initially denied visiting there, but photographs of him surrounded by children at the home, were later published. The States of Jersey Police say that an allegation of indecent assault at the home in the 1970s, by Saville, was investigated in 2008. There had been insufficient evidence to proceed. (In 2011 Jimmy Saville dies. He is mourned and tributes are paid - until months later allegations of abuse start to appear. By 2012 Operation Yewtree is launched into allegations of historic sexual abuse by Saville and many other people, including prominent celebrities. Hundreds of allegations are investigated against Saville, over 50 years, in hospitals and BBC premises with children and vulnerable adults.)

Monday 17ᵗʰ March. Gordon Claude Wateridge, a former warden at Haut de la Garenne, appears in court charged in connection with historic indecent assaults on children. He'd first been arrested at the end of

January.

March 28th The JEP suggest that as the Home was on a hill, the 'cellars' were more likely to be foundation cavities as many people on the island had suggested. Lenny Harper replied: 'The 'cellars' are the old ground floor, which became what they are during renovations.

31st March. It's later revealed that on this day Dr Higham from the Oxford Radiocarbon Accelerator Unit stated he believed the original remains was not bone. This information was not released to the public/media.

Tuesday 8th April. Jersey Police Press Release states: Further tests have failed to date the initial skull fragment. 'They do say however, that from a study of the material in the location where the find was made, the bone was placed at that location no earlier than the 1920s.'

'This leaves us with no knowledge of how, when, or indeed, where, the person died.'

Friday April 9th: The JEP request to publish a photograph of the 'skull fragment'. They report that Lenny Harper replies, 'No, this is human being and our advice is that we should treat the piece with dignity.'

Wednesday 16th April: Lenny Harper say they are very concerned about why two pits, including one containing lime, should have been dug in the grounds of the Home. Nothing was found in the pits.

Friday 18th April: Jersey Police announce the skull fragment predates the abuse inquiry period and would not be the subject of a murder investigation.

However, in the same press release, the police say 'a number of bloodstained items in cellars three and four' have been found.

Tuesday 22nd April 'Two Teeth found at Haut de la Garenne in cellars'.

Tuesday 29th April. Arrest of a man in connection with the abuse enquiry.

1st May: Letter sent by the Oxford Laboratory confirming the original find was not bone and almost certainly wood. Again this was not conveyed to the media.

5th May. Local Politician raises rumours that the skull fragment was not human with Chief Officer Power and suggests the record should be put straight.

Tuesday 13th May: Police announced they've found more children's teeth and bone fragments in the cellars and sent them to the UK for testing.

Sunday 18th May: Mail on Sunday reporter David Rose claims that the 'remains' had been identified by experts as being a small piece of wood or broken coconut shell.

Sunday 18th May: Jersey Police Press release in response to the MOS article. Lenny Harper summarises the findings of the laboratory examination of the fragment, and says that the laboratory says it would need further examination, rather than repeating the lab's actual statement that they did not believe it to be bone. This same press release also goes on to say that they have identified 20 pieces of bone and six children's teeth from the cellar. 'We expect the results of the dating next week and will be issuing a press statement about the teeth and bones on receipt of those results. At that stage we will know more about the possibility that there might have been unexplained deaths of children within Haut de la Garenne.'

This attempt to gloss over the findings of the initial remains and instead encourage the media and public to have the worst impressions, is later criticised in the Wiltshire Police Report.

18th May: In a separate Jersey Police press release detailing the finds by sniffer dogs, the police state: 'This area is of interest to the investigation team as being the location where it is reported that human remains MAY have been recovered previously during renovation in 2003. Further alert indications within the building by the dogs have been corroborated as being human remains and blood.'

Tuesday 21st May: Police press release updating on teeth and bone fragments found. 'Ten of these bone fragments were found yesterday (in an ashy area of cellar 3) and identified as being human, (Tuesday 20 May) while around 20 were found in the last two weeks.'

'The bone fragments found have been identified as being human.'

'Regarding the teeth, of the six we have sent to the UK, five of these cannot have come out naturally before death, and only one of the six has signs of decay. The rest have a lot of root attached. We have been told that teeth could come out naturally during the decomposition process.'

'Some of the bones exhibit signs of burning, and some show signs of being cut. This means that we COULD have the possibility of an unexplained death – and evidence of a dead child or children in the cellar. There was a fireplace area in the cellar.'

'What we do not know yet regarding the bone fragments and teeth, is who that person is, or how they died.'

Wednesday 22nd May: Mr Harper holds another press conference and holding a container with a tooth in it, says that evidence found by the team confirmed the remains of, 'a dead child or dead children.' He said bone fragments found at the home, some in an old fireplace, had been cut as well as burnt, he adds, 'This means we could have the possibility of an unexplained death and evidence of a dead child or children in the cellar.' Referring to the children's teeth, he said they could not have come out before death.

22nd May. The Express 'Children "cremated" at Jersey orphanage'. The paper goes on to report: 'Children may have been cremated in the cellar of a former Jersey orphanage, police said yesterday. A murder inquiry may be launched after 30 bone fragments were found alongside seven milk teeth in an underground chamber at Haut de la Garenne. The remains are said to belong to more than one child.

The paper quotes Mr Harper as saying: 'Whatever else, we have a dead child or dead children in that cellar. We do not know how they got there or how they died.'

27th May Jersey Police Press Release: 'There is one further matter we wish to comment on. Criticism has again been levelled at the enquiry team that the initial find in February was "sensationalised" in press releases. We would point out that at all times we have said that we did not know how, where, or when, the person concerned had died.'

Thursday 19th June: Police report they've found a total of over 50 children's teeth on the site.

Thursday 31st July A States of Jersey Police press release is issued clarifying the finds. They confirm they have 65 children's teeth and bone fragments which are in the UK for testing. The release says that 'Experts have told us they believe that the 65 teeth COULD come from up to five different children.'

Thursday 31st July The Daily Mail Online reports: 'At least five youngsters died in suspicious circumstances at the Jersey children's home of horrors - but no one will be charged with murder, police have revealed.

Their burnt and cut remains were hidden and secretly moved around, but police say it is proving impossible to accurately date when they died.

Announcing defeat yesterday, detectives said it was likely nobody would be brought to justice for their deaths.'

http://www.dailymail.co.uk/news/article-1040033/Remains-children-Jersey-care-home--killers-escape-justice.html#ixzz3yrr2AYUZ

Thursday 7th August: Lenny Harper retires from the force. This had been planned since before the enquiry started.

Wednesday 12th November. Jersey Police with Deputy Police Chief David Warcup, and the new man heading the Abuse enquiry, Detective Superintendent Mick Gradwell, hold a press conference.

Following a review David Warcup says 'It is unfortunate that we now believe that the information which was put into the public domain by the States of Jersey Police about certain 'finds' at Haut de la Garenne was inaccurate, and we regret this.' The States of Jersey Police are clear that these do not support suggestions that there have been murders at Haut de la Garenne. In particular;

A Piece of Child's Skull

-An anthropologist made an initial identification as this item being a piece of child's skull.

-The SIO made a decision to release information to the press about the find.

-On the 31st March 2008 Dr Higham from the Oxford Radiocarbon Accelerator Unit stated he believed the item was not bone.

-14th April the original anthropologist reviews her initial identification and says she no longer identifies it as part of a skull.

Shackles and Restraints

Jersey Police say these were in fact rusty pieces of metal.

The Bath and Blood Stains

The bath in the under floor voids has no water supply and has not been used as a bath since the 1920s when a brick pillar was constructed within it. Following detailed forensic microscopic examination, no blood has been found. There is nothing suspicious about the bath and no indication this bath has been used in the commission of any offences.

The Cellars

These are floor voids. They are not cellars and it is impossible for a grown person to stand up straight in the floor voids under Haut de la Garenne.

Teeth

There are 65 teeth found in the floor voids and 1 elsewhere. They are milk teeth coming from at least 10 people – up to a maximum of 65 people. Around 45 of the teeth originate from children aged 9 to 12 years and 20 from the range 6 to 8 years. There is wear on some of the teeth; these teeth generally have the appearance of being shed naturally.

Bones

170 pieces of bone which are mainly animal were found in the area of HDLG which was searched. Many more pieces of bone were found in the area of the grounds, all of which are animal.

-Of all that material, there are 3 fragments which are 'possibly' human; the biggest piece is 25mm long.

-2 fragments date 1470 to 1650 and the other 1650 to 1950

-These have not definitely been identified as human bone.

The Pits

These were dug in the late 1970s and are unexplained, but nothing suspicious has been found in either of them.

In Summary;
-No people are reported missing
-There are no allegations of murder
-There are no suspects for murder
-There is no specific time period for murder
-We are satisfied that there is no indication or evidence that there have been murders at HDLG

Wednesday 14th July, 2010. Police Chief Graham Power and Senior Investigating Officer Lenny Harper receive strong criticism for their handling of the enquiry following a report by Wiltshire Constabulary. The report's Executive Summary states: 'The media needed little encouragement to paint a graphic and horrific picture of institutionalised abuse of vulnerable children on the island. We are clear from the evidence that such reporting was condoned and even encouraged in a number of the States of Jersey Police press releases which variously described the *'partial remains of a child'*, *'skull'*, *'shackles'*, *'bath'*, *'cellars'* and *'blood'*, none of which transpired to be accurate.'

The report did say that the States of Jersey Police had been misquoted on a number of occasions, but that no evidence has been found that any steps were taken to address media misreporting.

Both police officers were said to be

inexperienced to deal with such an enquiry. Both men strenuously deny any wrong doing.

The Report also found that there had been lavish overspending by Mr Harper in an enquiry that up to June 2010 had cost over seven million pounds. In particular, the report picked out expense claims from Mr Harper which included a £90 a head meal at a London restaurant with a News of the World journalist who later printed a story headlined, 'All kiddie killers left were burnt bones and 65 teeth'.

On the publication of the Wiltshire Constabulary Report, Jersey's Home Affairs Minister apologises to the victims who came forward during the enquiry, for the raising of their hopes that justice might have been served after the huge time lapse.

6th December 2010 the Island's Chief Minister makes a formal apology to all those who suffered abuse in the States' residential care system, acknowledging that the care system has failed some children in a serious way.

Following the conclusion of an investigation by the States of Jersey Police, named Operation Rectangle, into historical child sexual, emotional and physical abuse in a number of institutions in Jersey: Operation Rectangle reported and recorded a total of 553 alleged offences between September 2007 and December 2010. Of these, 315 were reported as being committed at Haut de la Garenne Children's Home. Eight people were prosecuted for 145 offences and seven convictions secured. The Police identified 151 named offenders and 192 victims.

2013 A Committee of Inquiry is set up to look into how to improve the island's care system. It hears evidence from those involved in Operation Rectangle and many more. Its findings are due in 2016/17.

The Wiltshire Constabulary report:
https://www.gov.je/SiteCollectionDocuments/
Government and administration/R
WiltshirePoliceReportExtracts 20100713
ILeM.pdf

Acknowledgements

Thank you firstly to my husband, Matthew, and our boys for their patience in having to take second priority to this book. To my mother, Mavis, and my father, Len, for their encouragement through the years with my writing.

Thanks also to my mother-in-law, Patricia, for her support in reading and giving feedback on the manuscript.

A huge thank you to fellow writer and friend, Jan Caston, for her editing and whip-cracking, and for giving me excellent advice in the re-writing of Islands.

This book is also dedicated to the victims of abuse, those who need our support and vigilance; and to all those women who have suffered a miscarriage and struggled to deal with the emotional fallout. You are not alone.

Finally, thank *you* for reading this book. I hope you enjoyed it and look forward to sharing another story with you soon.

About the Author

Gwyn GB is a writer living in Jersey, Channel Islands. Born in the UK she moved there with her Jersey-born husband and their children. Gwyn has spent most of her career as a journalist, but has always written fiction in her spare time.

You can connect with Gwyn online:
Twitter: @gwyngb
Facebook:
https://www.facebook.com/GwynGBwriter/
Pinterest:
https://www.pinterest.com/GwynGB/
Instagram:
https://www.instagram.com/gwyngb/
Website: http://www.gwyngb.com

Gwyn's next book 'Lonely Hearts' is coming soon.

You can sign up to be notified when it's published and to receive special offers.
http://www.gwyngb.com/lonelyhearts

In the meantime, turn over the page for a free taster:

Lonely Hearts

1

Rachel

The garden is illuminated by thin leached light from the windows of the house, their curtains open for the purpose. The dark moon-less sky means a thousand shadows have been born - but only one has made her heart pound, turning her skin cold and sending the blood pumping in her veins.

She knows they're watching; just like she knew they were there last time.

Her hands start to shake slightly while she locks up the shed, determined not to leave her animals unprotected and vulnerable. Her breathing is shallow as she listens for the slightest sound from behind: a bush parting, soft footsteps on the lawn, the breath of another on her neck.

Like last time - there's nothing.

Nothing, except the gentle hum of suburban traffic and a baby crying in a house across the road, its high pitched wailing summoning tired parents. She is surrounded by houses, by families and couples going about their evening routines: TV, computer games, reading, arguing - all oblivious to her rising fear and what might be about to happen.

Rachel pockets the shed key and turns toward her house. It's only ten paces but the empty lawn gapes wide. Why are they here? It's been weeks since the last time and she thought they'd gone, scared off by the presence of a boyfriend in the house. It's almost as if they know she's alone tonight.

What if they're already inside? Slipped in unseen while she fed the animals.

The open doorway in front of her becomes a threat, lit up and welcoming to any passing stalker.

What should she do? Stay outside with the shadows in the open? Or trust the light and the doorway that will enclose her?

Fear wins. Her legs start to move as flight and adrenaline take over. If she gets into the kitchen, her mobile phone is on the table. She can almost see it from here.

She walks, each step an eternity, nearly twisting her ankle as she misses the edge where lawn meets footpath.

Rachel is just a few feet from the doorway, light bathes her face and makes her blonde hair glow. Her phone is just feet from her grasp.

2

Neil

Neil leans into the bathroom mirror, plucking the last grey hair from his eyebrow. The demanding youth culture of social media marketing isn't his only motivation to hold back the years.

It's as he drops his gaze to the sink, turning on the tap to wash away his age, that the knife enters his back.

He doesn't see who kills him. It wouldn't matter much if he did because he's as dead as the proverbial Dodo, and thus a useless witness, long before anyone thinks to check on him.

As he careers head first into the bath tub he knocks his bottle of Creed aftershave in with him; smashing and spattering the white porcelain with scent as well as blood.

The Coroner later comments, his is the nicest smelling corpse he's ever had the pleasure to be acquainted with.

By the time Neil's mobile rings in the sitting room, Rachel's phone number flashing up on the screen, his heart has stopped pumping. Neil will stay forever young.

3

Clare

Clare has an epiphany lying naked next to the man who's shared her bed for the past eighteen months. He is never going to make her happy. A fact backed up by the dull ache between her legs instead of a pleasure swollen post-orgasmic throb.

In truth, he's bored her for months but it's been convenient. The same reasons so many coppers get together: an understanding of the crap you have to deal with on a daily basis, and the shit hours. Unfortunately, Clare no longer wants convenience, she wants passion, and her own space. Neither of which she's been getting since Jack moved in.

He's also been getting a bit too heavy lately, broody even. Jack has started talking forward, not just weeks or months, but years.

'This would be a good investment,' he'd said the other night. They were sitting on the sofa, dinner finished, watching Game of Thrones when he just came out with it and handed Clare his iPad.

Clare expected him to show her a savings

account or the latest Indiegogo hit, but instead he offered up a local estate agency site with an ad that said, "Great neighbourhood. The perfect family starter-home." Clare hadn't known what to say. It was one of those rare occasions she'd been lost for words.

Thankfully, Khaleesi and her dragons took that moment to catch Jack's attention and she was spared any further awkwardness.

To be notified when Lonely Hearts is published, sign up here:

http://www.gwyngb.com/lonelyhearts